The Spirit Clearing

M.R. Tufo

CreateSpace Edition
Copyright 2012 Mark Tufo
Discover other titles by Mark Tufo
Visit us at <u>marktufo.com</u>
and **http://zombiefallout.blogspot.com/** home of future
webisodes
and find me on FACEBOOK
11.05.13

Cover Art:
Bookcovermachine.wordpress.com

CW01521568

Dedications -

To my wife whose constant belief and helpful suggestions has turned this idea into a story I'm proud to share with all of you.

To Katherine Coynor, Gloria Marin, Sara Smolarek, and Ken Keeler, my beta-readers gave me more advice and inspiration than I could have ever hoped for.

To John Ramsey Miller, just because I think you're the coolest cat I know!

To the brave men and women of the armed forces, I pray for your safety and am thankful for all your sacrifices.

Table of Contents

PROLOGUE

Hello Dear Reader, I hope you enjoy this latest installment in the alternate realities of our leading character Michael Talbot. I am very proud of this story as it is very different from anything I have written thus far. It is my sincerest hope that you enjoy reading it as much as I enjoyed writing it.

It was a cool fall evening the night Michael Talbot died. Why no one felt the need to tell him, only the fates will ever know.

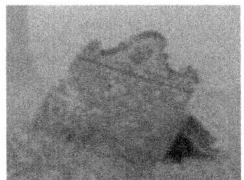

CHAPTER ONE – The Drive-In

The cars parked at the drive-in looked like they each had their own wood stove as smoke-funneled through cracked open windows. Management turned a blind eye at the numerous infractions as their tills filled with munchies money.

Mike was busy laying on coats of cheese sauce on his nachos when he listened in on a conversation better left unheard.

"I thought we were going to have to throw this food out," Steve Trandell, assistant manager at the I-128 drive-in, had said to his boss.

"There's a reason I did the stoner movies this weekend," Bob Brandle, the manager, told his underling. "These kids will eat anything."

"I know," Steve said as he handed over a hamburger to an eager eater, that he himself would not have fed to his dog.

***

"I don't think I could smoke any more of this if I had to," Paul said as he handed the oversized joint into the backseat where a glassy-eyed Dennis was staring deeply into his wax-coated cup of cola. He was cognizant enough to grasp the funny left handed cigarette, although more likely from muscle memory than true thought.

"Is that thing still going?" Mike asked, exasperated as he walked back up to the car with an armload of food that only the young and unknowing or the seriously starved would consider edible.

"Man, I'm glad to see you, I'm starving," Paul said as he reached across the seat to help his friend back in. "Dennis hasn't said anything since you left, I think we might have lost him for the night." Paul laughed.

The trio of friends had gone to one of the few remaining drive-ins still open in the early 80s on the East Coast. Trying their best to keep their doors open in an ever changing market, the facility had decided to do an all-night Cheech and Chong marathon, what they made at the admission gate was minimal, but that was more than made up for at the concession booth where lines of pimply faced teenagers paid entirely too much for small slivers of pizza, dried up corn dogs, stale nachos with old cheese sauce that smelled more like feet than anything else and flat sodas. Rounded out with chewy popcorn and butter-like sauce, the kids ate it as if it were five-star cuisine; but that had more to do with the influence of marijuana than the food itself.

**

"You know, this shit, really isn't all that good," Mike said around a mouthful of food.

"I know but I can't stop eating it," Paul answered.

Dennis still hadn't said anything from the backseat, but now his fixation had moved to the hot dog that could be more accurately described as 'lukewarm cat' in his hand.

"I'm gonna get a beer to wash down this turd in my mouth. You want one?" Mike asked Paul as he twisted to reach into the backseat and fumble around with the cooler.

"Sounds good," Paul muffled out.

"Hey, buddy," Mike said to Dennis.

Dennis slowly moved his gaze away from the hot dog to Mike's face. A smile immediately spread across his broad features. "Hey, Mike, where you been?" Dennis asked.

"I think the same could be said about you. You want a

beer?" Mike asked as he pulled his dripping can laden hand out of the frostiness.

"Beer?" Dennis asked as if he were hearing the word for the first time and was not sure of its meaning.

"You know the cold, wet stuff that makes you feel all funny in the head and makes you do really stupid shit around girls," Mike answered his friend.

Dennis had lost track of the conversation and was now watching the individual drops of water drip from Mike's hand.

"Dude, this thing is colder than hell, do you want it or not?" Mike asked, now full on smiling at how stoned his friend was.

"Man, I told you already I want it," Paul said from the front seat. "I'm dying of thirst up here."

"I was talking to Dennis," Mike answered.

"Is he listening?" Paul turned to see.

"I don't think so." Mike waved the can back and forth across Dennis' field of vision. Dennis' head would swivel to follow, but with a pronounced delay.

"Mike, give me the beer. He's sitting next to the cooler, if he wants one he can get it."

"I'm not sure he'd be able to figure out how to open it," Mike said as he reached into the cooler and grabbed another beer, turning back around for the start of the second movie in the three movie set.

***

Paul and Mike had met two years previous when Mike's parents had moved from his downtown Boston home and right into a Norman Rockwell painting that was a suburb called Walpole. They had become fast friends when they realized they both had a serious dislike for anything that resembled authority. Dennis had come into the mix the following school year when his father's job had been transferred from New York City to Boston. The only part of Dennis that Paul and Mike could not reconcile was that damn Yankees hat he insisted on wearing everywhere. Other than that he was one of the coolest kids they knew.

At the ripe old age of sixteen-and-a-half, Paul had been the first of the trio to get his license; it had taken three months and some heavy convincing of his father and stepmother that he was trustworthy enough to take the family car and his friends to the drive-in.

"This really is a sweet ride," Mike said as he tried to rub away the cheese sauce he had dripped onto his seat.

Paul started laughing as he watched Mike. "I don't think that's gonna work." Paul smiled as he handed over a napkin.

"Sorry," Mike said, looking up with pleading eyes.

"Don't worry about it, that's where Barb (his stepmother, but not really wicked, just no clue) sits." Paul and Mike both started laughing, it was no secret that Paul and Barb rarely saw eye-to-eye. She constantly tried to enforce her book learned child rearing authority and Paul thwarted her every attempt.

Mike felt a frantic tapping on his left shoulder and turned so quickly he was almost rewarded with a red hot cherry from the end of the joint into his left eye. "Shit, Dennis! You almost burned my eyeball," Mike jumped back.

Dennis didn't seem to notice as he felt his notification period was done and dropped the lit joint onto the seat.

"Dammit!" Mike grabbed for it quickly, but not before it burned a none-too-flattering hole in the fabric; it looked like an old puckered scar.

"If I wasn't so wasted I think I'd be concerned," Paul said rubbing his finger over the charred wound.

"Man, I'm sorry!" Mike fixated on the burn. He was fairly certain that, if he came home with a burn hole in his folks' fifteen-year-old piece-of-shit station wagon, he'd get thrown out. This was no old rolling Wally wagon – unless that was what they were calling 1983 Saabs these days.

"Mike, don't sweat it, we'll end up having a big family meeting about it and how this is a good learning experience," Paul said, still smiling.

"Your funeral." Mike took another toke he did not want. It was such an ingrained motion he completed it without even thinking. The conversation quickly subsided as the screen lit up and their attention was pulled in its direction.

***

Four hours later, Mike had to wake Paul up as the roar of multiple engines starting up disturbed his slumbering.

"Whoa, what time is it?" Mike asked, trying to pull the imaginary cotton from his mouth. He took a drag from the warm beer still wrapped in his hand. "Ugh, that was no help." Mike opened the door to pour the contents out. He peeked back in to the other occupants in the car. "Well, it's only a party foul if someone else is there to witness it," he said, the tepid liquid sloshing to the ground.

Dennis was passed out sideways on the backseat, he was using the cooler as the world's least comfortable pillow. Paul had at some point reclined his chair and was snoring loudly, a fine line of drool running down the side of his chin.

"Shit, wish I had known the seats went back that far," Mike said as he rubbed his stiffening neck. "Hey, buddy." Mike shook his friend.

"Yeah?" Paul asked, cracking one eyelid to see who dared disturb him.

"I think we missed the third movie."

"There was a third movie? What fucking time is it?" Paul adjusted his seat into a more driver-friendly posture, but not by much.

"Three," Mike said, looking back to the concession stand and the oversized clock hanging on the outside.

"Dammit, my curfew is two. I'm screwed."

Mike didn't think now was the time to bring back up the seat burn that was poking uncomfortably in his thigh. Mike's curfew was 'whenever he got home' thanks to a broken home, but he was in no way complaining. At least *something* good had come out of his parents' constant bickering.

Paul fumbled with the keys, starting the car. "Where's Dennis?" Paul asked, trying to reestablish some normalcy to his skewed reality.

"Backseat. He's crashed out."

"Dude, are you going to get in trouble?" Paul asked, concerned.

"Not me, man, my dad is up in Maine for the weekend and my mother is off playing cards until sometime late Sunday. I won't see either of them until then."

"I envy you sometimes, Mike."

"Don't, it's not all it's cracked up to be."

"What about him?" Paul asked, wondering if Dennis would feel the wrath of an angry parent.

"I don't think so, his folks are pretty lenient. Can't do shit about it now, anyway. You alright to drive?" Mike asked as Paul was about to put the car in drive.

"Fine, I think."

"Then you might want to take the speaker box out of your window first."

"That would probably be a good idea," Paul said rolling down his window and hanging up the heavy speaker onto the hook on the pole. "That would have sucked."

Mike cringed as Paul came within an inch of the speaker pole on his side.

"That was close," Mike said when they got safely by it.

"What was?" Paul asked as he looked bleary-eyed out the window.

"You sure you're alright?" Mike asked again, an uneasy feeling beginning to take root in his stomach.

"Never better," were the words Paul was shooting for, it came out more like 'nebah butter'.

Mike didn't know how to respond; he knew he was certainly in no shape to drive, and besides, he only had his learner's permit. *We'll be fine*, his inner psyche said, trying to calm his nerves. *We're teenagers, we're indestructible.* It wasn't verbalized, it was only a feeling – a feeling that had cost more than one young adult-in-waiting life and limb.

Mike thought Paul seemed mostly alright as they got onto the road outside the drive-in, he had only crossed over the double yellow lines twice... nope, three times so far. But that wasn't the scary part, it was when he would drift too far over to the right and begin to kick up dust, dirt, and debris on the shoulder of the road. The steel guardrail loomed large in Mike's field of vision every half mile or so as Paul cycled through his swerves.

It's like the damn thing is magnetic, Mike thought when Paul got particularly close to the rail again.

"I'm a little fucked up, Mike," Paul said, looking over to his friend with a sickly, grim smile.

"You might want to keep your eyes on the road, buddy," an alarmed Mike said when Paul kept staring at him as if he might have an answer that could help. Mike really didn't see what good him keeping his eyes on the road would really do, though; Paul's eyes were as wide as coin slots and what little was showing was blazing red.

"Music would be good, Mike...help me concentrate," Paul mumbled.

I would think driving your parents new Saab with your two friends in it would be enough, Mike thought, but kept to himself. A rising sense of dread kept percolating in his gut, there were many times over the following years that he wished he had heeded the prescient feeling.

Mike immediately moved to the stereo lest Paul have to take one of his white-knuckled hands off the steering wheel. Paul was hunched forward as if the six inches he gained from this position would help him avert a disaster.

"This is WAAF The Rock and Roll Air Force!" screamed through the speakers. Paul violently swerved into the oncoming lane trying to get away from the assault on his ears.

"Shit…sorry, Paul!" Mike yelled as he fumbled with the balance first and then the treble level before finally lucking out and getting the volume knob. "Man, my ears are ringing."

"My dad got the stereo upgrade package for this car."

"Damn, I guess."

"It's time to get the Led out," the rock DJ said. "It's after three in the morning I'm pretty sure my boss isn't listening. I'm going to play forty-five minutes of commercial-free Led Zeppelin." A bong bubbled in the background.

"Rock and roll!" Dennis yelled, sitting up for a half second, fingers splayed out in the traditional heavy metal sign. He may have even stuck his tongue out for dramatic effect, but it happened so fast Mike and Paul had not been able to see him clearly as he plummeted back down into his previous passed out position.

Whole Lotta Love was first up. Mike did not think this was the best song to garner focus, more than once he had found himself lost in the progressions of this hard rock mind trip of a song, over the last few months.

Paul passed with flying colors merely because he didn't bounce the car off of anything for the entire eight minutes and forty-seven seconds of the song.

Three songs later, Mike was feeling better about their chances of getting home unscathed. They had just passed over the town line 'Welcome to Walpole, Incorporated 1724', but instead, his feelings of impending doom kept growing.

In the Light started simultaneously with the high pitched squeal of tires as Paul misjudged a curve. The car lurched to the right as the wheels fought to seek purchase on the wet, leaf-strewn road. Paul twisted the steering wheel as far to the left as possible. Had not so many competing sounds been happening at the same time he would have been able to hear the power steering belts whining from the force being applied to them. Might as well have been a sheet of ice for all the hold his car had on the roadway.

Mike quickly looked to his right where his seatbelt hung uselessly, he placed one hand against the passenger side window and one against the center console as a copse of trees dominated everything on that side and in his sight.

"*Fuck!*" Paul screamed as he fought in vain against the inertia. The front tires spun uselessly as he applied more gas, hoping he would be able to force-of-will himself out of this death slide. The speedometer read seventy but time had almost stopped for the two teenagers who were painfully aware of their situation. As the right front tire slid off the road and onto dirt the car almost righted itself, Paul whipped the steering wheel back to the front, his foot still planted firmly to the floor on the accelerator (as the cops would write down in their investigation). The car rocketed straight forward, the road, however, did not.

The car slammed into a two hundred-year-old oak tree that had taken up this unfortunate piece of real estate. The front end wrinkled up, Mike felt himself rising up from his seat and did not have enough time to move his hands to protect his head as it made a violent collision with the windshield. A loud popping in his neck coincided with the shattering of the glass.

The car was still attempting to fuse with the tree as Mike found himself airborne. He was less and less concerned as the world around him began to darken, his head caught the side of the tree veering and shortening his previous trajectory. The world and all thoughts were black as he hit the ground.

Paul watched as Mike was launched from the car as if

he had an ejector seat underneath him, Paul would have also if not for the crushing force of Dennis' body as he slammed into the rear of Paul's seat and wedged him tight against the steering wheel. Paul wheezed as multiple ribs shattered, at least two puncturing his left lung. The pain was so intense his body thankfully shut down to prevent him from going into shock.

It was the smell that awakened him a few moments later. Burning plastic—something he was very familiar with. A month after Mike and Paul had met they had taken all their model cars, planes and *Star Wars* vehicles and used them in an epic battle replete with fireworks and lighter fluid. It was a symbolic burning of their youth, not that they realized it then but it was almost a rite of passage from youth to hooligan.

"That smells horrible," Paul said groggily, as he fought to come back to consciousness. "Mike?" Paul asked as he looked around for his friend. "Which one are you burn—" The intense pain in his chest flared, he took ragged breaths, unable and unwilling to take in the smoke-clogged air. "What…what is going on?" he muttered, placing his hands on the steering wheel, crushed onto his belly and collapsed rib cage. *This is bad*, he thought. But not as bad as the flames he saw licking up under the hood.

"Mike!" he tried to yell, his voice coming out a decibel or two louder than an ant farting.

Through the haze of heat shimmer, Paul saw the brown shaggy hair of his friend as he attempted to rise from the ground. Something wasn't quite right; the side of Mike's head looked caved in, blood poured down his face and neck, collecting on Mike's Ozzy Osbourne t-shirt where it eerily looked like it belonged. Add to that Mike's neck had a pronounced bulge and his arms were twitching erratically.

"Mike, help me," Paul begged as he watched in horror while his instrument panel began to melt under the intense and building heat. Paul looked back up and over the hood when he heard a soft thud as Mike's head lost the war against gravity, his upper body falling back to the ground.

Paul heard the volunteer fire-alarm sounding at the center of town and was distantly aware that it must be for them. A glimmer of hope sparked in him. "We're going to make it," he said with relief…just as fire crackled through the air vent.

Paul passed in and out of coherent thought, the volunteer alarm turned into outright sirens, but they sounded so distant. He hoped it had more to do with his cognitive thoughts rather than physical distance. Mike's seat was now on fire; the earlier burn mark completely erased. *At least Dad won't be mad about that now.* Paul winced as he thought it. The smoke was so thick in the interior of the car that what little Paul could breathe was now laced with carcinogens and poisons. It hardly seemed worth the difficulty of pulling that foul substance into his body.

"Mike, please," Paul pleaded one last time as the flame began to lick his right leg. Paul did not think he could be in any more pain until his leg began to sear from the blaze. His screams were cut short as a thick coil of flame entered into his throat and burned out his vocal chords, he had two heartbeats left with which to remember all the events in a life cut short.

Dennis had so violently struck the back of Paul's headrest he had never awakened; he had died shortly after Paul from smoke inhalation. He still looked as if he were peacefully asleep when the fire rescue crew pulled his lifeless body from the wreckage. It took them forty-five minutes to put the conflagration out and they had to use the Jaws of Life to extract Paul's charred remains. His mouth forever frozen in its final scream.

Mike was rushed out to Route 1 where the ambulance was met by Flight for Life. He was flown to Mass General where a team of doctors fought against nature. Three times he died on the table, and three times they brought him kicking and screaming back to the world of the living.

Please just let me die, he begged as he felt himself again being dragged back from the light. *The pain, the hurt, the darkness, it's too much.*

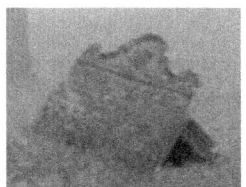

CHAPTER TWO - The Aftermath

It was Mike's sister Lyndsey who had initially received the news about her brother. She had been home that weekend from college and with friends the evening of the accident. One of the cops who responded to the car crash had recognized all three boys and told the hospital who Mike was. They had tried to reach the Talbot homestead at least a dozen times when they had finally called to talk to Officer McKinney to let him know they could not get in touch with the family.

Officer McKinney got into his cruiser and headed to Michael Talbot's house. Mike was a good kid as far as he knew; he had only been out here once for a disturbing the peace call when a particularly big party had raged, but even then the kid had been respectful. He had been implicated in the burning of the Principal's car, but no proof could be brought against him; and besides, Spindler was a prick. If someone had torched his car, too damn bad. McKinney had on more than one occasion been summoned to Spindler's office back when he was in school. *The self-righteous egomaniac got what was coming to him*, was all Officer McKinney thought when he had responded to the burned out hulk of a late model Cadillac last year.

He had made sure to act sufficiently concerned as he took the report and did his job thoroughly, looking for a culprit, but was internally pleased when he came up short in the suspect department. Mike and the dead Paul Ginson had been suspiciously close to the incident, as they 'studied' at the library, but they had an air-tight alibi, even if the window in the basement of the library looked like it had been recently disturbed.

He got out of his cruiser and placed his hat on his head. He took in and blew out a gust of air; this was the part of the job he hated the most.

He knocked three times on the door when a pretty college-aged girl with ruffled hair and sleep-wrinkled clothes answered the door.

"Oh, shit, what's he done now?" Lyndsey answered, instantly coming awake. "Mike, get your ass out here!" she turned to shout into the living room.

"He hasn't done—" Officer McKinney started.

"He's always pulling some bullshit when my parents are away," she said, turning back to face him. "Come on, Mike, he said he's going to come in and get you if you don't hurry up!"

"Ma'am, you don't understand."

"Oh, yes, I do. He just thinks he's all high and—"

"Miss, there's been an accident."

Lyndsey stopped in mid-sentence, her heart and head trying to reconcile the words the officer was telling her. "How bad?" she whispered, suddenly feeling like her legs weren't going to be strong enough to support her.

"Are your parents here?"

"Oh, God, he's dead!" she wailed. "I mean he's a little asshole, but he doesn't deserve to die." She started crying, leaning heavily on the doorframe.

"Are your parents home?" Officer McKinney asked again. Lyndsey just shook her head slowly from side to side. "Is there any way we can get in touch with them?"

***

By the end of the day the entire Talbot family was at the hospital. There were his three older brothers – Ron, Gary, and Glenn – and his only sister Lyndsey. His parents, Mary and Anthony, the latter of whom had broken long held speed records on the Maine turnpike to get back home, was there as well.

"You would have been here sooner if you weren't up in God's country doing who knows what with the shit-kickers," Mary said heatedly.

"For Chrissakes, Mary, is now the time for this?" Tony asked back.

"It's good to see some things don't change," Ron said to Gary grimly.

It was another three hours of tense silence before the neurosurgeon came out to speak with them.

"Mr. and Mrs. Talbot?" the doctor asked. The entire family coalesced around him.

"That's us," Mary said, uncharacteristically grabbing her husband's hand.

"Your son has suffered grievous wounds from the accident, we've revived him three times on the operating table."

Mary gasped and nearly swooned as Tony held her up.

"Is he alive?" Ron asked.

"He is, but we don't yet know the extent of the damage. He's in a coma."

Tony guided Mary to a nearby chair, the doctor followed. "We've had to remove bone from his skull in order to ease the pressure from his brain as it swells. He also has broken his neck and we have yet to be able to ascertain if he has motor function."

Mary began crying as did Lyndsey, seeking comfort in each other's arms. The Talbot men stood stoically, but more from shock than the denial of feelings.

"When will you know?" Tony asked, swallowing back the gorge threatening to rise up out of his throat. "When will you know if he can move again?" Tears were free-flowing from his eyes.

"Mr. Talbot, I'll be honest. Mike's not out of the

woods quite yet. Although my team and I are amazed at his will to survive. The next twenty-four to forty-eight hours will be crucial, but there's nothing any of you can do here. If you are the praying type, I suggest doing a lot of that and go home and get some sleep if you can. I will have the hospital notify you in the event that anything should change.

"Thank you, Doctor," Tony said, numbly sticking his hand out to shake the doctor's hand merely from force of habit.

***

"What do you think, Brent?" Terry, the anesthesiologist, asked the doctor who had just spoken to the Talbot family.

"I think he would have been better off if we had let him die," Brent said as he went to check on Michael's comatose form one more time before heading home.

***

I wanted to die, Mike thought as he lay huddled in the dark, damaged lining of his mind.

***

For twenty-three straight days the Talbot family alternated shifts at the hospital, keeping vigil on the ever still Michael. Occasionally, Michael's consciousness was close enough to the surface to hear some of the words being said, most times, though, he found himself walking alone in the endless void and expanse of his mind, searching for a way out.

'Sorry about not being there.' 'Did my son have any last words?' 'I might take next semester off.' 'I think he's a vegetable.'

Mike caught snippets of conversations, some as crystal clear as if he were involved in the dialog, and others as if he heard them under water, and ever he moved, not needing to rest as he wandered. The landscape was rippled with memories, sometimes he was six and huddled in his mother's arms as she shrieked with delight that 'The Indians were coming'. He smiled at this thought now, but as a youngster he could think of nothing more terrifying than some injuns coming to scalp him. His first kiss, he stopped to linger and smile at his clumsy attempt to plant his lips on Patty Preston's.

'We could harvest his organs.'

That caught his attention, it sounded as if someone were standing next to him and had whispered it in his ear.

'Let's face it, he's been a bag of bones for almost a month.'

'A month?' Mike asked, I bet Tara has broken up with me, probably going out with Paul now.

'He's not coming back.'

'I'm right here!' Mike shouted. No one was listening.

'Do you want me to talk to the family, see what they want to do?'

'I'll do it tomorrow, at least he'll do some good as opposed to laying here and taking up space.'

'Fuck you!' Mike shrieked. 'I'm a person, I can still feel!' Of that he was not entirely sure. He was not hungry. He did not sleep. 'What am I?' Mike asked. Blessed light began to shine around him, nothing more than a candle held a half mile away, but slowly it grew from the darkest obsidian to high noon. He would have shielded his eyes if he knew where his hands were.

"I'll be damned," Mike heard.

"Call his family," a female said excitedly. "I'm not going to lie, Mr. Talbot," the woman said. "I'm going to miss our conversations, you were the best listener I've ever had." She planted a small kiss on his forehead and he felt it! He would have done a small dance if he could have remembered how to operate his legs.

This time he did sleep, the fight to consciousness had exhausted him. He drifted off with the wetness on his forehead rapidly cooling as it evaporated.

Seconds, hours?—later, Mike forced one eyelid open. He had once bench-pressed two hundred and seventy-five pounds and that had been a breeze compared to the effort he was expending to do this small maneuver

"He's awake!" Lyndsey said excitedly. "What's the matter with his eye?"

"Shush," his mother said to her. "Mike, honey, can you hear us?" she asked soothingly.

Through the slitted left eye he could make out the outline of his mother, but she was blurry. As he struggled to open his right eye, his mother came into view as she should, the duality of the images had a disconcerting effect on him and he was afraid he was going to be sick.

"His heartbeat is beginning to race," his brother Glenn said. "What's that mean?"

Mike felt a small ripple leave his brain, travel down through his chest into his legs. By the time it cascaded into his toes it had grown like a tsunami; as the wave crashed, his body began to thrum wildly.

"Nurse! Doctor!" Mike thought it may have been his dad screaming the words, but by then he was in the full-on throes of a seizure. White foam poured from his mouth.

"What's wrong with him?" Lyndsey shrieked for maybe the fourth time.

"Please, we're going to need everyone out!" the triage nurse said forcibly.

Mike's body arced violently on the bed, so much so that the doctor feared he'd re-break his neck or possibly his back.

"Should we restrain him?"

Mike's world began to darken as alarms blared. "Flat

line!"

"Charging—clear."

Mike felt charcoal-like blistering heat points on his chest, his physical body again thrust heavenwards.

"Two-ten, charging. Clear."

The blistering heat came again.

The alarm stopped wailing, a rapid series of blips was followed by the traditional, thump-thump of a functioning heart.

"He's back," the doctor said. "What the hell happened?"

"I don't know. He was coming out of his coma and when he opened his eyes he went into cardiac arrest. I've never seen anything like it."

"How long was this kid down?" the on-call doctor asked.

"Twenty-three days," the nurse who had kissed Mike's forehead said.

"Alright, let's bring him back up to ICU for at least a couple of days, I'd like to run some tests and see if we can determine what just happened."

***

Mike was pretty sure it was night time before he thought about opening his eyes again. Foot traffic had died down significantly and he could only detect the softest of lights diffusing through his eyelids.

"Alright, we're going to start with the right eye first," he whispered. He slowly pushed his eyelid up, he could see a large window that faced the nurse's station a few feet past. He looked to his side at the large machine that had three lines moving across it, one was definitely for heart rhythm, the other he figured was brain waves and the third he had no clue. He was already becoming foggy with the effort he was expending.

"You ready for this?" he asked himself as he lifted his left eyelid. The world on that side was now coated in ethereal lights, shadows passed by his field of vision. His right eye took note of the spike in brain activity at the very moment he opened the left lid. He quickly slammed it shut, the uncaring line on the paper moved back down to what Mike figured was the 'normal' range.

"Coincidence, right?" he asked, again moving the lid slightly up.

The line moved as a heavy dose of vertigo set in, spinning the room on a tilted axis. His heart monitor began to thump wildly. He saw the duty nurse rise and look directly into his room. She picked up the phone and was calling someone. His brain and heart monitors were closing in on the red danger zones. He quickly squeezed his eyes shut; the monitors that sounded as angry as a disturbed hornet hive were quickly coming back down to regularity.

"What's the matter, honey?" the nurse asked. Hot tears streamed down his face. "Is it about your friends?"

"What about them?" Mike forced through a throat that didn't quite want to work.

"You don't know? Oh, dear." The nurse quickly vacated the room.

"Know what?" Mike croaked. His throat burned, he thought he might have seen a water bottle by the side of his bed but he dared not open his eyes.

Mike heard the door to his room open again.

"Michael, you awake? My name is Doctor Perkins, I'm the head of the ICU unit. Can you open your eyes?"

"Can I get some water?" Michael asked.

"Sure-sure," Dr. Perkins said as he hit the controls on the bed to get Mike into a sitting position. "Can you move your arms to grab the bottle?"

Mike looked desperately inside himself for the controls that would allow him to operate his arms but was failing miserably. "I... I don't know how to," Mike moaned.

The plastic straw was thrust a little too far into his mouth for his liking, but he drank greedily as the cool liquid flowed down his parched throat. Mike's forefinger twitched as the bottle was taken away too quickly.

"Still thirsty," Mike begged, ashamed he sounded so fragile.

"A little at a time. It has been a long time since you have had anything introduced into your system without the assistance of an IV."

Mike saw flashes of light flit across his eyelids as the doctor lit up a penlight.

"Can you open your eyes, Michael?"

"I can, I just don't want to."

"You've sustained a significant amount of damage to your left eye Michael. For reasons we haven't figured out yet, you have lost all pigmentation in it. Is that what is concerning you? There are contacts we can put in that will make it almost undetectable."

"I didn't even know about the pigmentation, doctor. When I open that eye, I don't see right. There's strange colors and shadows. It's as if I'm looking at a completely different world. And…and it's scary as hell."

The doctor laughed a little. "I'm sure it is, but I think with time your mind will begin to repair the images you are seeing and reconcile them with what is really there."

Mike didn't want to get into a philosophical debate about what was 'really' there. What his left eye 'saw' was just as real as what his right eye took in. He felt he was straddling two worlds, yet he had a foothold in neither. Mike feigned extreme exhaustion so the doctor would stop asking him to see what was not there. He laid awake another hour keeping his eyes clamped shut, the darkness behind his lids was much more palatable than the light beyond them. In time, he fell asleep, remembering right as he went under to ask again about his friends.

The following morning the ICU nurse came in to

inform him he was getting out of the ICU unit and would again be able to receive visitors and didn't he feel lucky?

He didn't.

The same doctor from the night before stopped in to sign Mike's discharge papers to be released from his ward.

"What about now, Mike, can I take a look at your eyes?"

"My friends first, Doc—where are they?" Mike asked.

There was a longer than normal pause as the doctor sought the appropriate words that wouldn't keep Mike any longer in his charge.

"Were they hurt as bad as me?" Mike asked, straining to keep his voice under control.

The doctor could think of no way in which to soften the blow. "They didn't make it, Mike."

"They?" Mike begged. "Oh, God, no." Tears squeezed through his tightly closed lids.

"I'm sorry, Mike, they died the night of the accident."

Mike opened both his eyes the vertigo rushed in to fill the void in his soul. Through one eye he saw a tear stained reflection of a caring individual the other, wild lights flickered all around the shadow of the man sitting in front of him. For the briefest of moments a red beam of light flickered on the side of the doctor's head drowning out all else.

"Aneurysm," Mike shot the word out not knowing why.

"No," the doctor replied, perplexed. "Your friends?"

"No, you," Mike said looking into the eyes of the doctor with one brown eye and one white.

The gaze was startling and the doctor pushed his chair away from the bedside momentarily stunned by what he felt were absolute truths in Mike's words. "Sorry," the doctor said, shrugging away the after-effects of what he felt, later telling himself it was merely stress. Although a month-and-a-half later when the blood vessels burst in his eye and he had time to have one final thought before his head crashed down onto the pavement outside the hospital, he realized Michael Talbot had been right.

Mike winced as the doctor flashed his penlight into his pigment-less eye. It wasn't the brightness of the beam that hurt, it was the shadow it cast onto his mind.

"I think we need to let your eye heal as much as it can on its own without any outside influences," the doctor said, rising from the chair. He wanted to put a patch over that all-seeing eye as much for his own sake as Mike's. "I'll be right back," he said, although it was the duty nurse that came back to fit him properly with the patch.

Mike felt much better an hour later as he was wheeled down to the regular part of the hospital, where his whole family had again gathered.

"Don't you guys have to work?" Mike said weakly. His mother laughed and cried simultaneously as she rushed to his bedside. Mike moved his right arm up to place it on her shoulder as her face was buried in his chest.

"He moved his arm!" Gary yelled.

Mike hadn't even realized he had done it until it was pointed out to him.

"You're so cold," Mike's mother said as she briskly rubbed her son's arms.

"Is it true about Paul and Dennis?" Mike asked. The room which was a moment ago alive with pleasure quickly dimmed to sorrow.

"They didn't suffer," Mike's dad said as he came up to the other side of the bed.

"I don't think that's what he was concerned about, Tony," Mary said snappishly.

"How do you know what he's concerned about? Are you all of a sudden a goddamned mind reader?"

"I know if you hadn't been up in shit-kickerville maybe this wouldn't have happened!" she shot back with a healthy dose of heat.

"Get out," Mike said barely above a whisper, but the words had a force behind them.

Mary and Tony both stopped their argument to look down at their son.

"Mike, I'm sorry," Tony said.

"Go," Mike said with resignation.

Anthony, a former Marine who had seen combat in World War II and now ran a heavy equipment construction crew, was a leader of men, acquiesced to that simple request without so much as 'well, how do you do'.

Tony walked through the door, and if he possessed a tail it would have been neatly tucked between his legs. Mary made sure she was second out the door as if that somehow mattered in their twisted little drama.

"They're just concerned, Mike, we all have been," Ron said, filling in his mother's vacated spot.

"I'm just sick of the fighting, Ron. I don't remember a time in my life where they weren't bickering like schoolyard children. I've asked Dad before why he didn't get a divorce. You want to know what he said?" Mike asked.

Ron nodded.

"He said he stayed because of us kids. I told him he wasn't doing us any favors. He got pissed and left the room. I felt bad, but it was the truth."

"Why are you telling me this, Mike?" Ron asked.

"Because maybe I realized you don't get second chances in this life and to compromise is to give up."

"You're a little young to be giving life lessons aren't you?"

"I saw the other side," Mike said, leaving that statement hanging heavy in the air.

Lyndsey waited impatiently for more. "You can't just say that and not continue," she said testily.

"There were no pearly gates, no Saint Peter in long robes, no fluffy clouds, no fucking harps, it was a gray world devoid of all color. I was alone, there was no group of ancestral loved ones coming to meet me. I was naked, cold and alone – how's that sound for an eternity?"

"Sounds more like a dream," the ever pragmatic Ron added.

Lyndsey was rapt to the conversation with fear and intensity. This went against everything all of them had been taught during their Catholic upbringing. Ron had completely rebelled and damn near broke their mother's heart when he told her he was agnostic. He believed in a higher power, just not necessarily Jesus.

"Does this look like a fucking dream?" Michael yelled, lifting his patch up revealing his pale eye.

Ron looked slightly embarrassed or perhaps it was chagrined, but he wasn't going to back down, either. "Mike, that happened in the accident."

"Don't get condescending with me!" Mike yelled. "Yeah, happens all the time doesn't it, pigmentation leaving an eye."

"Then what is it?" Lyndsey asked almost wishing she hadn't, but unable to stop herself.

"I was counted, and marked," Mike told them reverently.

"What, like your soul or something? That's ridiculous." Ron's voice was rising. It wasn't so much that he was refuting his brother as it was he wanted to deny the entire conversation's validity.

"Who counted you?" Lyndsey asked tremulously.

"You don't believe him do you? He bumped his head…hard. Who the hell knows what damage he did?" Ron said, turning to his sister, but she wasn't paying him any attention.

"Your aura is tinged with red, Ron," Mike said indifferently.

"Aw, so now you can see auras, maybe you should take your show on the road. What else can you see?" Ron asked sarcastically.

"I see lots of things…and not many of them are good."

Lyndsey moved slightly to her right, Ron blocking her direct line of sight to Mike. She had secrets to hide and until she knew what her baby brother could and couldn't see, she didn't want any part of it. Even still, she saw a look of surprise on Mike's face when he caught her eye. It happened so fast she thought she just imagined it.

"I'm getting the doctor, I think some counseling could do you good," Ron said. He turned to leave the room.

"Cocaine's a bad drug, Ron—wouldn't you agree?" Mike asked him.

Ron stopped for the briefest of moments then pulled the door open quickly stepping out of the room.

Mike put his patch back in place, he almost felt normal.

"We'll be back later." Gary followed Ron. Glenn gave a wave and was next out.

Only Lyndsey stayed behind. "I'm only nineteen, Mike. I wanted to have my own life first."

"It would've been a girl," Mike said, rolling over on his side, facing away from his sister.

The visits became less and less frequent, whole days would go by without a Talbot sighting. At first Mike was distraught, but as each passing hour went by, it seemed like somehow this was how it was meant to be.

It was close to two months after the accident when Mike was finally going to be discharged from the hospital. He wondered if he would have to take the bus to get home. His father waited outside in the loading zone as an orderly wheeled Mike out on a cold and blustery winter day.

"Mike," Tony said tersely.

Mike did not reply. He leaned his head against the cool glass, staring out the passenger side window. Only once did he lift his patch to see what the world had to offer outside the hospital walls. The darkness with which the world was enshrouded made this dreary day seem like a spring festival. He quickly made sure the patch was back in place before he opened his eyes again.

"You alright?" Tony asked. They were the only two words he uttered the entire car ride.

Once again, Mike didn't answer.

***

"Michael Talbot yet lives, Mr. Black," Simon Peter said to the dark entity before him.

Mr. Black produced a large dark ledger from his robes. He spent a moment shifting through the voluminous pages. "Ah, here it is. That is impossible. I collected him on October 11th at 3:33 AM. I can most assuredly tell you he is where he should be."

Simon Peter swept his arm, a vision of a small ranch home came into view, more importantly the lone figure sitting on the couch reading the Bible.

***

Mike looked around when he felt he was no longer alone.

***

Simon Peter swept his arm back and the image was gone. "Fix it."

Mr. Black, his face expressionless, gave a small bow and left.

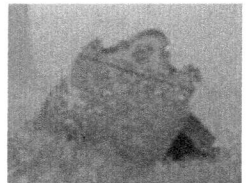

CHAPTER THREE – The Meeting

Mike stayed at home the last few weeks leading up to the Christmas break. Most of the time was spent in his room where occasionally, he would venture out to get some food. Not once did he sit at the table with his mother and father whose fighting had almost come to a standstill. It wasn't so much that they had made peace with each other as it was a grand détente. The silence was anything but peaceful; Mike could feel the tension mounting every day. Eventually, the collection of so many negative thoughts would need to be vented, but surprisingly, Mike just didn't give a shit. They were a toxic pair and for the life of him he could not figure how they got close enough to each other to produce five offspring. Maybe they used to drink heavily, he mused.

Lyndsey was the first to arrive on Christmas Eve. She was going to be home earlier in the week but she lied about having to make up some school work she had missed. She avoided Mike subliminally, she wasn't even aware she was doing it. When he would come into the kitchen she would go to the living room with a platter of meat and cheese, when he would come out to get something she would go into the kitchen to refill her glass of wine, which never seemed to be empty but not for lack of trying.

Ron completely skipped the traditional Talbot get together, saying he wasn't feeling so well. Well there was that and he was also elbow deep in two eight balls of his favorite recreational pharmaceutical.

Gary came about an hour later. He seemed the least affected by all that had happened in the recent past. Of the entire Talbot clan, he was the only one who wore a smile.

Glenn ever the trouble starter had made sure to find as pretty a psychic as he could so he could pass her off as his girlfriend. It had cost him a hundred and fifty bucks for her night of services but he considered it well worth the money and the potential for mischief she could bring to the dinner table. He had thought about 'coming out of the closet' this year even though he wasn't gay just to see the reactions from his family and then this had presented itself. He figured if it didn't go well, he would go with Plan B. It was going to be an interesting night in the Talbot household one way or another.

"Dinner in ten minutes!" Tony yelled as he placed the large turkey on the counter top. "Just got to let this rest for a few minutes then I'll carve it up," he said more to himself than anyone else.

As much as Lyndsey was avoiding Mike. This was more than made up for by the psychic Glenn had brought. She was constantly looking over at him; so much so, he was convinced his fly was open.

A few minutes later, Tony brought a large platter overflowing with warm succulent turkey to the table. Mary and Lyndsey were shuffling back and forth with various dishes and baskets of sides, including gravy, stuffing, green bean casserole, rolls, and everybody's favorite that nobody eats, the cylindrical jelled *can*berries.

Mike was last to the table. He had taken the time to return to his room and put the Bible he had been reading back. It had been his eighth go around with the Book of Revelations.

"There's no seat," Mike said, looking at everyone getting ready to eat.

"Sure there is, just sit down at one. I set the table earlier," Mary answered, never looking up.

Lyndsey stole a glance at her brother and then at everyone at the table. "There isn't, Mom," she answered sheepishly.

"There has to be—" Mary stopped short. "Oh, I'm sorry, honey," she said never looking directly at Mike. "I didn't know Glenn was going to bring a guest."

"Her name is Denise, Mom, and we're in love," Glenn hammed up.

Mary didn't swallow a bit of that, she was just biding her time until she figured what her son was up to. The boy could get in trouble in a padded room with nothing more to occupy his time than a wet sponge.

"That shouldn't have mattered," Mike said. "Ron cancelled after you put the place settings down."

A shiver ran up Mary's spine and it was even more unnerving because she didn't know why. Mary got up to get another plate and Tony rose to find a folding chair.

"Don't worry about it. I'm not all that hungry." Mike left the dining room. His mother did not protest and within another minute the conversation became as lively as ever with a constant smattering of laughter.

It was forty-five minutes later when Denise knocked on Mike's bedroom door. He had been wondering when she'd get the nerve.

"Hi, Mike, do you mind if I come in?" she asked as she peeked her head around the door.

"You might as well. I've got a feeling you will no matter what I say," Mike answered. He was sitting up in his bed reading the Bible, searching for answers it did not contain.

"Do you know I'm a psychic?" she asked.

"Well, it was either that or a pedophile," Mike told her.

She laughed. "So you caught me looking at you."

"I would have went with ogling or even sight rape, but if you want to call it looking…that's fine."

She laughed again. It was the first time since the accident that Mike almost felt like doing the same.

"I can't get a true bead on you, Michael. It's like

you're not supposed to be here."

Mike was not liking the intense scrutiny and was trying to deflect some of it. "I could say the same about you."

This time she did not laugh, but kept peering as if she were concentrating on a particularly difficult trigonometry problem. There was no mirth in her gaze. "It's just that no matter how I try to look at you, I'm always getting a sidelong glance. I...I can't 'see' you head on and I don't know why."

Mike lifted his patch. Denise instantly paled.

"Ohmigod," she gasped. Backing up, she asked if he would please put it down.

She was just regaining some color when Glenn waltzed into the room. "Come on, Denise, I didn't pay you all that money to babysit. You need to come out and tell some juicy fortunes while we eat dessert."

"Sure-sure," she said, taking one long glance back at Mike as she was willingly escorted from the room.

***

Mike actually looked forward to resuming the school year. He hoped it could restore some normalcy in his life. And partly it did, but he could not shake the echoes of his two best friends. Their memories reverberated at every turn. Home room was one of the worst as Mike continually found himself turning to the empty seat behind him waiting for Dennis to ask him what they were going to do for lunch or if he thought Beckie Windenthal's tits were bigger today. And they did seem so, he wanted to tell his departed friend.

"Mike. Mike, honey," his homeroom teacher, Mrs. Jenkins, said. "The bell has rung. It's first period."

It took Mike more than a few moments longer to respond, Mrs. Jenkins got up to see if he was alright. She was within arm's distance when Mike's gaze refocused from the thousand yards out it had been.

"Where is everyone?" he asked, confused, looking up

at his concerned teacher's face.

"The bell has rung—do you need me to write you a note?" she asked.

"For what?" he asked just as the second bell rang.

"I've got to go, Michael, I have study hall in the cafeteria. Hold on and I'll write you a pass."

Mike absently grabbed it and headed out of the classroom and straight out the nearest exit. He found himself at the frozen, snow-covered football field where he, Paul, and Dennis had led the Walpole Rebels to a near perfect season. He stood there on what he assumed was the fifty yard line, oblivious to the snow he was almost knee deep in. The quiet was soothing as a light snow began to fall and a northeasterly breeze began to stir.

Mike could hear the approaching footfalls but kept his gaze heavenward.

"You come here often?" Yvette Nickerson asked. She had been Paul's girlfriend for six months up until the accident. And in adjusted high school time, that was damned near an eternity.

Mike knew on some level Yvette was hoping for some levity in her choice of words but he answered dryly. "I used to," Mike said, never moving his gaze. He finally looked at her. "But I won't, not ever again."

"Did he say anything about me…when…when he died?" Yvette asked.

Mike wanted to shout and swear at her. *Yeah bitch it's all about you! While he was roasting like a fucking duck in a deep fryer he was yelling his undying love, you stupid fuck!* He shook his head. "I was unconscious, Yvette. I'm sure he did, though."

"I miss him, Mike."

"Me too," he told her.

"Heather tried to kill herself," Yvette said. Heather and Dennis had only been going out for a month or so and even in adjusted high school time that wasn't a ton, but she was kind of a drama queen. "Her mom found her in the bathroom with cuts on her wrists."

"Cross or length wise?" Mike asked.

"What?"

"Were the cuts across the veins or up slicing them in two?"

"What's the difference? And it was cross wise." She motioned on her own wrist which direction the cuts had gone.

"Cross wise is someone just seeking attention. If she really wanted to do herself in she would have split the vein open lengthwise like a pea pod. The blood drains out a lot quicker that way and it's much more difficult to repair."

"What is wrong with you? Don't you care?"

"Not really," Mike told her honestly.

"I thought we could mourn together," Yvette said angrily.

"Why? It won't bring them back."

"You're an asshole!" She stormed away.

"Well, at least that's something," Mike said, again returning his gaze skyward. He stayed there long enough for snow to start gathering on his eyelashes, when the niggling in the back of his head let him know he wasn't alone.

"I know you're there."

"Impressive," a voice said from underneath the bleachers.

Mike looked hard but could not see from where the voice issued.

Jandilyn Hollow came out from behind and approached. She was pretty in the 'I am going to get you in so much trouble' kind of way. She was type-cast as the school slut, but Mike had always assumed that was the talk of jealous girls who were mad at how easily beauty came to her.

"Are you sure your reputation can stand being seen with me?" she asked, taunting him as she approached.

"At this point, I think it might be the other way

around."

"What?" she mocked. "The great and mighty Talbot has fallen from his perch—what in heaven's name shall we do?" She placed her hands theatrically against the side of her face.

"That's pretty good," Mike said, lifting one corner of his mouth in a wry smile.

"Sorry about your friends. I didn't really know them, but they seemed nice enough."

Mike ignored her entreaty. "Is it true what they say about you?" he asked her.

"What do you think?"

"I think it's a bunch of horseshit perpetuated by a bunch of small-minded, bitchy girls."

She laughed. "That's much closer to the truth than they would have you believe," she said, still approaching. "Is what they say about you true?"

"I wouldn't know. Not many people are talking to me, lately. And whatever it is, I'm sure there's some truth to it."

"Are you still dating Tara Big-titties?"

"Bigelow?" he snorted. "No, when she found out I was most likely never going to play football again she dumped me.

"She's a bitch."

"I agree," Mike told her.

"Are you going to ask me out?" Jandilyn asked.

"I wasn't planning on it."

"Do you drive?"

"I doubt I ever will." He pointed to his patch.

"Oh, right. Alright, I'll pick you up at seven on Friday."

"What?" Mike asked. "I didn't even ask you out."

"Don't worry, you'll have fun." She began to walk away, stopped, then turned. "But not *that* much fun." She smiled and left.

Mike had to admit, he appreciated the view from this angle. By the time he went back into the school the sixth and final period was beginning. He hung out in the locker room, staring at Paul's locker, number sixty-nine. Paul had paid Freddy Griffith two packs of smokes to change with him.

"Gotta love the sixty-nine, Mike," Paul had bragged as they sat on this very bench.

Mike wasn't sure. He was no virgin, he just hadn't had an opportunity yet to try this particular position. Anything more than a hand job, or a blowjob was kind of tough in the front seat of a Buick Skylark. And the couple of times he and Tara had actually found a spare bedroom at a party it was more the thrusting of the inexperienced than anything exploratory.

"I miss you, Paul," Mike said, staring at the lock now protecting belongings that would never be claimed by their rightful owner. More than likely they would be put in a box and given to Barb who would probably donate them to the local Salvation Army. But would even *they* want a used jock strap; and who would buy it? Mike did not want to dwell long on that thought.

He couldn't help but fixate on that latch. His heart began to stutter in his chest. Mike's vision started to tunnel, he didn't want to pass out here. The students inside the gymnasium playing dodge ball would be done in another fifteen minutes and if they found him sprawled out on the floor it would just sprout a bunch of questions he wasn't willing or able to answer.

"Just open it," he said aloud. Mike knew the combination, the locker room was a lot closer to most of Mike's classes and Paul had given him the combo so he didn't have to lug his books all over the place.

The lock was warm to the touch when Mike grabbed it. It felt as if it had been in the firm grasp of someone moments ago. "I figured it would be ice cold, or maybe that's just me. Twenty-nine right, seven twice to the left, back up to two." Mike was sure the lock wouldn't open, as he pulled down gently, the clasp let go like it had a hundred times before, now he wasn't so sure there was anything in there he wanted to see. "It's smelly fucking gym shorts, Talbot—what are you doing?" he asked himself as he lifted the handle, the door squealed open, sounding like a crypt door in much need of some oil.

The smell of a long forgotten lunch assailed Mike's nose. That or Paul had taken a shit in there, which was entirely possible knowing his friend. "No, he would have done it in somebody else's." Mike picked up the baggie of whatever type of food had liquefied and hastily tossed it in the trash.

"Books and dirty clothes. What was I expecting?" Mike asked. But his roiling gut said there was more to look at. He pulled the books out carelessly, under the Chemistry book was the familiar bright orange yellow envelope that housed developed pictures. Mike had to force himself to grab the sleeve of pictures, he had no idea what to hope for when he began to thumb through the photos, but it certainly wasn't anything he had been expecting. "These are pictures from Nina McInerney's party last summer. I took some of them. Why didn't he ever show them to me?" Mike asked as he got a pang of sorrow every time the frame was centered on either Paul or Dennis. "These are just normal pictures, not even incriminating. None of us are holding beers or bongs—that would be way worse."

But something was wrong with them, he just couldn't put his finger on it until the third go round through the stack. By then the first bell had rung signifying the end of the last class of the day. Sweaty freshmen resplendent with red ball welts flooded into the locker room. No one questioned his presence or why he was going through the 'dead kid's' stuff. They walked around him as if he were merely another physical object they needed to navigate.

Mike was still standing there when every last kid had

vacated the school grounds except for those unlucky few that were spending some quality time with the principal. He had sat back down on the bench looking for something in the photos that would release him from the visual nightmare he now grasped in his hand.

It was the portraits of Paul that had first caught his attention. The first one he was going to catch a Frisbee. The sun was over his right shoulder and was so bright it almost washed out the entire image, the rays licking his body in a hundred fiery kisses. In the next Paul was standing by the grill. When Mike had stopped to take the picture, Paul saw him and started to ham it up. Mike thought he may have been yelling something about his sister wanting to date him. But the snap of the shot had coincided with a flare up from the grill and from the angle Mike had taken the picture it appeared that Paul's left side was ablaze and his taunting yell now looked like a scream for help.

Mike was feeling anxious. Every picture of Paul at the party in some way showed him with fire. Mike finally thought he had broken the trend at the last one. Paul had his arm draped around his girlfriend, and then Mike's heart dropped when he saw Larry Sullivan in the background laughing as he was trying to light his cigarette. As a joke, someone had turned up the butane so it looked more like a small flame thrower than a coffin nail igniter.

"It's just a coincidence," Mike told himself to steady his nerves. "But did Paul see something in these pictures and that's why he didn't want me to see them?"

There were four pictures of Dennis, the first showed him right after taking a bong hit (the bong was not present in the photo). But Mike knew it was in his hands out of frame because he had just handed it to him. Dennis was struggling to hold the hit in, tendrils of smoke leaked from his nose and mouth. In the second photo, Dennis had been manning the grill, a large plume of smoke had almost completely obscured him in the image. The other two revealed anomalies just as significant.

"What do mine look like then?" Mike asked, his hands visibly shaking. The first one showed him sitting under an elm tree in Nina's backyard. "Nothing weird about that, right?" he asked, scanning the entire image for fire, smoke, evil clowns or leprechauns. He felt somewhat better but the feelings of dread would not abate.

He flipped through until he found the next one of him, his grip so tight his fingers began to hurt. Sweat beaded up on his forehead and began to flow down his head. He was holding up his non-criminal red plastic cup as a toast to the picture taker, Paul. This time he was in the center of the yard, he knew this because he had taken a break from the Frisbee game of 'tips' to get a swallow of his beer, the sun had been blazing bright and there wasn't a cloud in the sky, yet he was bathed in shadows. Mike quickly stood up, tossed the pictures back into the locker and left the school. His mind was racing.

"It was just a plane flying overhead or a giant fucking bird," Mike muttered, his hands buried deep in his coat pockets as he walked home.

Mike got home an hour later, still not able to give any rational explanation for what he had just seen. The house was quiet except for the sobs coming from down the hallway. He quickly walked toward his bedroom where his door was slightly ajar. He slowly pushed the door open, his mother was sitting on the bed, his pillow in her arms, tears free-flowing as she rocked back and forth, crying about her baby.

"Mom?" Mike asked with concern. If she heard him she did not respond. "Mom!" he said with more force.

Mary looked up, black streaks of mascara ran in runnels down her tired face. For the briefest of moments Mike saw the confusion in her eyes as she looked at him. "Mike?" she asked tremulously, then stood up. "I thought you were dead!" She sobbed anew. "I was taking a nap and I had a dream. It was all the same as the night I got the call from your sister. Everything! Even the damn nasty Swedish meatballs your Aunt Teresa brought to the card game. I rushed there, and when the doctor finally came out, he said the third time you had died on the operating table they were not able to resuscitate you! It…it was so real, I…I thought you were dead. I even dreamed about all the times since the day of the accident I had come in here and cried, holding your pillow to my face, hoping I could smell just a little bit of you. When I awoke, I thought it was the truth." She hung her head.

Mike had a discordant thought go through him that perhaps it would have been better if he had died. At least that way the loved ones in his life could grieve and move on, and he could stop always walking in the shadows. An icy cold finger scratched up his spine.

"Maybe it is," Mike said softly.

Instead of responding, Mary arose from the room and brushed past him without a backward glance, leaving a trail of tears in her wake.

***

Mike finished the rest of his school week, noticing all the teachers were willing without a second thought to give him a coveted hall pass. Sometimes he went to class and would venture out midway through; an act that would have brought severe penalties before the accident didn't even garner a glance now. He mostly wandered around the school, but never once going back to the locker room. He hoped Gradity, the janitor, had thrown the damn pictures away.

He didn't run into Jandilyn again that week and almost chalked her up to a hallucination right until she beeped her horn promptly at 8:15 PM.

"Nice car," Mike said. "You're late."

"It's my mom's and looking this good takes time," she said, waving her hand in a circular motion around her face."

He had to admit she did look beautiful.

"Where we going?" Mike asked.

"You're taking me out, remember?" When she saw the look of mild terror on his face she pressed on. "You mean I have to pick you up and pay for the date? You'd better put out." She laughed.

Mike couldn't tell if he was embarrassed, flattered, amused, or mortified. All of those emotions vied for his attention. They ended up at a mom-and-pop coffee house, Ye Old Stomping Grounds.

"I love coffee. You?" she asked as they got out of the car.

Mike didn't think it mattered much what his response was, they were going in either way. And besides, she was paying. He shrugged his shoulders as she held the door open for him.

"This date is over if you ask me whether you look fat or not in those jeans," Jandilyn said as she went up to the counter. "Double espresso latte, heavy on the whipped cream and whatever my silent friend back there orders," she said, pulling out a pink *Power Girls* wallet.

"Nice," Mike told her. "I'll take a large iced coffee."

"How uncouth," Jandilyn said as she handed the 'pop' of the mom-and-pop a ten dollar bill.

Within five minutes, they were sitting at a booth on the far side of the small establishment. Mike suddenly felt self-conscious as Jandilyn was studying him intently.

"Why did you want to go out on this date?" he asked her, finally lifting his eye to meet hers.

"You really are a good-looking cat," she said, almost ignoring Mike's initial question.

"Jandilyn, stop looking at me like that. It's uncomfortable."

"Sorry," she said, shaking her head as if awakening from a trance. "You were just standing in the middle of that field and I knew there was something different about you. You were no longer the jock, party animal asshole."

Mike raised his eyebrows at the 'asshole' remark.

"It's the truth," she said, defending her words.

"Jerk, maybe, but asshole?" he questioned.

"One girl's jerk is another girl's asshole." Jandilyn stopped. "Did I really just say that?"

Mike was grinning. "At least now I know how you got your reputation."

She reached over and punched him in the shoulder. "You looked vulnerable out there, that was the Mike I wanted to get to know." She seated herself back in her booth.

"Did you see anything else?" Mike probed, wondering just how deep her insight might go.

"There's a sadness about you that's more than just the deaths of your friends."

Mike let go of his iced coffee as if that was what was chilling his heart.

"I answered your question, now I want to know why you agreed to come out with me."

"I was looking for a good time." Mike put up his hands when Jandilyn started to rise and come over the table again. "Wait, I'm just going by what was on the bathroom wall."

"Funny." She smirked.

"Truth?"

"That would be nice."

"You're the first person since the night of the accident that has looked at me rather than through me. I don't know how to explain it Jandilyn, but I don't feel like I belong here."

"Nobody feels like they belong in Walpole, this is just a way-station to bigger and better places."

It was much more than Walpole, Mike thought. Any place with a physical address would not feel right and what scared him was he didn't know why he felt that way.

"What's it like to only have one eye?" she asked, again studying his face.

"You shouldn't be shy, if you've got a question just ask," Mike said as he swallowed down a heavy swig of his coffee.

She snorted. "Sorry, my mom says I'm too blunt for my own good." She waited for a response.

Mike kept waiting and waiting, hoping she would drop the subject he did not want to talk about. After a lengthy silence he knew she wasn't going to be dissuaded.

"I have both my eyes," he said, hoping that would suffice but knowing it wouldn't.

"Why the pirate get-up then? Halloween's already past."

"I think it makes me look cool."

"You're being trite."

"I'm not sure I know what that means."

"Well, if you weren't getting your head knocked around playing football all those years, you might know."

"Fine." Mike slowly lifted the eye patch, the kaleidoscope of colors he saw sitting across from him made his head swim, dizziness threatened to make him fall out of his bench seat which would have been less than impressive on a first date. He immediately put the patch back in place, but the damage was already done to a stomach that would not settle down for another two hours.

Jandilyn was plastered against her booth as if she had been exposed to a micro-burst hurricane that had merged her into her red vinyl seat back.

"What the fuck was that?" she asked, her complexion pale, her lips a trembling blue.

"I've got to go home," Mike said, rising from his seat and spilling the remaining iced coffee across the table. He started heading for the door, oblivious to Jandilyn's open-mouthed stare.

He was a half mile away from the café walking

tersely when Jandilyn rolled up next to him in her mother's Volkswagen Cabriolet.

He didn't even notice her as she matched his pace. She rolled down the window. "Mike, get in. It's freezing out there and you've got another six or seven miles."

Mike looked over at her. It was freezing, actually significantly colder than that at ten degrees Fahrenheit, but he felt none of it. All he could think about was Jandilyn's disgusted, fear-frozen face as she stared into the abyss of his colorless eye.

"I'm sorry about the way I reacted. I…I mean I've never seen anything…I mean felt anything like that."

"Felt?" Mike asked softly.

"Please get in the car. I'd like to talk about it."

"That's the thing, Jandilyn, I'd rather not." He stopped so he could face her.

"Alright, I promise I won't say another word about it unless you bring it up. Just get in."

Mike thought this was dubious at best, but he also knew she wouldn't leave him out here. And he'd be damned if he walked the whole way home with her following in the car. The car ride was an uneasy silence. Mike could tell Jandilyn was close to chewing through the side of her cheek trying not to talk. It probably hadn't helped that she was cracking on a double dose of caffeine, either.

Mike hadn't said a word as she pulled up to his house, the porch light was out as if everyone who should have been in, already was. He didn't say a word to Jandilyn as he exited the car and shut it behind him. Jandilyn watched him for a moment longer and then sped away. He never turned to watch her go. Mike walked through the front door and walked back out when he heard his mother sobbing from the direction of his room.

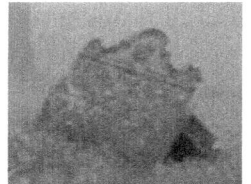

CHAPTER FOUR – The Meeting Part Two

It was Friday of the next week when Jandilyn was finally able to corner Mike.

"Do you even go to this school?" she asked breathlessly. "I've been trying to find you since Monday. You're like a ghost."

Mike let those last words hang for a moment as he thought about them. "You know this is the boys' bathroom, right?"

"I know, I tried to catch you before you came in." She looked around. "I wish I could pee standing up. I hate public rest rooms—who knows where someone else's ass has been?"

Mike had never thought of that, but now that she brought it up, it was pretty disgusting. He filed that away for future thought. "Jandilyn, what do you want?"

Jandilyn looked hurt. "You know I've been going to your classes, asking your teachers where you are, most of them look at me like I'm crazy or they just shrug their shoulders. I don't get what's going on, Mike. Your homeroom teacher always says she thinks she wrote you a hall pass, but usually can't remember. I don't even know why you stay at the school, you're never in class."

"Where else can I go?" Mike asked with hurt in his voice.

The door to the bathroom pushed in.

"Go find somewhere else to tinkle!" Jandilyn shouted. The door pulled shut quickly. "Must have been a freshman."

"I lost more than my friends in that accident, Jandilyn."

"You can get through this, Mike, and I'd like to help."

"I saw the horror in your face, Jandilyn. I think I scare the shit out of you."

"Then I guess we're in the right place." She spread her arms. "What time do you want me to pick you up tonight?"

Mike sighed and dropped his head a bit. "You're not going to leave me alone, are you?"

"Probably not, the restraining orders people have filed on me didn't stop me, I don't see why your feeble attempts to push me away will work."

"Same time will be fine," Mike said. The smallest hint of a smile cracked his lips.

"I'll let you get back to your business, but I'd put down a couple layers of toilet paper if you're going to sit."

Mike waited until the door closed before producing the joint he had palmed when she had burst through the door like her hair was on fire. He lit the end and inhaled deeply, savoring the sweet smoke. When he exhaled he spoke. "Hi, Paul. Is it better where you're at?" He shuddered when he thought he heard a softly whispered 'no'.

After school, Mike took a detour to a place called Indian Hill, it was rumored to be an ancient Indian burial ground, but was more famous for being a party haven for teenagers. It was a fifty acre field surrounded on all sides by pines, oaks and elms. It had for a while been Paul, Dennis, and Mike's personal playground. Mike sat under a giant oak that stood as a lone sentinel in the center of the field. The trio had come up here many times in the last year; it was their oasis from the 'real world', a place to get away. Mike placed his hands against the monstrous tree. He could almost feel the life force thrumming through the trunk. Tears ran down his face as he pressed his forehead against the rough bark.

"I hurt so bad." He wept. The tree stayed stolid, but Mike could swear he felt something stir under his fingertips.

He pulled back quickly, looking closely at the tree. He saw nothing there, but something seemed to dash in and out of his peripheral vision. He turned quickly to try to catch it. When he didn't, he attributed it to an overactive imagination and trudged his way home.

It was after six when he got back, his parents had just finished eating and his mother was at the sink with hunched over shoulders as she presoaked the dishes, preparing them for the dishwasher. His father was sitting at the table with his head in his hands. Mike shut the door and walked down to his room, neither parent acknowledged his presence.

Jandilyn beeped her horn promptly at 9:12.

"You're getting worse," Mike said as he slid into the passenger seat.

"Hungry?" she asked.

"You know you have a bad habit of ignoring me?"

"I packed a picnic."

"Well, I'm glad we got that part of the uncomfortable conversation out of the way. You do know that most people do picnics at noon?"

Her eyes asked 'do we look like most people?'

"Fine, where are we going?"

Mike's heart almost stopped when she spoke. "Indian Hill."

"Were you there today?"

She looked over at him when she caught the tremor in his voice. "No, were you?"

"For a little bit. How do you know about that place?"

"You and your friends aren't the only ones who go. In fact, I've seen you three a lot up there." She laughed when she saw Mike's expression. "Relax, I won't tell anyone about where your secret fort and stash of booze are."

"How the hell could you follow us around and we not know?"

"I'm good at hiding in the shadows."

Mike shivered, thinking back to Paul's pictures.

"You know it's not exactly summertime," Mike said, trying to dissuade her from her present course. He had a feeling this just might not be the best idea.

"It's like forty-five degrees, damn near t-shirt weather for New England," she answered, his words having had little effect.

She was right; they were in the midst of an Indian summer. There was no snow on the ground and some plants had even foolishly poked their petals out, not realizing that a Massachusetts February was usually the harshest month of the year. They'd learn or they'd die.

Jandilyn parked her car under a small copse of trees next to the train trestle. From there they could look up to the Hill and right now it was as dark as a deep closet in a scared child's bedroom. Who knew what horrors were within its confines?

"You ready?" Jandilyn asked Mike, but he was under the impression she was trying to bolster her own courage.

"Let's get this over with," Mike said, getting out.

"Why, thanks," she said, reaching in the back to grab the bag of food she had prepared.

"I didn't mean it that way," Mike said. "I just don't think this is the best place to go right now."

"You don't really believe this is a burial ground do you?"

Mike really did. Jandilyn headed down the path that paralleled the train tracks for a couple of hundred yards before going down and then back up toward the hill. Neither spoke as they made the trek. Mike grabbed the bag and Jandilyn grabbed his free hand as they ascended. Mike, for one of the first times in months felt at peace. It was an uneasy peace, but it was a peace, nonetheless.

They sat under the protective branches of the giant oak. Jandilyn had brought a candle and a small blanket, which they sat on comfortably close. She produced a couple of sandwiches and Pop-Tarts for dessert.

"You do know the stomach is the way to a man's heart?" Mike asked as he took another bite of his peanut butter and jelly sandwich.

"This is fine cuisine," she said playfully.

"Is this what I have to look forward to if we get together?"

"I hope," she said as she snuggled closer.

Mike had his back against the tree. He wrapped his arms around Jandilyn who leaned up against him. Mike stiffened when he heard noise off to their right. So did Jandilyn.

"Did you hear that?" he whispered.

"It's the Indians come to gather us up," Jandilyn said in her spookiest voice.

"Not funny." Mike stood up.

"Hey, I was comfortable," she said as they could hear the noises getting closer and now they could even hear some murmuring voices. Mike had wished he had the foresight to blow out the candle, but whatever was heading their way had already seen it and were being drawn like a zombie to a brain. *Weird analogy*, he thought.

"So then I kicked him in his—" the voice drifted clear as a bell.

Mike didn't hear the rest because of Jandilyn's indrawn breath.

"What's the matter?" Mike asked, picking up on her distress.

"Old boyfriend. We should leave." She blew the candle out and grabbed Mike's hand.

"You're kidding, right?" But he didn't stop her.

They immediately froze when they were painted in the powerful beam of a flashlight.

"Whoa there, pardners. Where are you two off to in such a rush?" the owner of the flashlight asked.

Mike could hear at least one, maybe two other people snicker behind the taunting words, but he had been effectively night-blinded by the powerful torch. Jandilyn began to inch her way behind Mike. He was not getting a good feeling about this.

The flashlight swept over their blanket and still smoking candle, discarded sandwiches and juice boxes.

"Aww, that's so cute, isn't it?" the flashlight holder asked his buddies. And like a pack of hyenas, they laughed in response.

"Yeah, so cute."

"Kind of romantic really," the other said.

"How fast can you run?" Jandilyn asked, her body trembling behind him.

Mike had been pretty fast in his day, but with his lack of depth perception he'd be on the ground before he could go a hundred yards.

"Go," Mike said. "I'll be right behind you."

"You're lying. They'll hurt you bad."

Mike doubted they could hurt him any further than he felt most of the time, but he was talking metaphysically not physically. He figured they could hurt him plenty physically.

Flashlight man was within twenty feet now and the window of escape had closed. Mike could feel the intensity of the beam shift a bit from his face to over his shoulder.

"Jandilyn?" asked the voice.

"Durgan," she said resignedly.

"What is my girlfriend doing out in the middle of the night with this one-eyed turd?"

"One-eyed turd," Buffoon Two mimicked, laughing with a sneer.

"I'm not your girlfriend," she said softly.

"One would almost think you were walking out on me."

"Don't you get it?" she asked with some force. "We went out once. I realized how big of a fucking jerk you were and never went out with you again."

Mike was having a hard time understanding why she

was poking the beehive, so to speak. The flashlight finally went off, it was long moments before the sliver of moon could cast its pale light upon the unfolding scene. Mike hoped it was some sort of trick of light or the perspective from which he was looking at Durgan, but the guy was huge.

"You should have told me you went out with the Incredible Hulk," Mike said to Jandilyn softly.

"I'm so sorry," Jandilyn said as if she already knew how this part of the movie was going to play out.

"You know what happens to guys that try to go out with my girlfriend, don't you?" Durgan asked Mike.

"The giving of undying gratitude from the girl?" Mike asked back.

There was a long silence as Durgan tried to wrestle the meaning out of the words.

"What the fuck did he just say?" Durgan asked one of his henchmen.

"Something about not dying," one responded.

"Wrong answer," Durgan said to Mike. "Because they most certainly will."

"So you're really into Rhodes Scholars then?" Mike asked Jandilyn.

"That's funny, Mike, but this situation isn't." She shivered behind him.

"What are you two whispering about?" Durgan asked, coming closer.

"I was asking her about the theory of relativity," Mike said. It was the first thing that popped into his mind.

"That's right!" Durgan spat. "I'm gonna hurt you so bad your relatives are going to feel it."

"Were you drinking when you agreed to a date?" Mike asked.

Jandilyn didn't respond but he thought he could hear her nodding.

Mike gently pushed Jandilyn away as Durgan came closer. Mike had to crane his neck up to see the steroid-induced madman's face.

Mike had played football since he was old enough to put the pads on. He was never a big kid but there was a strength to his frame that belied his size, more than one opponent had underestimated him and paid the price. *Now or never*, Mike thought as he made a fist and swung for the fences.

Durgan had been completely caught unawares as Mike's fist slammed into the side of his face. Either the punch had to travel too high or the trajectory just didn't allow for enough force but besides a slight stagger backward Durgan seemed unaffected.

"Fuck me," Mike said, bringing his fist close to his chest, it felt like he had punched granite.

Durgan put his left hand up to his face, a shocked look crossed his features. "I can't believe you really did that. That takes some balls, man, it really does. I had thought about maybe just scaring you enough until you wet your pants so my girlfriend would see you for the girly-man you are, but then you go and hit me. Now I'm going to have to beat you into the dirt."

"Yeah, beat him into the dirt!" his goons yelled.

Mike never saw the strike from Durgan as it came up his blind side. The pain was excruciating, red dominated his field of vision as he fell to the ground.

Jandilyn came forward to help Mike up. Mike held his hand out to make her stop. Blood flowed from his lip as he pushed himself off the ground.

"Damn, you can take a punch, too!" Durgan smiled as he struck again from Mike's left side. The eye patch spun away wildly as Mike again found himself on the ground.

"You got him good, man!" Mike heard through a thickening cobweb of semi-cognitive thought.

Mike pushed himself off the ground, absently wiping the sod sticking to his busted lip, the taste all too reminiscent of his bygone football days.

Durgan leaned down. "There's no shame in staying down."

"No shame," Mike echoed, standing all the way up, swaying as if in the midst of a gale.

Mike was relieved when Durgan plowed his fist into his solar plexus, one more punch to the face and he was afraid it would cave-in.

"*Stop!*" Jandilyn screamed. The goons were laughing, Durgan wasn't.

"All he's got to say is uncle and to stop dating my girlfriend and I'll leave him alone."

Mike was on the ground desperately sucking for the elusive air that had been forced from his body. He hitched as he again began to stand. "Uncle?" he asked. "What are you? Eight?"

The next punch caught him again in the stomach, he was now in a vacuum where air was not present. Mike began to see bright pin pricks dance in front of his eyes as his body fought for air.

"You're killing him!" Jandilyn yelled, coming down to Michael's side. Durgan pushed her over with his foot and she rolled a couple of feet away. Mike pulled a sliver of air through his gritted teeth. He again stood up.

"Man, do you see that?" one of the goons asked.

"What?" the other goon asked. "See, what?"

A smaller light than the one Durgan used now clicked on in Mike's face. Mike thought the weight of the light alone might make him fall onto his knees.

"What the fuck is wrong with you?" Durgan asked, backing away, as Mike assumed the light was now shining on his pale eye.

"Busted…lip…maybe…concussion," Mike worked out.

"Your eye, man," Durgan said, pointing as if Mike weren't painfully aware of it. "The…the light doesn't shine on it, it kind of sucks it in. Shut the fucking thing off!"

Durgan said as he pushed the light from his friend's hand.

The flashlight hit the ground and went out. Nobody moved as everyone readjusted to the moonlight.

"Had enough?" Mike was able to get out in one breath.

"Whatever, man," Durgan said, clearly scared, but not wanting to let his cronies know. "You can keep her, she doesn't put out anyway. Let's go." The trio streamed by Mike, careful to stay more than an arm's length away.

Mike found himself swaying from their wake.

Jandilyn stood up and rushed over to Mike's side. "You alright?"

"Is it Tuesday?" he asked her.

"What?" she asked, wondering if he had possibly just suffered some brain damage.

"Because that's where I feel like I've been knocked into," he answered back.

"Is that a joke?" she asked as she led him back to the blanket.

"Sorry, they're usually better than that…having a hard time thinking clearly at the moment."

Jandilyn sat Mike down and wet a napkin with some juice-like substance from the little cardboard box. She very gently wiped the dirt grass and blood from his lip.

"Does that hurt?" she asked wincing.

"Only when you touch it," he said as he rested his throbbing head against the trunk of the tree, his eyes closed as she applied her ministrations.

"This is going to fucking kill then," Jandilyn said as she placed the most tender kiss he would ever feel on his lips. A spark of electricity from the contact coursed through his body.

"Did you feel that?" he asked as she pulled back.

"I did," she said, slightly out of breath. "You're my hero."

"Yup, I can take a beating like no one's business."

"Shut up," she told him as she tenderly kissed him again.

They stayed like that for another hour; she would occasionally kiss him as she tended to his cuts and abrasions.

At some point she had re-lit their candle and now held it up between them, Mike slightly turned and closed his left eye.

"Don't," she said, putting her hand softly on his chin.

Mike turned to face her, his heart pounding wildly. Here was someone he cared for and seemed to care for him also. He couldn't afford to lose her.

She did not pull back as she stared long and hard into both his eyes.

Shadows danced around her but all of that was drowned out by the shimmering bright pink light dotted with red that surrounded her like an oversized cloak.

"I've never met anyone like you, Mike," she said, still staring intently at him.

"Probably a good thing. We're going to have to go soon, I think there's a rock under my butt trying to get intimate, and not for nothing, but I would like a little more food than a peanut butter and jelly sandwich."

"You have a problem with my cooking?"

"I think maybe you should take Home Ec next semester."

"I wouldn't have taken you for a sexist." She laughed, helping him up.

Mike shrugged and immediately regretted the move as his bruised gut let him know exactly what it thought about that.

"You're a mess," Jandilyn said as she quickly picked up all the night's offerings and placed them back in the bag.

Mike tried to be as chivalrous as possible by not applying too much weight on Jandilyn as she became his crutch, but vertigo, lack of depth perception and a mild concussion had him staggering as if he had funneled a twelve pack, and that last was a feeling he had been acquainted with.

Crossing over the train trestle had been a particularly slow endeavor. Mike could only manage a step or two before he would need to take a rest, the dizzying height to the rushing water below was playing havoc on his misfiring synapses.

"I feel like I'm eighty," he said to Jandilyn.

"You're not going to make it that long if you don't get off this thing," she said looking back down the tracks where she wholeheartedly expected a train to come roaring any minute.

"Relax, the trains don't run this late." And almost as if in a direct response, a distant train whistle blew.

"Why, Michael Talbot, I think that is your first lie to me," Jandilyn said in mock shock.

"There'll be more, no need to celebrate this one. Hurry up and get me off this thing."

It was five full minutes after they were both sitting in Jandilyn's mom's car that the sixty-two car freight liner passed them by.

"I don't think even you could take a punch from that thing."

"Probably not. Home, James, my pillow beckons."

Jandilyn drove him home and helped him up the steps and into his house.

"Is no one home?" she asked, wondering why the house was in pure black out mode.

"My parents are."

"They don't leave a light on for you?" she asked.

"I don't think they believe I'm coming home." *Ever.* Mike's head was now in full tilt mode as he opened the front door. He could barely keep his eyes open. Eyes closed meant less spinning. If he had looked, though, he would have seen the figure that was darker than the surrounding gloom standing in the corner of the room.

"I'm good from here," he told Jandilyn.

"You sure?" she asked suspiciously. "Or is this lie number two?"

"This is going to be a depressing relationship if we count the untruths."

"Relationship?" Jandilyn asked. "You still want to go out with me?"

"I could ask you the same. Go home. We'll talk tomorrow." Mike gripped the loveseat, doing his best to keep from toppling over.

Jandilyn stood up on her toes and once again kissed him softly. "Goodnight, hero."

Hero, Mike thought. *That's hilarious, the only thing between me and the rug is my death grip on this seat.*

The door shut softy. A chill raced through Mike as he bumped from wall to wall down the hallway to his room. He knew somewhere from his football days that he should not go to sleep with a concussion for at least twenty-four hours; he was too tired to care. He noted that his pillow was wet with the tears from his mother as he fell into a blissful peaceful sleep, Jandilyn's name upon his lips as he dozed.

The remainder of the school year went by without incident. Mike mostly drifted from class to class if he showed at all. The majority of his time was either up at Indian Hill mourning the passing of his friends or with Jandilyn who kept the 'grays' as he came to call them at bay. With summer rapidly approaching the couple became inseparable. Not that either one had a plethora of friends who would give them too much of a hard time about it anyway.

***

"What do you mean you don't want to go, Jandilyn? You worked hard to get an internship at the Museum of Modern Art and it's in Paris. You won't get another opportunity like this," Gina Hollow said to her daughter, her exasperation clear. "It's about that boy isn't it?"

"His name is Mike, mom," Jandilyn said, almost rolling her eyes at a mother who didn't get it.

"Boys are a dime a dozen, Jandilyn. This is a once in a lifetime chance."

"Not this one, he's different," Jandilyn said, defending Mike.

"Does he have a penis?" Gina shouted.

Drew Hollow had walked into the room to find out what was happening and just as quickly left when he heard the 'P' word.

"Mom!" Jandilyn shouted back.

"Because if he does, then he's just like three billion other swinging dicks." Gina was upset and was having a hard time reining her tongue in.

"Could you be any more crude?" Jandilyn asked. "We're in love and that's all that matters."

"Did he tell you he loved you before or after?" Gina was full-throated shouting now.

"Not that it's any of your business, but we haven't done anything," Jandilyn answered evenly.

Jandilyn's dad did a small fist pump in the other room, thankful for his daughter's intact virtue.

"Well, you can be assured that when you do he'll be done with you and your chance to go to Paris will be long past."

"He needs me, Mom," Jandilyn said.

"It's one summer, Jandilyn, you need to think this through." Gina tried a more rational approach. *And maybe that loser will off his morose self.* Gina had tolerated Mike because her daughter seemed infatuated with him, but now he was actively destroying her daughter's future and she could not idly sit back and watch the disaster as it unfolded.

"I have thought it through," Jandilyn said, trying to put finality to the argument.

"This has been your dream for the last three years and now that you've achieved it you don't want it? I gave up so much in my life when I shacked up with your father, I don't want you to do the same."

Hey! Drew thought, *I'm right here!* But he remained silent, this was not an unfamiliar argument that was directed at him. They had also been high school sweethearts, both had intended on attending college but Gina had gotten pregnant and both of their lives had been forever altered, not that either complained about the outcome but, it had been a difficult first few years.

"I'm not like you," Jandilyn said. "I *know* what I'm doing," she stressed.

"When it all comes crashing down on you, I won't tell you 'I told you so', but I'll be thinking it," Gina said cruelly.

Brutal, Drew thought. He didn't know his wife had that sort of mean streak in her. He wondered what she said about him behind his back to her friends. He shuddered. *Better to not think about that*.

Gina stomped out of the kitchen and right past a surprised Drew. If she noticed him she made no acknowledgement, her anger had tunneled her vision.

"You alright?" Drew asked his daughter. She had her back to him and he thought she might be crying.

"Do you think I'm doing the wrong thing, Dad?" she asked, slightly hitching.

"Affairs of the heart are a serious thing. If you truly feel that strongly for the boy, who am I to say differently? Do I think you are giving up a great opportunity? Yes I do, but I don't think it will be the only shot you have. You work hard for what you want, Jandilyn, and very rarely do you let anything stand in your way. This summer is going to be a living hell for you, though. Your mother isn't going to let this go anytime soon. And if something should go south with you and this Mike character you had better at least pretend to keep going out with him."

Jandilyn laughed at that. "Thank you, Dad," she said,

turning around to give him a hug.

Yup I wouldn't change a thing, Drew thought as he held her close.

As the summer wore on, the heat outside did little to defrost the icy build-up between Jandilyn and her mother. Drew noted that the further Gina pushed away the closer Mike and Jandilyn got. He could not fathom how his wife wasn't privy to this parenting fundamental. More than once he had tried to broach the subject with her or at least diffuse the tension and she had told him in no uncertain terms if he ever wanted to have sex with her again then he'd better back off. Gina was not one for idle threats. Much to his chagrin, he acquiesced.

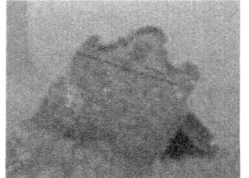

CHAPTER FIVE – Senior Year

Senior year was a blur. Mike did not attend one football game even though the season was dedicated to him and his dead friends. The Rebels went 3-5, their worst season in a decade-and-a-half. He barely managed to go to a class or two a day, he wasn't even sure why he bothered. Scratch that—he knew exactly why and her name was Jandilyn Hollow.

"Mike, I know you have Science next what are you doing on this side of the building?" Jandilyn asked as she exited her advanced English class. She feigned anger badly, her heart raced every time she saw him.

"I was lost and now I'm found," Mike told her, oblivious to the stares from their classmates.

The couple had become somewhat of a topic of discussion. Mike had fallen far from his perch but still the 'inners' couldn't believe how far down he would stoop to go out with the class pump. Mike had taken two of his classmates to task about rumors they were spreading about Jandilyn. They both had recanted their statements in blood.

***

"Why are they saying these things about you?" Mike had asked Jandilyn one day a few weeks previous. Jandilyn had been washing his bloodied knuckles.

She didn't look up as she applied some salve to his cuts. "I got in a fight with Renee McMahon back in the ninth grade—it started then."

Renee McMahon's father owned McMahon

Mortuaries, 'Where all your loved one's final needs are met'. The family was from money and Renee liked to let everyone know. She was the captain of the cheerleading squad and class vice president. Her nose was so upturned she had to go to the chiropractor weekly to realign her spine.

"The ninth grade? Isn't it over yet?"

"Oh, I'm sure it's over, but we haven't talked since then. Once the word is out that you're a slut, there's no return."

"But why now?" Mike asked, wincing as she pulled a piece of a tooth out of his index knuckle.

"Are you really so naïve?"

"What?"

"You do remember that, until recently, you were a *co-*captain on the football team."

"Dating a cheerleader," Mike finished with chagrin. "Jandilyn, I'm so sorry."

"Don't be, it isn't anything I haven't heard before, plus I get the added bonus of you," she said, kissing him on his cheek.

"What does she care? What do any of them care? None of them wanted anything to do with me after that goddamned accident," Mike said with vehemence.

"You were one of them, Mike. You were in the 'in' crowd. You had everything, at least as much as high schoolers are concerned. Maybe they didn't want to believe all they had could be taken just as quickly. Better to shun you than to try to accept what had happened."

"Wow, are we all that shallow?"

"Did you ever talk to me before the accident?"

"No," Mike said, bowing his head.

"Stop, Mike, don't go getting all soft on me. It's us now, we're a team, you and me. And you've got to promise me something." She looked up at him with her sky blue eyes.

"Anything."

"No more fights."

"Shit, I was going to add that exclusion."

"Mike!"

"Jandilyn, they are lying pieces of shit. I'm defending your honor."

"I don't need my honor defended, Mike. It's still completely intact."

"One more?" Mike asked.

"Mike!" she squealed as Mike turned and grabbed her midsection. He attacked her feverishly with tickles. He forced her onto the couch where he could use his body weight to hold her in place. "Stop…I…can't…breathe!"

Mike bent down and kissed her.

"Now you've definitely taken my breath away," she said as she wrapped her arms around his neck pulling him down on top of her.

***

"You need to get to your next class," Jandilyn said as Mike walked her to her locker.

He wanted to ask her why he should bother. Every teacher was passing him with a 'C' or better, and for the most part, he never attended. He didn't know if they were doing him any favors or not—the free time it afforded gave him entirely too much time to think.

Mike didn't show up for graduation. That would have entailed sitting on the football field for the commencement speeches and he still couldn't bring himself to do it.

He was sitting on Jandilyn's porch when she and her parents came home from the ceremony.

"Where were you?" Jandilyn asked, flushed with excitement to finally be free of the oppression that was high school, especially for those on the outside looking in.

"Hello, Michael," Mr. Hollow said stiffly.

He had hoped Jandilyn would finally come to her senses and let the 'damaged' boy go, ending the yearlong frost between mother and daughter. He had to admit the kid had brought a sparkle to his daughter's eye, something that had been in serious decline since freshman year. But enough was enough, she was poised to venture forth into the world and Mr. Hollow was afraid Mike might be the anchor his wife said he was.

"Hello, Mr. Hollow," Mike said politely, but his eyes were on Jandilyn as he stood.

"Did you even graduate today?" Mrs. Hollow asked him.

"Mom, you know he did. They called your name twice," she said, turning back to Mike. "How come you didn't go?" She grabbed his hand.

"Seemed like a waste of time," he told her.

"But sitting on our front porch for God knows how long seemed better?" Mrs. Hollow asked as she pushed past and went into the house.

Mike was about to answer, 'Yes, yes it was,' but Jandilyn placed her index fingers against his lips and shook her head with a big smile. "Don't you dare," she said softly.

"Well, he's here now," Mrs. Hollow shouted from inside the house. "Ask him if he wants a drink of water."

"See, she's getting better." Jandilyn smiled.

"She probably wants to spit in it." Mike laughed.

"You're horrible." Jandilyn laughed with him.

"But funny," Mr. Hollow said as he walked past, a ghost of a smile on his lips.

Mike's face froze in shock when he realized he'd been overheard.

He stayed a little while longer, congratulated Jandilyn but he had other, less pleasant business he needed to take care of.

"You won't stay?" Jandilyn said as they sat at the kitchen table.

"No, I want to go see Paul and Dennis' parents."

"Want me to take you?"

"No. Stay with your folks, celebrate—we'll talk later."

"You sure?" Her mother was already pulling her away.

Mike left Jandilyn's house, his spirits teetering on a filament fine balance point. On one side he was happy for Jandilyn on the other he was distraught at the realization he could not celebrate this day with his friends. Each step he took to Dennis' house reminded him of everything he had lost. It was an hour later as his final footfall brought him to the driveway that led up to the two-story Tudor home. Dennis' home had been party central mainly due to the fact his parents' house was lake front property resplendent with a pier and a small sandy beach. More than one teenager had dove off that small wooden dock sans clothes.

Mike thought about walking into the backyard but he didn't think his heart could take it. He walked up the flagstone pathway to the front door, all the shades were drawn and the house was dark. He silently hoped nobody was home.

Maybe if I just knock softly no one will know I'm here, he thought as he opened the screen door. He rang the doorbell instead, quickly shutting the screen door as a layer of protection from whatever lurked inside.

Mike heard some shuffling and a muffled 'ummph' from inside.

"Dammit. Dammit," he said under his breath.

Mrs. Waggoner answered the door, cigarette in her left hand and in the right she held a large glass with ice and an amber-colored liquid that looked suspiciously like scotch. "Whaddaya want?" she said, taking a drag from her cigarette and chasing it down with the scotch.

"Hello, Mrs. Waggoner."

"Eh." She belched.

Mike wanted to rip the screen door open and give her a hug. This was once the woman he called his second mom and she had gladly accepted the responsibility.

"I just wanted to see how you were doing," Mike said, thinking now about how that this might have been the stupidest thing he'd done in a very long time.

"You come here to just rub it in my face that you're still alive!" she spat. "But no, now that I'm looking at you good, you're not really…are you?" She cackled. "I can almost see right through you."

"Please m—"

"Don't you dare!" She pointed her cigarette-laden hand at him. "My son is dead! And if you had any brains left you'd have joined him!" The front of the house shook from the force with which she slammed the door.

Mike was too shocked to know whether to cry or vomit. He stepped off the porch and headed to Paul's. "Well, at least I don't think it can get worse," he told himself, failing miserably to prop himself up.

"Fuck," Mike said as he mentally prepared himself. Paul's home in contrast to Dennis' appeared cheery and welcoming, the front door was even open, allowing a fresh breeze to circulate throughout the home. Mike walked onto the porch and knocked on the aluminum door.

"Hello, Michael," Mrs. Ginson said from off to his side. She had been sitting on the deck reading a book.

"Hello, Mrs. Ginson," Mike said.

"What brings you here?" she asked coolly.

"I just wanted to pay my respects," Mike said, wishing desperately he had worn a hat so he could take it off and wring it with his hands.

"Consider them paid," she said, turning back to her book.

"Is Mr. Ginson home?" Mike asked.

"He's where he always is at this time of the day."

Mike stood there for a moment, wondering if she was going to clarify. When he figured she had reached the end of the paragraph she was pretending to read she looked back up

"The grave. He's at the grave. He's always at that damned grave site."

"I'm so sorry," Mike said.

"Paul was our only son, it should have been you who died."

Mike almost rocked on his heels from her words.

"Your parents probably wouldn't have missed you at all. It was nice of you to stop by," she said, resuming her place in the book.

Mike missed the first step entirely as he left, nearly losing his balance and toppling over. He wanted to go back to Jandilyn's, to the only person who could bring him out of this *Twilight Zone* episode, but her mother wasn't much more welcoming than the two he had just dealt with and he didn't know if he had it in him for round three. He went home and lay on his bed. A day that had started with such promise for so many of his classmates was nothing but a nightmare for him. He couldn't imagine being able to sleep anytime soon. He awoke some hours later to the tapping of a large crow perched on his window sill.

"Go the fuck away," he said, picking up a small trophy from his Pop Warner Football days, threatening to throw it through the screen.

The crow seemed to know he wouldn't let loose the shiny object, but it cawed once, opened its beak as if it were smiling and alit from the ledge.

***

It was two weeks after graduation, Jandilyn's head resting on Mike's chest as they lay in his bed.

"Your mom really doesn't care about me being here?"

"I don't think she even knows I'm here," Mike said in earnest, although he had a few months previous put a lock on his door to keep his mother out.

More than once he had awoken to the sight of her

standing over his bed with a confused look upon her face, as if wondering who he was. It had freaked him out to no end and it was after the third time that he had gone down to the local hardware store to rectify the problem. She had tried the handle only twice over the following months and then had stopped trying to get in altogether.

"What's wrong with them, Mike?" she asked, propping her head up with her hand. "It's like they're mourning."

"I don't know. I really don't." Part of that was a lie; he had some sneaking suspicions, but he was in no mood to share his dour thoughts.

"I think the contact looks great—does it bother you at all?" she said, smiling up at him.

Mike had tried a few months ago to see if leaving the patch off would in some way make the two separate halves of his vision unite again. His experiment had failed miserably within the first few hours, the resultant migraine headache had caused Jandilyn to break no fewer than seven traffic violations as she drove him to the hospital. The doctor who had seen him there suggested the prosthetic contact that would match his right eye but would completely block light from coming in.

"I don't miss the pirate patch. That's for sure. Want to get some lunch? I'm starving."

"We can go back to my house and I'll make something."

"I was hoping for something with a little more substance than a baloney sandwich."

She smacked him gently. "Do you sometimes wish I lived up to my reputation?" she asked as she stood up.

Mike smiled as he noticed how slyly she was trying to gauge his reaction without looking like she was. He made a big show of exaggerating his features to show disappointment. "I deal with it as best I can. My dad has a lifetime subscription to National Geographic and there's always the Sears catalog with the women's underwear section."

She smacked him a little harder this time. Besides some potential world record-breaking kissing marathons and some heavy petting, Mike and Jandilyn had not done the deed.

"I don't think I would have gone out with you if I had known just how pious you were."

"Pious? You're calling me pious! I'm going to start wearing ankle-length dresses!"

"You'd still look good," he said playfully.

Her face saddened a bit.

"Jandilyn, I love you. When we do it—when we're both ready, we'll do it. I'm in no rush."

Jandilyn scrunched up her eyebrows.

"Okay, that last bit might be a stretch of the truth, but it doesn't change the fact of how I feel about you. You saved me."

Her face beamed.

"Come on," she said, grabbing his hand. "I know how to make grilled cheeses now."

The bright sun beamed down into the car as Jandilyn retracted the cloth roof, but Mike could not shake the feeling that something was barreling toward him.

"You alright?" Jandilyn asked, noticing his discomfort.

"Heartburn," he told her.

"We haven't even eaten yet."

"I was thinking about your cooking."

"Funny."

As they pulled up to Jandilyn's home, Mr. Hollow was coming back across the street holding the mail in his left hand and waving enthusiastically to his daughter, a broad smile across his face. When he looked at Mike the smile faded ever so slightly. Mr. Hollow had been nothing but amicable to Mike, but there was always an underlying current of wariness as if he expected Mike to strike at any moment and he would be there to put him down.

Mrs. Hollow, on the other hand, was just openly hostile, but Mike thought it was getting marginally better. At least she just left the room when he entered instead of making snide comments.

"Maybe we should just go," Mike said as Jandilyn pulled into the driveway.

"Something came in the mail for you," Mr. Hollow said, waving a large envelope in front of her.

"OhmiGod," Jandilyn said so fast it sounded like one word. She quickly exited the vehicle and snatched the letter from her father's hand, sending the rest of the mail sprawling. Her father laughed. She scanned the outside quickly then thrust it back at him. "I can't open this! You open it!"

"Not a chance, kiddo." He laughed and shook his head.

Mike got out of the car and stared at them, feeling more like an outsider as each word was spoken. He turned to the house where Jandilyn's mom was looking at him. She did the sign of the Holy Trinity and then let the curtain fall back into place a chill rippled across his brow.

Mike looked back to Jandilyn as he heard the telltale sound of an envelope ripping open.

"Dear Miss Jandilyn Hollow," Jandilyn muttered softly as she read, a trait Mike found endearing. "We are happy to inform—" That was all she read before she started jumping up and down.

Her father embraced her in a bear hug and swung her around. "Congratulations!"

Now Mike knew what he had been feeling in the car.

"I'm in, I'm in!" she shouted again. "I'm in, Mike, I'm going to UCLA Berkeley!"

"I heard," Mike tried to answer as enthusiastically as possible.

"Where are you going to college?" Mr. Hollow asked Mike as he finally put his daughter down. She read through the rest of the letter and subsequent enrollment paperwork. Mike hesitated to respond. "I've seen you play, you must have some prospects, some partial scholarships."

Mike's head dropped.

"I'm… I'm sorry, I just got wrapped up in Jandilyn's news, I forgot."

"What's the matter?" Jandilyn asked a huge smile nearly spreading ear-to-ear.

"Your old dad might be getting a little daft I think," Mr. Hollow said with a nervous laugh at the end.

Mike's stomach was churning. He was proud for his girlfriend and was dreading the thought of losing her. Mike at this moment wished he were as invisible as he sometimes felt. If he could have just walked off into the sunset he would have done so.

"This calls for a celebration!" Mr. Hollow said, getting pulled back up in his daughter's emotions, his earlier embarrassment swept under the rug.

"Dad, I have to fly out for orientation in two weeks," Jandilyn said dismayed. She looked over to Mike, the realization of what was taking place finally dawning on her.

"Jandilyn, I'm going to head home, you need to be with your family. Do some planning,"

"We haven't eaten lunch yet, though," she said.

"I've lost my appetite," he said, trying to smile.

"Oh, you've had her cooking too then." Mr. Hollow laughed.

Mr. Hollow was trying to help soften the mood and Mike thanked him for that.

"You guys have a lot to talk about and I feel a killer headache coming on," he lied. It wasn't coming on, it had already hit with full force.

"Then at least let me take you home," Jandilyn said.

"No, I really think the air will do me some good."

"You sure, Mike?" she asked, coming over to him and grabbing his hands. The pages she clutched in her right hand would do more than separate them from the inches they were at the moment.

"I love you," Mike said softly as he placed his forehead against hers.

"Same," she returned, glancing over quickly at her father, a blush of embarrassment as she noticed her father trying his best to not be involved in this scene.

"I'll call you later," she said.

"Sounds good," Mike said as he turned and started back the way they had just come.

Mike heard the Hollows' door open and Mrs. Hollow disingenuously yell out. "Oh that's a shame he's not coming in."

"Mom, I got accepted!" Jandilyn fairly squealed as she raced up the stairs to show her mother, completely oblivious to her mother's outward disdain for Mike.

"UCLA, that's great," Mrs. Hollow said a little too loudly as Mike tried his best to get out of earshot without looking like he was running. "I hope that's far enough away!"

"Far enough away from what?" Jandilyn asked, Mike was finally out of range of a response if one came.

Mike's range of emotions varied from angst to depression. Jandilyn was his life. His best friends were dead, the platoon of close friends he'd had before the accident who could have stepped into a best friend role had all marched out on him, or him on them, he wasn't sure. His family who had always been a stalwart from any advancing storm had cracked and splintered from the storm waves he had caused. Of all his siblings, he had only seen his sister once in the last six months and that had been barely. It had been a half day at school or he would not have even seen her half-hearted attempt at a wave as she pulled out of the driveway as Jandilyn was pulling in.

Mike was lost in his thoughts and did not notice the Blue Chevelle as it slowly approached him.

"It's the freak!" One of the passengers in the car said. "You gonna get him this time?" the hyena voice asked.

Durgan slowed as he pulled next to Mike. He had his attention now. Mike thought a beat down might do him some good right now.

"Mike," Durgan said, acknowledging him with a small nod before gunning his engine and leaving him in a smell Mike had come to loathe, burning rubber.

Mike turned to watch as the car rapidly retreated from his vision. "What a weird fucking day," Mike said as he headed for the only place where he thought he could get some solace.

**

Within twenty minutes he was back at the train trestle. He had learned to compensate for his lack of depth perception, but that still didn't mean he liked it. He took his time crossing. When he finally made it to the other side he took his first comforting breath in almost five minutes.

"That sucked." He walked over to the pathway that led up to the Hill proper. No matter how much he wanted it, he knew without a doubt Jandilyn was not watching him this time as he ventured off to the right and into the denser woods. The large rope swing swung gently. Mike grabbed the coarse hemp and thought about swinging on it, but without Paul and Dennis to laugh and joke as they swung perilously close to the trees on the downward arc, what was the point?

The leaves above his head rippled as a calm breeze passed through. Birds sang and crickets, unaware of the time, chirped. Mike climbed up the side of the Hill he was on, dragging the rope with him. When it had gone as far as it could, he watched its descent as he let it go, remembering a time when Dennis had been riding the rope, his hat had flown off and Dennis had made a valiant stab at it with his right hand to try and snag it out of the air and missing. The funny part had been when Dennis also reached out with his left hand, the only part keeping him tethered to the rope. He had been successful in retrieving his hat, but then he was free flying, which was not necessarily a good thing when there was not any water to break your fall.

Loud 'umphs' and 'ugs' had been punctuated by spirited laughter from Mike and Paul.

"What the fuck are you doing?" Paul had been asking as he ran down the hill to make sure his friend had not done anything too serious as he had tumbled across the pine needle-laden ground. Except for some dirt skids and minor scraping Dennis had lived, at least for a few more months.

Mike had been too busy laughing on the ground clutching his stomach to be of much help.

"I got it, didn't I?" Dennis had said defiantly as Paul helped him to stand.

"It's a Yankees hat. You should have left it there," Paul told him, brushing leaves off Dennis' side.

The empty rope came to a standstill; there was no laughter this time. Only the slow empty creak as the thick hemp rubbed the bark raw on the bough it hung from.

***

"I'll be back in less than a week," Jandilyn said, smiling at Mike.

"I know that," Mike said. "It's after that has me concerned."

"Mike, you know I love you," she said as she stopped her packing.

"Jandilyn, I'm going to be a 'townie', you're going off to school. At first, we'll have this kind of yearning long distance relationship, we'll talk every day, maybe even write each other for a month, maybe two. But then you'll get some friends, one of the asses might even be a boy," Mike said, getting jealous of a person who didn't even exist yet.

"Didn't you once say USC was interested in you?" Jandilyn asked hopefully.

"It wasn't for academics." Mike laughed ruefully. "It was when they thought I might be able to help them on the field. Even before the accident, I'm probably a little too small for a class A program."

"Come with me, Mike," Jandilyn said as if that made the most sense in the world.

"What? I didn't get accepted, I didn't even apply."

"Not to the school. Do you think they only let students into California?" she asked, smiling.

"I…I can't—what would I do?"

"What are you doing here?"

"Taking up space," was his solemn response.

"Do you even know how much you mean to me?" she asked as she gripped the sides of his face in her hands.

"You're squishing my face," he said through fish lips.

She kissed him hard. "Think about it, it'll be a fresh start. I've got to imagine you see the ghosts your friends have left behind at every turn. It'll do you some good."

Mike was going to object that his parents would protest, but would they? Maybe it would be a relief for them, they could finally mourn his passing without his constant reminders that he was still there.

"I'll think about it," he told her honestly, although he was pretty sure his mind was already made up.

CHAPTER SIX – College

September 1st, Jandilyn and her parents flew out to California to get her situated in her new off-campus apartment. Jandilyn's parents had protested loudly and long about her decision to move in with 'that boy'. She would hear none of it.

"He's a good-for-nothing! No job, no future! He'll drag you down with him."

She didn't respond, what was the point? They would never understand that he had saved her as much as she had saved him. She couldn't even contemplate a life without him and really saw no reason to.

Her plane was touching down in the Earthquake state just as Mike's Greyhound bus crossed over the Massachusetts border and into New York. Mike hoped the flatulent fat man next to him was getting off somewhere before the Mississippi or it was going to be a *long, long* ride.

Other than the noxious fumes, Mike was feeling good. His father had given him three thousand dollars, saying he had been saving that for his college education that he wouldn't be needing anymore.

"Gee…thanks, Dad. I think?" Mike said as he accepted the money.

Mike had walked to the center of town to pick up the bus. His father had gone to work and his mother had decided to not get up in time to see him off.

Mike had his father's old Marine Corps duffle bag, one gym bag full of clothes, a few prized possessions, and that was it. He wanted to leave as much of the past as he could behind. Had he known just how tethered to it he was, he wouldn't have even tried.

He looked out the window as Walpole passed by, his heart panged a bit, but he knew in three days he would be meeting up with someone who would be able to make it all better. He had just settled down to the latest Stephen King book when a rotund man smiled embarrassedly at him as he sat down.

"No place else to sit," the man had said with a greasy smile. "Ben Grogan," the man said, sticking out an equally greasy hand.

When the man saw Mike's look of horror at the proffered hand he attempted to wipe it off on his dirty khakis. "KFC. It was kind of greasy." Ben finally pulled his hand back in when he knew the kid he was sitting next to was not going to shake it.

The bus slightly settled as the man took his seat, all the arm rest, and part of Mike's chair.

"Wonderful," Mike said, turning his head toward the window. They had been riding for about an hour and had finally hit the Mass Pike after a few stops. The fat man had got off at one of them to replenish his ass-gassing stores. Two Pop-Tarts (cherry) five Slim Jims and a diet Coke. Mike was wondering if it would look funny if he were to wear a bandanna around his mouth and nose in a desperate bid to filter out some of the stench.

Ben had attempted a Silent-But-Deadly discharge of methane and had mostly succeeded except for the eight on the Richter scale vibrations sent through Mike's seat.

"You're kidding me with that, right?" Mike asked.

Ben shrugged his shoulders as if to say, 'What can I do?'

You can start by not shoving that processed shit into your fat pie hole! Mike wanted to shout in response. Instead, he turned his head to the window where a slight draft of air streamed past, he hoped it would keep the worst of the odor away from him. "I bet fucking zombies smell better," Mike said softly.

Mike's forehead was against the cool glass and he was mostly not focusing on anything as it whirred by. A sight a few feet deep in the woods that lined the highway would have launched him from his seat if he wasn't wedged in tight from Ben.

"Paul?" Mike asked alarmed, craning his neck back as the bus sped past. Mike's face drained of color as he thought the specter (what else could it be?) waved, but it was impossible to tell if it was in greeting or departure.

"Sorry," Gaseous Grogan said, wrongly assuming Mike's rapid color drain had to do with his bodily emissions.

Big Ben thankfully got off in Toledo, Ohio. The rest of the voyage, as passengers came and went, left Mike blissfully alone. He had no more encounters but the vision of Paul did not fade until he saw the smiling face of Jandilyn at the bus depot. Her sunny disposition was in direct contrast to the cool rain pouring down.

"I didn't think it rained in LA," Mike said as he stepped off the bus and into Jandilyn's arms.

"It doesn't, it's been gorgeous up until this morning. How was your ride?" she asked, grabbing his hand.

Mike told her about 'Gaseous Grogan' in all its gory detail. She laughed at his rich colorization of the drama.

"It wasn't that bad? Was it?" she asked, steering him out of the large terminal.

"How's your apartment?" Mike asked.

"Well, it was lonely, but it should be alright now," she said, looking up at him.

"Are we taking a cab? Because I'll pay, I don't think I ever want to get on a bus again."

"Look," she said, pointing to a little red car excitedly.

"Is that yours?" Mike asked.

"My parents got it for me. It's the finest car coming out of Korea!"

"I think it's the only one," Mike added, but it sure

beat the hell out of sharing his seat with anyone.

"Is that all you have?" Jandilyn asked when she realized Mike was only holding two bags.

"Besides you, it's all I need."

Fifteen minutes later they pulled up to a square box of apartments, the kind most people would drive by without even acknowledging their existence. The yellow brick exterior was only broken up by the five tiers of windows.

"It's not much," Jandilyn said, watching Mike as he stepped out of the car, looking up at the building.

"It's home," Mike said as a smile spread on his lips.

"Fifth floor," she said.

"Of course it is. Elevator?"

"What do you think? Still happy you came out?"

"Well, honestly…not as much anymore," Mike said, careful to dodge the resultant swing. "When do your classes start?" He stepped into the apartment.

"Monday. Come here, I've got to show you something."

Mike followed her down a short hallway that led into the only bedroom. An oversized bed dominated the room. It had a green and white comforter and an abundance of pillows. Mike went over and placed his hand on the bed. "Very soft, I like it," he said, turning around to see Jandilyn. "How the hell did you do that?" He asked as he stared at a scantily clad Jandilyn. "I really think I'm going to like it here." Jandilyn ran into him hard enough to drive him back onto the bed.

"Good!" She laughed and planted kisses on his lips.

They spent many moments exploring each other. Two hours later, every pillow had become a casualty, not one had remained on the bed during the sometimes frenetic, at other times slow and sensual, marathon love-making session.

Jandilyn got out of bed, her slim bare form swaying as she walked to the door. "You hungry?" she asked over her shoulder.

"Famished." But he wasn't sure if he meant for food or for her.

"Want some bacon?"

"Who doesn't?"

"I'll go make some."

"Wait, aren't you going to put some clothes on?" Mike asked, leaning up on his elbows.

"I thought we'd have a little snack and then get back to the task at hand."

"Okay," Mike said speculatively. Within a couple of minutes he was laughing to himself as Jandilyn swore repeatedly every time bacon grease splattered. Mike got up and quickly found the bathroom, he had intended to get her a towel, but thought the robe hanging up would be a better find.

He came into the kitchen, Jandilyn had scooted her legs and abdomen as far from the old stove as she could. She looked like she was in serious need of a chiropractor.

Mike came up and draped the robe around her shoulders; she quickly tied the sash around herself.

"Thank you. Not one of my best ideas," she said as she licked her hand. "Could you watch this for a second, I've got some toast going."

Mike wasn't thrilled, he figured he could take a hit or two on his arms and maybe his stomach, but how much pain would he be in if the hot grease traveled a little farther south?

"I'll kiss it and make it better if anything happens," Jandilyn said lasciviously as she watched Michael's thought processes playing out in front of her.

Mike was assaulted with numerous splatters, but none ever ventured lower than his left breast…even if he white-lied and told Jandilyn that it had.

***

That first week Jandilyn had gotten adjusted to her

new school and Mike had scoured the local newspapers in search of a job that required absolutely no skill. He was almost resigned to asking folks if they wanted 'fries with that' when he stumbled upon an ad 'No experience necessary'. "Sounds right up my alley," Mike said. 'Night watchman, graveyard shift. Anaheim. Call after 8 p.m., ask for Jed.' The ad listed a number.

"I'll give it a shot," Mike said as he stepped out onto their small patio overlooking the smog banks of L.A.

***

"What's your name, kid?" a grizzled old man asked Mike as he sat in a blue plastic chair in the break room of the warehouse. A large pink Tab machine hummed in the corner along with a sandwich dispenser that hadn't seen new food since the Carter administration.

"Mike. Michael Talbot."

"Jed Planter." The old man extended a hand that Mike grasped firmly. "I can see you dressed up for the occasion."

Mike smiled a little embarrassed. The best he could wrangle out of his limited clothing was a newer pair of jeans and a t-shirt that did not contain a heavy metal band emblazoned on the front. "Sorry, we just moved here."

"Who's we?" Jed asked.

"My girlfriend and I."

"East Coast?" Jed asked. Mike gave him a questioning glance. "Accent," Jed explained.

"Oh."

"I'm from Denver myself, not sure why I came out to California. Been here damn near thirty years, though. Oh, yeah, I remember why now," Jed said with a faraway look. "Betsy Hoegler." He gave a mirthful smile. "What's your story, son?" Jed asked.

Mike damn near told him everything—the accident, his recovery, how he was ostracized from school, how

Jandilyn had probably saved him and how he couldn't imagine life without her and that was why he was in California. He hadn't meant to divulge so much and Mike certainly didn't let him know about his handicapped left eye, but Jed seemed like such a fatherly type and it really had been cathartic to tell someone.

"When can you start?" Jed asked.

"Wait—what? That's the interview? I got the job?"

"Well, if you don't want it."

"Whoa, I never said that. That seemed pretty easy."

"Let's face it, we're not assembling rockets here and I'm tired of interviewing men as old as I am. It will be nice to live vicariously through someone much younger than myself. But—" Jed turned all serious. "If zombies come, I expect you to defend my back while I run away."

"Zombies?" Mike asked, wondering if Jed had all his marbles securely tucked away in his brain bag.

"Have had a thing for them ever since I saw *Night of the Living Dead*. Ever seen it?"

Mike shook his head.

"We'll watch that on our first night as part of orientation."

"We can do that?"

"Listen, son, this is a warehouse for coffee beans. I'm sure there's a few million dollars' worth of product here at any given time, but ain't no one going to steal it." He laughed. "When can you start?"

"Yesterday," Mike said enthusiastically.

"You are planning on being here for a while, right? Because if I have to listen to one more ex-cop tell me how degrading being a security guard is…well, I'll leave it at that. Do you drive?"

Mike shook his head. "I haven't driven since the accident."

"I could see why," Jed replied, not aware that it wasn't that Mike didn't want to drive, it was that he couldn't.

"You take the bus here?"

"I will be, but my girlfriend brought me here tonight."

"Tell her to come in. Nobody should be outside in the dark alone. This is a lonely area."

The words had an instant effect on Mike. A finger of panic poked into his abdomen. "Alright," he said, standing up abruptly, sending his chair skittering across the orange linoleum flooring.

"We've got about an hour of damned paperwork to go through and then you two can go home."

Mike didn't hear the last of the sentence as he was already out the break room door. Intense feelings of doom and despair covered him like a heavy wet blanket. Cold sweat began to form in pockets on various parts of his anatomy. His left eye was throbbing, something it did sometimes only when the contact was off. His feet wouldn't move fast enough. *Am I dreaming?* he thought more than once as he looked down at his traitorous feet.

He quickly passed by the welcome station and the man he was replacing. Ted Stanton looked better than warmed over death, but in degrees only highly specialized equipment would be able to determine.

Ted awoke from his slumber just long enough to wave at a kid passing him by, who for the life of him he couldn't figure out why he was here. Or who he was for that matter.

Mike was coming up to the two sets of glass doors that led out to a small parking lot. Jandilyn's car sat by itself. Mike's heart lurched, *It's already happened.* He sagged, not knowing what 'it' was just yet and he didn't know if he had the courage to find out. The front of Jandilyn's car was facing him, but the interior was too dark to make out anybody inside. Once he pushed through the second set of doors he began to run to the car, his heart hammering in his throat. Something in the front seat leaned forward, the stark white sodium lights in the parking lot caught just enough contour to illuminate a yellowing skull, Mike pulled up short when he saw what was superimposed over Jandilyn's face like a trick photograph at a carnival and then it was gone.

Jandilyn's smile vanished from her face faster than a cheetah on the Savannah. "What's wrong?" she asked, getting out of her car.

"I'm sorry…nothing," Mike said, visibly shaken. "The light…I don't know."

"Mike, tell me. You look like you've seen a ghost."

"I thought something had happened to you," Mike said, hoping his heart would stop misfiring sometime soon.

"Well, I broke a nail," she said holding up her middle finger. "But I've got a feeling that's not what you're talking about."

"Not quite. I'm better now," he said, grabbing her up in his arms, trying to burn the image of her skeletal face from his mind.

"You're shivering."

"Probably an earthquake," Mike said, stepping back trying his best but failing miserably to put a smile on his lips.

"You look like a sneering dog," she said, laughing at him. "I'm fine, Mike! I mean, it's going to cost me fifteen bucks I don't have to get this nail fixed but other than that—"

"I love you, Jandilyn."

"Well, I'd rather hoped that had already been established," she said. "You ready to go home now?"

"I got the job, the old guy Jed wants me to fill out some paperwork. He thought I should come and get you."

"Congratulations, honey!" She grabbed his arm in hers and they walked back in. Ted was snoring softly.

Jed found himself warming up to the kid by the minute. Part of it was his girlfriend, who besides being a knockout was a genuinely warm-souled person. But there was also something else about the kid he couldn't quite put his finger on. There was something missing in the story he had told. Jed didn't think it was any of his concern as long as the kid showed up every night so he himself could get a proper night's sleep, then he would be A-Okay in Jed's book.

Ted and Jed had struck a bargain that while they were both on duty they would take turns staying awake. Ted hadn't made it ten minutes into any of his shifts before drifting off. Jed had almost gotten caught when his boss had come to do his yearly spot inspection. He hadn't gotten a good night of sleep on the job since. He let out a small laugh.

"Something funny?" Jandilyn's eyes sparkled as she was sorting through the plethora of paperwork Mike was skimming through and signing.

"Just nice to be around some youngsters as nice as you two. I've seen some of the less desirables your generation has to offer." He laughed.

"Well, you might change your mind if you get to know us better," Jandilyn said.

"Maybe I will," Jed said, giving Mike a stern eye.

"It's all her, Jed, she's the bad seed," Mike said.

"We'll see. Hurry up and fill this stuff out."

"Gun safety course?" Mike asked, holding the form up.

"The security agency is going to issue you a gun," Jed said. "Is that a problem? Are you two a couple of those tree-hugging types—make love not war?"

"Who wouldn't rather make love than war, Jed?" Jandilyn asked.

Jed stopped for a second. "Okay, valid point. Do you have a problem with a gun, Mike?"

"I've just never shot one. I don't want to blast any of my toes off."

"That's what the class is for, plus you get paid for it."

"Okay," Mike said dubiously. He was concerned that his lack of stereographic vision was going to make it extremely difficult to qualify on a range.

Forty minutes later, the paperwork filled out and signed, Mike and Jandilyn were getting ready to head out the door.

"Hey, Mike, next week you're on your own for the gun safety course, but the following week I'll pick you up for your shift," Jed said just as they reached the door.

"You sure?" Mike asked.

"You're only about ten minutes (he lied it was closer to twenty, but the kid looked like he could use a break) out of my way. This way I'll have someone to tell all my old stories to."

"Thank you, Jed," Jandilyn said, coming back and giving the man a small peck on the cheek.

"Get out of here," Jed said, blushing for the first time in maybe twenty-five years.

"Would this be a bad time to ask for a raise?" Mike asked.

"I'll see you next week, wise ass."

"You don't know the half of it," Jandilyn said, smiling as she walked through the door Mike was holding open for her.

Jed was approaching the visitor's station. "You have to sign in," Ted said, startling himself out of a deep sleep. "Oh, hi, Jed. I thought we had guests."

"We did, Ted."

"Did they sign in?" Ted asked, but his eyes were already on the downward slope.

"Sleep good, my friend." Jed laughed.

Mike hesitated as they walked across the lot to Jandilyn's car. He could almost feel the entity sitting there waiting for an opportune time to again lean forward, it's eyeless gaze boring holes into him.

"Mike?"

"I'm fine," he said. "Must be dinner."

"What?" Jandilyn said indignantly. "I make the best Ramen noodles this side of the Mississippi."

"Come on, let's find a diner or something, I'm starving," Mike said as they got in the car. He was certain what had been there had now departed.

"You know we're on a budget," Jandilyn told him.

"My treat, plus I just got a job. We should celebrate."

"I'm just warning you, I plan on eating a lot."

"I wanted to talk to you about that," Mike said seriously. "The other night when you asked if those jeans made you look fat, I lied."

She slugged him in the arm. "Fine, I'm starting off with chicken fingers, some steak and eggs, with a side of bacon—nope, a plate of bacon. You're going to have to roll me back to the car."

***

The gun safety course went better than Mike had expected. His one-eyed shooting style was not the preferred method his instructor taught but it was hard to dispute the results. Mike was consistently hitting nine out of ten shots center mass. With certificate securely in hand, Mike had called Jed with the number he had supplied at the interview.

"I passed," Mike said excitedly. Not introducing himself or even making sure it was Jed.

"Who's this?" came the gruff voiced question from the other side of the telephone line.

"Sorry, is this Jed?" Mike asked sheepishly.

"Just bustin' your balls, son. The instructor is a close friend of mine, he let me know how you were doing. He said you're a natural with the gun. I'll pick you up around seven on Monday."

"Thank you, Jed."

Jed could feel the heartfelt attachment in those words as the kid said them. Something even worse than the deaths of his friends had happened in that accident and he hoped someday Mike would trust him enough to let him know.

"*De nada*. See you in a couple of days." Then they hung up.

***

"Hey, kid, how you doing?" Jed asked as he rolled up two minutes earlier than expected. Jed noted with amusement that Mike looked like he had been waiting impatiently for fifteen minutes before he arrived.

"Nice ride," Mike said, hopping into the restored 1970 Mustang.

"It should be for what it cost to fix up."

Mike was fairly bumping around in his seat.

"First job?" Jed asked.

"How'd you know?"

"Relax, kid, this is an easy gig. Crappy pay, even crappier benefits, but like I said…easy."

"How long have you been doing this, Jed?"

"In my other life I was a minor politician, Selectman, Mayor. Real small town," he added when Mike was about to question him on that. "Most of the town was kin and I still almost lost. Did that sort of thing for most of my adult life and just kind of finally got disenfranchised with it."

Mike was looking at him funny.

"They were all fucking hypocrites, every last politician I came across. Preach for the people while they lined their pockets. I didn't want any more to do with it. I found the least stressful job I could that did not involve handing out stickers at a store front. Luckily, my wife comes from money. So to answer your original question…about a dozen years by now. Sounds like a long time by your standards, but it goes by pretty fast when you're my age."

"My folks used to say that."

"Used to?" Jed stressed the words.

Mike was looking down at his hands. "We really don't talk much since the accident."

"Do they blame you?" Jed asked.

"I wasn't even driving, Jed," Mike said abashedly.

"They'll come around. They will. Let's change the subject. You going to make that wonderful girl you introduced me to an honest woman?"

Mike laughed. "This isn't the forties, Jed! And I'm only eighteen."

"At eighteen we had our first born and I was running for treasurer in my hometown."

"Damn, Jed, I haven't even got a dog yet," Mike answered.

"That's the problem with you kids—'there's always tomorrow'. What about today?" Jed asked.

"Between me and you, Jed, I fully intend on marrying that girl, I've just got to get my shit together. You know, get a career going."

"You're not intending on staying here?" Jed asked in mock horror. Mike's face fell. "You're way too easy, kid. I wasn't expecting you to retire here. You give me at least a year I'll be thrilled."

The rest of the ride was in an easy silence Mike relished. Besides Jandilyn, he had not enjoyed that with anyone else in close to two years.

***

"Well, here we are, kid, your new home away from home," Jed said as they rolled up into the parking lot.

For a brief second Mike got a moment of dread as he looked up at the building. It looked exactly the same as it had the last time he was here, now it just felt different. 'Expectant' was the word that bubbled to the surface, like it had been waiting for him for a very long time. Mike shivered.

"You cold, kid?" Jed asked. And just like that the abhorrent feeling vanished.

"I think someone just walked across my grave."

Three thousand miles away, a police sergeant was

investigating a minor accident in the same location Paul had slid off the road and into a mighty oak. The scars in the bark still not healed.

"Come on, I'll take you on the grand tour." Jed used his keycard to get in. The resulting beep awoke Ted whose feet were propped up on the desk twenty feet to their front.

"Aren't there cameras?" Mike asked, wondering how Ted could consistently sleep on the job and not get in trouble.

"Oh, there are, but unless something happens the tapes get recycled every three or four days. We haven't so much as had someone stop to ask for directions after hours. Oh…wait, there was a guy about five years ago, a security guard. He was pilfering coffee. Dipshit had a hole in his pocket, I followed the trail from the warehouse to the break room and he must have had two pounds of beans in his pockets. He was shoving them into baggies in his locker. What's even funnier is we get a huge discount on coffee if you want some, a buck fifty a pound I think is what we pay."

"You don't know?"

"I can't stand the stuff. I used to have a cup or two in my day, but you'll understand when you make your rounds in the warehouse, the smell is so overwhelming. It'd be kind of like working at McDonald's, at first you wouldn't be able to get enough of them free French fries and then pretty soon you start to gag when you even think about them."

"Gag when thinking about McDonald's French fries? Are you a communist, Jed?"

"Come on, smart ass, I've got to get you your very own Rayon uniform, I suggest washing it repeatedly because they are itchy as hell right out of the package."

"If nothing happens here, why the guns?"

"Because the stuff is still worth a lot of money. I'll be honest, though, I'm not taking a bullet for a bean and you shouldn't, either. Someone comes in here and they're determined to rob us, we're letting them. Don't look at me like that. All the coffee is insured. If anything were to happen the company would recoup all of their losses, the only reason there are armed guards is because it brings the insurance premiums down to an acceptable level. Does Ted, even with a gun, scare you at all?"

Mike shook his head. "I don't even think he could hold it up, so unless I was trying to look up his inseam I think I'd be alright."

"You're funny, Mike, we're going to get along fabulously. Let's go get your burr infused shirt and pants."

Mike went into the locker room, removed his clothes and dressed in what he could only construe as some form of Russian torture. "This is ridiculous!" Mike bemoaned as he scratched all over his body. "I feel like I fell asleep on a fire ant nest."

"The tie looks nice, now you can take it off."

"Thank God," Mike exclaimed as he nearly ripped the noose from his neck.

"That uniform change is the best thing our union has done for us."

"Union?"

"Barely. Don't sweat it, it's voluntary."

Mike started scratching his pants vigorously. "I wish you had given me this uniform the other night, I would have made sure to wash the hell out of it before now."

"Oh, no, son, you don't get it. This is part of the initiation, the rites and passages of the Security Guard. Even old Ted had to go through it, although he slept most of the night."

"On his first day?"

"Narcolepsy."

"Didn't anyone think to ask him if he had any disabilities that might prevent him from performing his job?"

"They did, they didn't care. They just needed a body and that's really just about all they got." Jed laughed.

"I'm not sure if I should laugh or not."

"Laugh, it's good for you. Come on, let's walk. It'll

take your mind off the incessant itching."

Mike thought that was highly doubtful, if anything it would only irritate the ants all over his body. He walked as stiffed-armed and legged as possible so as to avoid scraping against the offending material, that felt more like sand paper than any wearable clothing.

From the locker room they took a right, which led down a brightly lit corridor fifty feet long that ended in a set of double swinging doors. Next to the door was a clipboard with a sign-up sheet clipped to it.

"We are required by the insurance company to make rounds every two hours. I'll let you in on a little secret…most nights I write down all of my times on this here sheet when I get in." Jed grabbed the pen and began to fill in times alternating, with first his name and then Mike's. "Very ambitious of you and on your first night to boot," Jed said, letting the clipboard bang back against the wall. He pushed open the door next to them.

The bitter aromatic smell of tons of coffee assailed their nostrils. "After you," Jed said, almost holding his breath.

"Wow, you weren't kidding," Mike said, walking into the vast warehouse. "How long do they store this stuff here?"

"Some of it they age for a little bit, depending on the bean. But for the most part, any particular pallet isn't here for more than a few days. This place is crazy in the daytime, forklifts all over the place. But at the moment you can tell it's pretty quiet, just pallets and pallets of coffee beans."

Mike went over and looked at the boxes piled high.

"You don't plan on putting any in your pockets are you?" Jed asked jokingly.

"More of a Mountain Dew fan myself. I guess I just never realized there was this much coffee."

"Interesting stuff, huh? Do you like to read?"

"Not so much, gives me headaches," Mike answered absently, rubbing his left eye.

"Well, you better find some hobby you enjoy doing or these nights are going to drag on forever."

"I'm sure I'll be able to keep busy just scratching tonight."

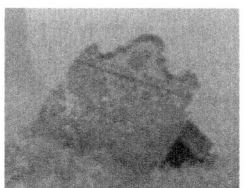

CHAPTER SEVEN – The Encounter

"How'd your first night go?" Jandilyn asked.

Mike almost told her about his hesitation regarding the building when they first got there, but he hadn't thought about it since that brief moment at the beginning of his shift so he couldn't figure out why he wanted to say something now. "Besides this torture device," Mike held up his wet uniform pants, "it was pretty good."

"Didn't you already wash them this morning before I went to class?"

"And three times since."

"You need to get some sleep before you work tonight."

"Lack of sleep isn't going to be a problem. Jed pretty much told me naps are mandatory."

"Maybe I could come over and we could nap together."

"That sounds great," Mike said, pulling her close. The pants rubbed up against her arm.

"You have to wear those?" Jandilyn laughed as she looked at the small scrape on her arm.

"The shirt is worse."

"Have you used any fabric softener?"

"Wait… there's something called fabric softener? You're kidding, right?"

Jandilyn reached on top of the machine and grabbed a big blue jug.

***

"Oh, this is heavenly," Mike said, rubbing his arm. His uniform had been through four cycles before he finally had to get ready for work. "I wish I had more time to let my pants dry, though." Mike started to duck walk out of the apartment.

"You look pretty threatening when you walk that way." She laughed.

"I think you and Jed have teamed up to make my clothes as uncomfortable as possible."

"Please don't tell me you're becoming a conspiracy theorist?"

"Not yet, but there's still time."

"I'll see you in the morning," she said, planting a big kiss on his lips.

Mike lingered, the kiss extending.

"Jed will be outside in a minute," Jandilyn said, backing away from Mike. "And if you go down there with that showing," she pointed to his pants pup-tent, "he's going to think you have a thing for older men."

"Great," Mike said with chagrin. "Wet pants and a stiffie, this oughtta be fun." He resumed his now hunched-over duck walk.

"All you need now is a cigar and a hat, Groucho, and you'll be all set."

"You did this to me."

"You can pay me back in the morning." She leered.

"Whassa matter with you?" Jed asked as Mike got into the car.

"My pants are wet."

"Have a little accident, did you?"

"Funny, the dryer doesn't work so good."

"When we get in, you can put on a new pair until those dry."

"Hell no, I'd rather be wet than put new ones on."

Jed sped off with a laugh. "Don't blame you."

"Where's Ted?" Mike asked as they walked in and

the visitor's desk was empty.

"He's gone now. No, not dead," he added for clarification when Mike looked over. "He was just waiting for his replacement so he could truly retire this time."

"So how's this work?" Mike asked as he squished down into Ted's now vacated seat.

"Well, we sit here, play cards, maybe some cribbage. Have some idle chit-chat, do some reading and periodically you'll go make rounds."

"Me?"

"Yeah, you wouldn't want to have these old bones keep getting up and down would you?"

"No, I guess I wouldn't. You do look mighty frail."

"Not so frail that I'm not going to have half your check by the time payday rolls around," Jed said as he pulled a deck of cards out of his pocket. "Do you know how to play Texas Hold 'Em?"

"Is that poker?"

"Oh, we're going to get along fabulously."

"How is this happening?" Jed asked two hours later, with a heavy degree of sadness, putting his hand on his forehead. He was down five dollars and didn't think the kid had any clue what he was doing. "You'd better go do your rounds while I rethink my strategy."

"Damn, at this pace I really don't need to work, I'll just take your money."

"Don't make me regret hiring you."

Mike left the duty station in high spirits. He took an immediate left that led him through the break room and toward the corridor that housed a couple of offices, he jiggled the door handles to make sure they were locked and then headed the rest of the way down the long corridor to the double doors.

The one on the left was partially pushed open about a foot; it was difficult to see that far down but he had the distinct impression someone was peeking around the door, watching his approach.

The hallway's bright. I would be able to see them, Mike thought as he slowly kept walking. He stopped when the door swung to the shut position. *Okay, that was kind of creepy*, Mike thought as goose bumps rippled up his arms and the back of his neck.

"Jed's fucking with me," he said softly. "Probably got Ted doing this. If I puss out he's gonna bust my balls." Mike looked to the camera behind him that got a good shot of the entire corridor and flipped it the finger. "Kiss my ass," he said with exaggerated mouth movement.

Mike was not feeling nearly as confident as he had portrayed to the camera as he walked the rest of the way down the hall and pushed the double-hinged doors open. The warehouse was bathed in ghostly white from the safety lights perched every twenty-five feet or so up on the walls. The first thing Mike noticed when he entered was the absence of the coffee smell, it was something very subtle, something he remembered from his chemistry classes—at least when that stuff still mattered and he actually attended. "Rotten eggs—it smells like rotten eggs in here." The word 'sulfur' came to mind.

Now Mike was shivering. "Shit, it's cold in here, don't remember that from the other night." He cupped his hands and blew into them. If he had been paying attention he would have noticed the breath coming out of him. *Must be the wet pants*, he thought, even though they had finished drying while he was busy taking Jed's money.

His attention was pulled to his right as he heard a loud clanging noise. "This isn't all that funny, Jed," Mike said. "If it's about the money, I'll lose on purpose the next few hands. It's not my fault you suck at the game." He waited for a response. The clanging happened again this time it was somewhat muted.

"This sucks," Mike huffed as he headed toward the noise. He wished he had grabbed the large flashlight that was sitting on the desk next to Jed. He walked over toward the loading docks. The dozen or so doors were all the metal roll up variety, each had a chain attached to a pulley that could either be run manually or with a motor.

"Well, at least I know the source of the sound," Mike said as he looked around. One of the chains to his left was moving slightly. But what caused it? *Ted! It has to be Ted. But I would have seen his ass shuffling off or more likely he would have fallen asleep right here waiting for my arrival. It has to be Jed. Is he mobile enough to do this, though? Okay, so he's probably in his fifties, he looks fit enough. There must be some other way down to the warehouse, so he hustled his ass down here and now he's doing some new initiation.*

"Fine, I'll play your game!" Mike shouted, trying to bolster his flagging bravado. "If I catch your ass, I'm going to treat you like any other thief." *I don't even have cuffs*, he thought. *I can make them stand in a corner while I call their mothers.*

A blade of light illuminated the warehouse. "Hey, kid, everything alright?" Jed yelled from the doors on the far side. "You've been gone for a while."

Mike looked up to the chain still swaying back and forth. "I thought I heard something!" Mike answered. "There's no way he circled around me and I didn't hear it. No fucking way unless he's a damn ninja," Mike mumbled.

"Come on, kid, I want to see if I can make my money back before the end of our shift."

The door where the chain was moving rippled a little bit as if a stiff breeze were blowing outside, although it had no effect on any of the other doors. The wind forced through a small opening by the latch whispered his name along with the ominous words 'your time has passed'. Mike moved as quickly as he could toward the light without breaking into a run. He wasn't quite as sure this was a practical joke, but if it was he wasn't going to give Jed the satisfaction of saying 'Gotcha!'

"What's the matter, Mike?" Jed asked with seemingly true concern. "The smell of coffee beans already getting to you?"

Mike scanned Jed's face hard for any signs of exertion from running or trying to hide his inside knowledge of what was going on. But they had just played fifteen hands of poker and Mike knew Jed did not possess a poker face.

"Heard a noise, just checking it out."

"Anything?" Jed asked.

"You tell me."

"A joke? Not me, kid, I get a big enough kick out of the new uniforms. It could be rats, we've had problems from time to time. They don't much care for the coffee, but a lot of the damn dock workers are constantly leaving food around. I'll leave a note for the receptionist that she should maybe call the exterminator again."

"The chain that rattled was three feet off the ground, if that was a rat I want hazard pay." *And they sure as hell didn't open that double door*, he thought but didn't say out loud.

"I'll put in your request, but don't hold your breath. Sign the sheet that you were here. Let's go back to the desk, in fact, just sign it that you were here all night. I don't want you getting rabies or something on your first week, Jandilyn will be pissed at me."

That was just fine with Mike. The rest of the shift went by without incident, Mike even increased his winnings by another six-fifty. He kept waiting patiently for an 'aha' from Jed which never came. No matter how he tried, he could not shake the niggling feeling from the back of his head that nothing even remotely similar to rats had been in that warehouse, although he completely forgot about the sulfurous smell.

By the time Mike got home that morning the entire event was a distant memory.

"Same time tonight?" a red-eyed Jed asked.

"Looking forward to it, I'll be able to retire soon at this pace."

"Keep talking, funny boy, you'll be crying poor mouth by the end of the week."

"Thanks for the ride, Jed." Mike trundled up the five flights to his apartment. Jandilyn was right where he hoped she would be, snuggled up on the bed. He moved some of the pillows she had been hugging and nestled himself up in their place. They made love so long she was late for her first class.

"Not cool, Mr. Talbot," she said as she ran around the apartment getting ready.

"Shhh," he said. "I'm trying to get some sleep, that's some exhausting work I do, keeping the national coffee supply safe."

She tossed one of the heavier pillows in his direction.

"You throw like a girl."

"I'll be home by four."

"I'll have dinner ready."

Mike was dead asleep when his dream began to turn south. He was up on Indian Hill enjoying a picnic with Jandilyn and she had gone to pick some wild flowers. He started to get concerned when she didn't return right away. He watched as the fruit she had been eating began to at first brown from exposure and then begin to dry in the noon sun.

"Jandilyn!" he had yelled. But her name was picked up and blown away by a small breeze that increased in force until his clothes were rippling. The small blanket they had been sitting on was threatening to uproot itself, it was being held down by rapidly decaying food, the block of cheese they had been eating had molded over, dried and split.

"Jandilyn!" Mike shrieked again. A large metal chain barely missed his head as it swung past. Mike looked up, the chain had been looped around a large branch, the ends catching in the wind.

"Probably rats," Jed said, looking up to the top of the chain.

"Jed? What are you doing here?" Mike asked in alarm.

"Jandilyn, sent me," Jed said through a mouthful of broken and bloody teeth.

"Where is she?" Mike asked, panic welling up in his throat.

Jed just kept smiling his horrific smile, a large hairless tail was wriggling out through a gap in his now shattered teeth. Mike grabbed Jed's shoulders and pushed him up against the tree.

"Tell me where she is!" Mike screamed, shaking Jed, his head striking the bark.

The clicking sound as Jed's head struck the tree even in the context with which it was in, struck some nerve in Mike that was even more frightening than everything else that was happening around him. The faster Mike shook Jed the louder the clicking noise became until he heard the tree break. But that wasn't quite right, it sounded like the tinkle of glass. Mike awoke with a start. He looked over to the bedroom's lone window. A sharp black beak was poking through a small round hole in the center pane.

"What the hell, bird!" Mike yelled.

He threw the blanket off and walked to the window. The large black bird pulled its beak free but did not yield its spot on the ledge. It watched intently as Mike crossed the room. Mike stopped when he got closer, the bird had one black and one white eye.

"It can't be," Mike said, more as a statement of fact to calm his own nerves. Mike wanted to open the window and punch the offending bird in the head but something told him this would be an unwise decision. "Probably got encephalitis," he said to the bird, but he wasn't even sure if birds could catch that disease.

The bird swiveled its head first so its black eye got a good long look at him, then it turned so its unsettling white eye could get a gander. When it seemed satisfied it took off for parts unknown.

Mike surveyed the damage, the hole was little bigger than a BB shot but spider web thin cracks radiated out from the hole. It would need to be replaced.

"Well, scotch tape is going to have to do for now," Mike said as he covered the hole and the small cracks to hopefully prevent further damage.

He swept up the small pieces on the ground into an electric bill envelope and then tried to reconcile his disturbing dream along with the appearance of a bird that eerily had eyes similar to his. He wondered if it shared the same visions as well.

"It's just a coincidence, it has to be."

"What is?"

Mike jumped up. "Shit, woman, you scared the hell out of me. What are you doing home?"

"I thought I'd surprise you, if you want me to leave I can go back," she kidded.

"Not a chance."

"What happened here?" she asked as she came up to the window. Mike shivered as she traced one of the cracks with her finger. That did not seem like a great idea.

Mike wavered between telling her the truth and going with the made up BB shot explanation. But combined with his inability to lie and her expert bullshit detector he'd be caught before he finished his story and then he'd have to explain why he was lying.

"It was a bird," he said, deciding to go with the minimalistic truth.

"A bird did this?" she asked incredulously. "Did you piss it off?"

"I really don't know what its problem is—*was* (he added hastily). I was sleeping and the damn thing was tapping on the window. He woke me up." *Well it was partly that and the fact that I thought something real bad had happened to you.*

"What kind of bird was it?" she asked, her expression getting grave.

"Hummingbird," Mike answered quickly.

"Mike."

"A big fucking crow or raven, I guess." *With one dark eye and one white eye like me.*

"And it was trying to get in?"

Mike didn't need to say anything, the proof was in the pudding, he was still holding the makeshift dustpan containing the small bits of glass in his hand.

"What, Jandilyn? What's going on?"

"Have you ever seen this bird before?"

Not the bird but the eyes, yes, he thought, but said, "How would I know one bird from another?"

Jandilyn eyed Mike suspiciously. "I'm afraid for you, Mike. There's something here I'm missing or something you're not telling me."

Mike was thinking back to his dream and Jandilyn's disappearance. That combined with the appearance of the bird was not sitting easily in his gut. "Sometimes a bird is just a bird," he said, but the words felt dirty on his tongue even as he spoke them.

"I might believe you if you didn't look like you had swallowed a worm while you said it."

Could the hairless tail poking out of Jed's busted mouth have actually been a worm? Mike thought. The similarities were too close.

Jandilyn was going through her catalog of internal knowledge. "Okay, let me think. Ravens actually get a bad rap in modern American mythology."

"I love when you use big words," Mike said, trying to steer the conversation away from its obvious conclusion.

"I was saying that most Americans think Ravens and Crows are harbingers of doom and death."

"Wonderful."

"But they're wrong."

"Wonderful!" Mike said, his inflection changed to the positive. *Please let this be the end of the conversation.*

"Their presence is actually one of light and hope. I'm pretty sure—I'll have to go to the library on that."

"Let's just go with that."

"No, that's not all, Mike."

It never is, he thought sourly.

"A bird in the house means something totally different, that *does* (she stressed does), mean something bad, I'm just not sure."

"It wasn't inside."

"Maybe not all of it, but it wanted in."

"Jandilyn, maybe it just had rabies…or distemper," he added when she shook her head.

"Mike, has anything been happening lately?" she asked.

Besides the huge rat peeking at me from behind the door and the heavy chains swaying in the nonexistent breeze at work? And the freaky wind words? Absolutely nothing.

"Nope," Mike lied.

"You've got that swallowed worm look again."

"Any chance of a different analogy? My stomach is a little queasy at the moment."

"You sick?" she asked with concern.

"Not yet, but if we keep this conversation up, probably."

Mike was happy when Jandilyn finally let it drop.

"Let's go out," Jandilyn said, a smile coming across her face. "I bought some stuff for a picnic."

As long as it's not at Indian Hill and Jed isn't there.

***

The remainder of the week went by without notice. No giant blackbirds tried to gain entry into their apartment and the rat specter did not reappear. Mike did not go into the warehouse, it was all he could do to go to the end of the hallway and sign his name on the sheet. By Thursday he finally wised up enough to remember to add all of his rounds at one time as opposed to doing it every two hours. The remainder of the night he would cautiously glance down the length of the hallway hoping-the door was not cracked open and a hazy black figure looking out at him.

"I cannot believe I owe you twenty-two fifty," Jed said as their Friday night shift was coming to a close.

"I want it in large bills," Mike told him. "Don't go trying to pay me in pennies you've been saving since the Kennedy administration."

"Good man Kennedy was. I wish he had stayed alive long enough to do some of the good he had planned on," Jed said with a faraway look in his eyes.

"Even he wouldn't have been able to help your poker playing this week," Mike quipped.

"I'm going to start charging you gas money, this week alone was most likely thirty bucks."

"Well, then come on we've got enough time for one more hand and I can break even."

"Funny boy, tell me again why I hired you?"

"Because I'll actually do the rounds and you can sit here and take your frequent naps."

"Oh yeah, there's that." Jed dealt one more hand.

***

"You alright, kid?" Jed asked as he dropped Mike off. "You seem a little distracted even for you."

"I'm good."

"Women troubles? I've learned if you nod a lot when they're talking and say 'I'm sorry' and 'yes dear' whenever appropriate you can avoid about ninety-nine percent of issues."

"Thanks for the advice, but I guess I just have a hard

time believing anything from a man who can't even beat his student in poker."

"Poker is much like life, Mike, it has its ups and downs, I'll be on top soon enough."

"We'll see. See you next week, Jed, thanks for the lift."

"Have a great weekend. Don't spend all my hard earned money in one place."

"Hard earned?" Mike asked.

"You know what I mean."

"Sure." Mike waved as Jed pulled away.

Jed stuck his hand out and gave him the middle finger. Mike couldn't help but laugh. Mike walked up the steps, not until the third floor landing did his good feelings leave him like rats from a burning ship. He bounded up the remaining two flights, fumbled with his key, and stepped into the apartment.

"Jandilyn?" he asked not too loudly in case she was asleep. He could see their bedroom door from where he stood, a steady stream of sunlight was coming out from underneath the closed plank. His heart eased as he saw shadows dancing through the gap between door and floor.

Good, she's up, Mike thought as he took off his shirt. He walked down the hall and opened the door, the bed was perfectly made as if no one had slept there the previous night, the bathroom door was open, and the light was out.

"Jandilyn?" Mike asked again, only this time much more anxiously. "This isn't really funny." There were not many places to hide in a room that on a good day was twelve feet wide by twelve feet across. The bed was a platform bed resting on some space saving drawers, no place to hide there. So that left the small closet or the dark laden bathroom. "I know you're in here, I saw your shadow under the door."

Maybe it's rats, Jed said in Mike's head.

The door was open to the closet and there was not enough room to hide anyway. Mike looked to the bathroom.

This wasn't Jandilyn's M.O.; she wasn't much into practical jokes. So if she weren't here, first question was where was she? And secondly, who or what was in the bathroom? *What?* Mike thought, *Why would I think a what?*

Mike was concentrating so hard trying to see through the murky light in the bathroom he missed the throw pillow on the floor as he stepped down, the silk cushion slid like a greased snake through a lubed pipe. Mike's right foot flew forward, his ass impacted hard enough with the ground to throw his head back which made his teeth clatter when the back of his skull made contact with the thin carpet.

"Dammit," Mike pulled his head up off the floor. His contact had dislodged from his eye and he was now staring at something in the bathroom that was staring back at him. "What are you?" Mike asked as terror closed his throat.

The entity quickly dissipated almost as if once it knew it was being witnessed it was time to go.

"Mike, you alright?" Jandilyn asked from the doorway.

Mike turned quickly, vertigo setting in as his dual vision tried to take in all he saw. On one side was his girlfriend as everyone would see her and through the other was the myriad of colors ever swirling around her. "Might be rats," Mike said and collapsed.

Mike was in bed when he awoke. He was unsure how long he had been out, but the sun was still shining brightly through the window. His head hurt but not overly, his eye was covered with his old pirate patch and he had no pants on. "This feels suspiciously like a date rape," Mike said as he hefted himself up on the pillow.

"Good to see you awake," Jandilyn said as she was coming back down the hallway with an ice pack. She had a smile on her face, but it was deeply lined with worry. She sat on the bed and placed the bag against the back of his head. "You looked like you had a seizure, Mike."

"That would explain a lot," he said.

"About what?"

"I said that out loud?" he asked, truly irked he had done so.

"Too late to stuff the cat back in the bag," she said.

"What if we just tie the end off so it can't breathe?"

"That would mean the cat was still in it. When did you become a non-lover of cats?"

"When I discovered they were the gatekeepers to the underworld."

"Who the hell told you that?" Jandilyn asked disbelievingly.

"I read it somewhere."

"Comic books don't count. God, you're good, sometimes I forget just how good," she said.

"What are you talking about?"

"Your ability to change the conversation. It's so subtle and inane that one doesn't even realize that you have completely derailed the train onto a whole new set of tracks. You really should think about politics."

"I'd make a great comptroller."

"Do you even know what that is?"

"Not really, but it sounds like something that would have been in *The Terminator*."

"Mike," Jandilyn said, exasperated.

"Sorry, I guess I'm really trying to figure it out myself. The bedroom door was closed but I swore you were home so I came down here…hey, where are my pants? Are you trying to take advantage of me?"

"I might if you tell me the rest of what you're avoiding."

"No, you probably won't, but here goes. I had reason to think you were home. Does that make sense?" He was doing his best to give her the information without saying it. To say it aloud gave it a power, a sense of reality and he wasn't sure if he was up to the task of wrestling with that right now.

"Sure, you thought I was home. Normally, I would be, but I had to do some errands before I go to the library. I've got a paper due next month and I wanted to get started on it."

"Whoa, that's friggin' weird," Mike said.

"What?" Jandilyn asked with concern.

"You have a paper due next month and you're starting it now? Holy crap."

Jandilyn smacked him in the arm. "Not all of us are procrastinators. I think you might need some incentive." She stripped off her t-shirt.

Mike sat all the way up, reaching for her sheer bra-clad breasts.

"Not a chance." She laughed. "Not until I get the rest of what you are so desperately trying to not tell me."

"How about we make love first and then I'll tell you," he said, never taking his eyes from her chest.

"Up here, Mike," she said, gripping him under the chin and moving his field of vision up to her eyes.

"Who are you?" Mike asked as they made eye contact. "And what have you done with those wonderful mammaries?"

"You're incorrigible," she said, meaning it, but laughing at the same time.

"That's not cool that you are you using fancy college words on me now."

"Remember these?" Jandilyn asked, squishing her breasts together.

"How could I forget?" Mike asked again, dropping his gaze.

"Now look at me."

Mike ripped his gaze from below. "Fine, Jandilyn." He sighed. "I thought you were home because I would have sworn on a stack of Bibles, I saw you—I mean your shadow—walk past the door." Mike was looking at Jandilyn's face but it would have been impossible to not notice the goosed flesh that sprang up on her arms all the way to her shoulders.

"And when I found you on the floor?"

Mike dropped his gaze to his lap. "My contact fell out and I *did* see something."

"Are you sure? I thought you couldn't really see anything out of your left eye."

"I'm sure about what I saw."

"Where?"

Mike pointed to the bathroom.

"Why is it always the bathroom?" Jandilyn sighed. "How am I ever going to put make-up on again in there?"

"Good thing you don't need it."

"You might think so, how you going to feel about week two without a shower, though?"

"I'll probably have you sleep out on the couch."

"Is it still in there?"

"It seemed to leave when it realized I could see it."

"It was intelligent? This is not getting better. Talking about things is supposed to make it better. That's what my mother always used to say."

"Pretty sure this wasn't what she was thinking about when she said that." *Plus, she's a bitch*, Mike thought.

"Face your fears was another one," Jandilyn said as she got up, heading toward the bathroom.

Mike watched as she took an unnaturally long time to get to the doorway. She took a heavy breath reached in and turned the lights on. "Huh!" she cried in triumph. "There's nothing in here! Do you see anything?" she asked looking back, with a scared expression on her face.

"It's a great view from here," Mike said.

"Mike, I'm not a big fan of the supernatural, could you help me out a little bit?"

Mike slowly lifted his patch, shrinking away from the sun light. "Well, you still look good," he said with some discomfort. "And you're alone," he said as he dropped the patch back in place.

"Could you stay in here with me while I take a shower?" Jandilyn asked with a small quiver in her voice.

"The only thing that could beat that would be season tickets to the Red Sox."

"That's better than this?" Jandilyn removed her bra.

"It's the Red Sox, Jandilyn."

"And this?" she said, stepping out of her jeans.

Baseball was completely forgotten except for the bases being traversed in the small shower.

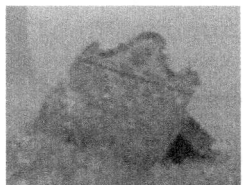

CHAPTER EIGHT – Roger

"Wow," Jandilyn said a half hour later. "That's probably the best shower I've ever had."

"Probably?" Mike asked. He was stretched out on the bathroom floor breathing heavily, a puddle of water spread around him.

Jandilyn shuddered once as she pictured the clear water a muddy red for the briefest of seconds. "You should towel off, you'll catch a cold."

"If that means I could stay home for a day and do that again, I'd catch the damn flu."

"Are you going to get up? I have to get ready now."

"The view from this angle is incredible."

"Mike!" She kicked him lightly in the side.

"I feel used right now."

"You'll get over it."

"Maybe, but I'll be damaged goods from here on out. No one else will want me."

"Good," she said "Because you're all mine." She leaned down and kissed him as he was sitting up. "By the way…I found your contact. I placed it in its case on the nightstand on your side of the bed."

He wrung out the wet patch as best as possible, put the uncomfortable chaffing piece back on, and after a vigorous towel drying he hopped into bed. He watched Jandilyn who had decided to get ready with the door open. The colors swirling around her were soothing.

"Mike, how am I going to sleep here without you?" she asked as she applied some eyeliner.

He didn't have a good answer for her. But something

came to him, whether she took comfort from it was a different story. "I don't think they're here for you, Jandilyn."

"*They*, Mike?" she asked, turning around to look at him rather than through the mirror.

"It's Saturday, where are you going?" Mike asked completely ignoring her question.

"Study group, library, remember? Half the class is supposed to be there."

"You really take this school stuff seriously."

"They?" she repeated, never taking her eyes off of him.

"God, Jandilyn, you've got some blonde hair, I would have thought you would have forgotten by now. Fine, there was something at work, Jed thinks it's rats, I'm not convinced." He spent the next few minutes detailing the events at the warehouse.

"You think this has to do with you?"

"I'd swear I heard it say my name by that garage door."

"That's it, I'm getting a priest."

"What? Like in *The Exorcist*? I'm not possessed. I think. I don't even like split pea soup and I sure can't turn my head around in a three sixty. I'd love to try the floating bed trick, though," Mike said looking off into space.

"I'm going to get this place blessed."

"Do they do that? And what about the warehouse?"

"Well, that poses a problem," she said trying to work it out in her head. "Maybe I'll just get you blessed."

"I am not demon spawn."

"My mother begs to differ."

"Really? I thought she liked me. She always laughs at my jokes."

"Those are sneers."

"I always thought they were a little toothy, I just figured she had some sort of condition."

"What condition involves flashing canines?"

"Vampirism, I mean she does look really good for her age."

"Gee, I can't imagine what she doesn't see in you."

"Wait, was that a backhanded compliment?"

"Sleep on it, I'll be back in a few hours."

"Goodbye, love," Mike said as he nestled his head on his pillow.

"Never goodbye, Mike, that has too much finality attached to it."

"Godspeed then?"

"How hard did you hit that tree?" Jandilyn asked. "How about 'cheerio'?"

"We're not British and I can't stand the cereal. How about 'you are the air I breathe and until you come back to me I will never be able to catch my breath?'"

"A little lengthy."

"It's the truth, though."

"I hope this will keep you until I get back," she said and placed a tender kiss on Mike's lips.

"It'll do for now." He smiled and was almost asleep before Jandilyn could get the apartment door closed. A droplet of water on the back of the patch was irritating him enough that he lifted the soggy material to wipe it away. He just happened to have his left eye open. The colors encompassing Jandilyn were muted, unsettling, and if he was being honest with himself, even disturbing. Mike jumped out of bed as the lock clasped into place. He had been exhausted moments earlier and now he began to dress quickly and with purpose. The library was no more than a mile-and-a-half from the apartment. He could get there in twenty minutes; Jandilyn would really only beat him by ten minutes once she parked. Mike put his contact in and headed out.

"Nothing can happen in ten minutes," he said aloud, trying his best to shun the memory of the car accident that hadn't lasted more than three seconds.

Mike made it to the library in fifteen minutes.

Jandilyn's car was close to the front of the massive structure. *Not many kids want to do higher education on a Saturday morning*, he thought. *She probably stopped for coffee, most likely hasn't been here for more than a minute or two, if she catches me skulking about she's going to kill me.*

"How the hell am I going to figure out what floor she's on?" Mike asked as he craned his neck to look up the twenty floors of tome-lined stories.

If Mike had a watch it would have read exactly forty-seven and-a-half minutes later when he tiredly stumbled upon the study group, although to call two people a group was pushing the limits of that definition.

Mike walked on to the twelfth floor. He could hear some quiet talking off to his left, but straight ahead he saw a large table that could hold as many as a dozen students, but right now there was only Jandilyn who had her back to him and a strikingly good-looking guy Mike thought looked like a bigger version of Tom Cruise. His heart thudded in his stomach, the oversized Tom Cruise doppelgänger briefly noted Mike and then dismissed him like a big fish in a small pond is apt to do. Mike veered sharply to the left and into a large column of books, the titles all revolved around Medieval literature. Mike didn't think any of them told how to deal with a broken heart.

He wondered if he were to remove his contact and spy on them what would the colors of betrayal look like? He went to the far end of the column he was at and found a way to circle around and get a better look at them. He found a decent vantage point not more than twenty feet away and he was hidden by a large row of catalog shelves.

Jandilyn was busy pouring over her array of spread books; Tom's twin was barely paying attention to his book propped up on the desk merely for effect. Every chance he got he stole a glance at Jandilyn. A few times he would even rise to stretch to see if he could get a better vantage point down the front of her shirt. Mike thought his blood was going to begin to boil over. He wouldn't be surprised if hot liquid began to leak out of his ears.

He wanted nothing more than to confront them, but what would he say?-What *could* he say? He had followed her and technically she still hadn't done anything wrong. "Except be in the motherfucking library alone with Mr. Movie Star," Mike said in hot, hushed tones.

"God, I'm starving," Top Shit said as he over exaggeratedly grabbed his smooth torso.

"Go get something." Jandilyn looked up at him.

"How about we both get something?" he asked. A smile flashed across his lips, but Mike saw something much more sinister Jandilyn missed.

"Roger, I've got way too much work to do."

"I'll buy. Come on, we'll be quick. My car is in the garage. We'll go grab a bagel or something and come right back."

"I am kind of hungry. This coffee is burning a hole in my stomach."

Mike had the distinct impression he was going to throw up in his mouth as he watched his life pack her books up and stuff them into her stretched-out book bag.

"I'll get that," Roger said as he grabbed her bag before she had a chance to respond.

Mike noticed just the slightest hint of hesitation in her movements, and his heart soared for it, but when Roger turned and asked her if she was coming she followed behind.

They stood at the elevators, Mike ducked quickly as Jandilyn turned around as if she felt something. The elevator 'binged.' Mike stood as he watched the doors close.

He was a moment away from going home and packing his things when he decided that he wanted the satisfaction of a direct confrontation. Besides, he thought he'd go insane if he had to stay at the apartment and wait for her for any extended amount of time.

Mike raced down the stairs to level G1. "Oh, come

on, how many levels can there be in this garage?" Five to be exact but he only needed to check out two more before he came across Roger and his soon-to-be ex.

It had been much easier searching the subterranean parking structure, Mike could count the number of cars on one hand, and a couple of those were labeled as University property.

He heard a car door slam and knew without a doubt that was them. He slowly started plodding to the car, his heart now not so infused with the hot magna as it had been earlier, now it was filled with cold dread. His life was about to be over, not in the traditional way, but it would be a death all the same.

Mike was about to say 'fuck it'. Maybe he'd just pack his shit up and go slinking into the night. That was until he heard the loud thwack followed by a very loud "Bitch, you've been teasing me with those tits for weeks now."

Mike heard Jandilyn's cry as he sprinted for the car. He had just got to the driver's side door as Roger ripped Jandilyn's t-shirt in two.

Mike ripped a fingernail off in his haste to get the door open. He had enough adrenaline surging through his veins he thought he'd be able to rip it off the hinges like Superman even if it was locked.

It wasn't locked.

"What the fuck?" came from both Roger and Mike almost as if they had rehearsed it.

Mike took in the scene quickly, the left side of Jandilyn's face was a deep red from the slap and would continue swelling for a few more hours. Her shirt, which had been one of her favorites that she had bought just last weekend, was barely holding on as a large rip that started from her neckline traveled past her navel where two lone strands were holding on for dear life as if to protect her modesty.

Jandilyn looked up and over Roger's shoulder at

Mike, her left eye already shutting from the swelling, a look of panic and confusion on her features.

"Listen, asshole, this is none of your fucking business. You should probably leave before someone gets hurt," Roger said as he began to fold himself out from his late model BMW.

Jandilyn why are they always big? Mike questioned her silently. If he let Roger on solid footing, the size disparity would become apparent all too quickly. Mike, without hesitation and not truly thinking things out, hopped back about six inches and launched himself forehead first into Roger's upturned face as he was coming out of the auto. The pain Mike felt was excruciating, it wrapped around his entire skull and rocketed down his spine. That was nothing compared to the damage inflicted on Roger; it would be many surgeries later before he regained some of his movie star good looks.

Roger's nose was laid almost flat against the right side of his face, his eyes had already begun to blacken and sink in where the delicate orbital bones had been shattered, blood could not get out of his system fast enough. Roger sat back, choking as viscous fluid ran from his destroyed nose and into his mouth. He took ragged breaths of air as he tried to work through the pain, his exhalations sent blood spray onto his dashboard and front windshield.

"Are you alright, Jandilyn?" Mike asked, leaning down so he could see her. His left eye was squeezed shut from the pain and he had his right hand up to his forehead trying to ascertain if he had split his skull open.

She still looked somewhat dazed, either from the blow or the events that had just transpired. She reached over and rocked Roger with a slap that came from somewhere deep in the corner of Fenway. "Now we're even!" she yelled.

Roger's eyes closed. Mike thought at first he might be playing possum to avoid any further retribution, but on second glance he thought Jandilyn's strike was the last straw that had sent Roger hurtling off the edge of consciousness.

She quickly got out, making sure to kick the passenger door shut and leave a sizable door ding. She ran into Mike's arms. "How?" she asked. "Are you alright?"

"Are my brains leaking out?" Mike asked, showing her his purpling skull.

"I don't think so, I'm not sure you could afford to lose any," she said now sobbing.

"It's okay, honey, it's okay," Mike said over and over. They slowly walked away from Roger's car.

Mike had the receptionist at the library call the police. He was certain if he hadn't that Roger would find a way to turn this around and blame the assault on Mike and Jandilyn.

Mike was sitting on the rear bumper of the ambulance, an ice pack in hand and he was applying it gingerly to his aching head.

"So tell me again what happened," the cop asked for the third or fourth time. Mike was having great difficulty focusing.

"You might have a concussion, kid. You sure you don't want to go to the hospital?" the EMT asked.

Mike shook his head slowly. Any faster and he swore he could feel his brain moving and the pain became unbearable. "This is the last time," Mike said, defiantly. "Then my girlfriend and I are going home."

The cop was silent, neither confirming nor denying Mike's intentions.

"Jandilyn, with a K." Mike elaborated when he realized the cop wasn't writing anything down. "You've got your pen and your little notebook—why aren't you taking copious notes?" Mike asked.

"Don't you worry about me…I'm just trying to corroborate your story."

"So you're saying you pretty much know what I'm going to say, you just want to make sure I say it the same way? Am I right?"

The cop again did not reply.

"I'm done," Mike said, getting up off the bumper, he had to catch himself from falling back as he did so.

"You're done when I say you're done," the cop said evenly.

"And people wonder why folks have issues with authority. Go fuck yourself," Mike said.

The cop started to reach for his handcuffs. "Sergeant Gibson!" a plain clothes detective yelled as he approached. "Do you have everything you need from the witness?" The detective grabbed the small notebook.

"Almost, sir," the cop said, hating to have to kowtow in front of Mike.

"I think we're done here," the detective said, looking through the notes quickly. "We have your contact information if we need anything further, Mr. Talbot. Why don't you get your girlfriend and head home?"

Mike didn't say anything as he turned to leave. He had to fight a real desire to stick his tongue out at the uniformed officer. He walked over to Jandilyn who had a small blanket draped across her shoulders. She was talking to a female detective and she was holding an identical ice pack to her cheek. She smiled when she saw him coming even though it most likely hurt to do so.

"We've got him now," the female detective told Jandilyn. "You were lucky, we found these in the car." The detective held up a roll of duct tape, clothesline, and a large body bag size sheet of plastic. "I think he meant to kill you."

Mike's head ached even more when he realized just how close he had come to losing Jandilyn. "You ready to go home?" he asked, extending his free hand to her."

"Yes, very much so," she said, getting up from the detective's car.

"We'll be in contact," the detective told Jandilyn.

Jandilyn nodded and tightly gripped Mike's hand as they walked to her car.

"I'm shaking so bad, Mike, I don't think I can drive."

"I'll give it a shot."

"Comforting," she said as she placed her head on his shoulder. "I just barely escaped one life-threatening event, what makes you think I'd be so lucky a second time?"

Mike's mile-and-a-half drive home was almost as scary as their earlier encounter. He was all over the road, nearly sideswiping a parked Ford pickup and then overcompensating into the oncoming lane of traffic.

"Oh, dear God," Jandilyn said, completely forgetting her ice bag as she clutched at any hand hold that might help spare her from any further damage.

Mike had his tongue out and clenched his jaw tightly as he tried his best to concentrate on the task at hand. When they finally came up to their apartment building, Jandilyn's color and Mike's, for that matter, had drained. Mike jumped the curb as he thankfully brought the death ride to a halt.

"I can barely see." Mike turned to Jandilyn.

"That was plainly evident," she said as she vacated her car almost as quickly as she had Roger's. "Can you promise me we'll never do that again?" She came around to help him out of the car and up the stairs to their apartment.

"The driving or head-butting Roger?" Mike asked.

"Both."

When they had finally sat down on the couch Jandilyn looked over to Mike. "What were you doing there, Mike? Don't tell me what you told the cops—there's no way you thought I was cheating on you. And *no*, I wasn't," she added when Mike's eyebrows shot up in a question. "Roger set the whole thing up. He said he had told the entire class. Then when I got there he shrugged it off as being Saturday morning and nobody wanted to get up early and study. I almost left but I've got so much work, I figured what could it hurt? Sure, he's a little bit of a jerk, but he's also pretty smart."

Mike let his head drop a bit before he answered. "I

was about to go to sleep when you were leaving, I just happened to check out your gorgeous backside to lull me into sweet dreams and then I just lifted my patch for half a second. The colors surrounding you looked wrong, there were angry reds, tinged with black and some swirling deep purple that looked the color of bruises. It didn't look right, Jandilyn. I'd never seen that before and I was concerned. I ran down to the library and spent about an hour looking for you."

"Did you see us at the table and then get up to leave together?"

Mike nodded.

"That would look a little suspect. Mike, do you believe I love you with all of me, with everything that I am? Sometimes I don't know where I end and you begin that's how closely I feel intertwined with you. You're my hero… again."

"It's what I do," Mike told her, half joking.

"Are you precognitive? Did the accident somehow allow you to see into the future?"

"I don't think so. I think I can see energy—the energy that surrounds us all, I just don't normally know what it means."

"He was going to kill me, Mike, his eyes were flat like a reptile's. Do you think that's what the 'black' was all about?"

"Probably."

They both shuddered, although their apartment was relatively balmy inside.

"How am I going to go through life like this, Jandilyn?"

"You're just going to have to make sure your contact is in all the time."

"If it had been today, we wouldn't even be having this conversation."

"Mike, I can't begin to tell you how grateful I am that

you saved me, but we can't live our lives afraid to do anything. We're not supposed to know when our time is up."

"But if I have the ability, aren't we obligated to try to stop it?"

"No, because then you start to disrupt the natural order of things," she said tenderly. "You have to promise me on all that we are you will not take that contact out again."

He agreed on principle. He didn't want to argue with her, Mike could count on one hand and have fingers left over how many times she'd let him win a fight. But he planned on making sure he snuck a peek at her through his left eye as often as possible.

That night Mike went into the bathroom with the sole intent of taking a shower. He did something he had rarely done since the accident; he stared at himself in the mirror without bandages, patches or a contact covering his eye. He choked back a strangled scream as he peered at his reflection.

On one side he looked like the normal Michael Talbot, albeit a little more tired and worried than the one from yesterday. But this time he was surrounded by a pulsing undulating cloak of black, occasionally a flicker of silver rippled through like mercury coated lightning but mostly it was blackness.

"You alright, Mike? You sound like you just choked on a cat," Jandilyn called from the bed.

"Good," Mike answered monosyllabically.

He knew he was going to die, now he was left wondering in what fashion. He waited for his heart to stop beating, wondering how much pain he would be in when his chin slammed off the corner of the vanity as he plunged to the ground. He wondered if he would be blocking the door with his lifeless body. Would Jandilyn beg him to let her in? Was it fair that he should save her only to die in return? He thought it was more than a fair trade, but he was going to miss her all the same.

"I thought you were taking a shower?" Jandilyn asked

when she didn't hear the water turn on.

Mike stood there waiting for the inevitable to happen. "Is today not a good day to die?" he asked himself.

"What?"

"Sorry," Mike answered, turning the shower on quickly to avoid any further discussion. Mike walked on eggshells the remainder of the weekend, waiting for the end to come. When a piano didn't land on his head Monday morning, he was no closer to an answer about what the black shroud meant, but he was still alive when he got into Jed's car that night.

"What the hell happened to you?" Jed asked, fixating on the angry purple greenish knot on Mike's forehead.

"Got into a wicked bad pillow fight with Jandilyn." Mike responded.

"Did she put a bowling ball in hers first? Damn, kid, that looks like it hurts."

"Would you mind, Jed, if I maybe told you about it someday…but not right now?" Mike asked with pleading eyes.

"Sure, Mike, sure," Jed said as he pulled away from the curb.

Jed was concerned for Mike. The kid hadn't said more than a handful of words the entire week even during the few games of cards they played. Even not paying attention, Mike cleaned his clock at poker. The rest of the time Mike had spent writing in a yellow legal pad he had found in one of the visitor kiosk drawers.

"That must be one hell of a shopping list," Jed said on Friday when Mike was digging through the drawers again, looking for a blank pad. The one he had got on Monday was full and sitting upside down on the desk.

"Got a second?" Mike asked.

"Actually, about five hours," Jed said, pointing up to the large clock.

Mike laid out everything that had happened Saturday

except for the part about what his left eye saw and about what he glimpsed in the mirror that evening. When he was through, they still had four and a half hours left on their shift.

"Holy shit," Jed said, taking in a breath with a distinctive whistle to it.

"Yeah, that's what I thought."

"You're an idiot to think that girl would cheat on you."

"Again, that's what I thought."

"You kicked his ass good then?"

"Believe it or not he's in worse shape than me."

"Should have killed him, Mike. Should have just put him down like the rabid sick man that he is."

"Maybe, Jed, but that wasn't my first concern. It was Jandilyn's safety."

"Well, I guess paranoia pays off sometimes," Jed said, reflecting on the entire thread of their talk.

"Jed, I was this close to losing her," Mike said, holding his thumb and forefinger a hair's breadth apart.

"You didn't, though, Mike. That's what you need to focus on. You didn't. Don't think about what might have been. Think about what is. That's much more important. Many people waste their lives mourning what has past, never once enjoying what is present, and dreading the future. That's no way to walk through this life. We live and learn from the past only to help us walk into the future, to reside solely in what has already happened leaves us wholly unprepared for what comes next."

"Maybe you missed your calling, Jed."

"How so?"

"Those are some mighty philosophical words."

"You think I could have been the next Descartes, maybe Socrates? Well, I'll tell you what, kid…night guardsman pays better and I have dental."

Mike laughed for the first time since Saturday. "Thanks, Jed, I needed that."

"Good, now sit down, I need to make some of my money back."

"How much do you owe me?"

"Let's just say the gift I was going to get my granddaughter for her birthday is now on hold."

"I take installments. I mean, of course I'll have to charge interest."

"Wonderful. Sit your ass down."

***

They fell into a routine like that, Mike would write furiously most weeknights whilst almost simultaneously taking Jed's money except for one day late in December when Jed had finally broke through and come out on top.

"About time!" Jed had screamed, standing up quickly from his chair, hands raised high. "Hallelujah!" he said enthusiastically as their Friday shift came to an end.

"Jed, I hate to be the bearer of mediocre news, but you're only up by a dollar sixty-two," Mike said.

"That's not the point, not the point at all. I can finally hold my head high this weekend."

"This been wearing on you a little bit?" Mike said, putting the poker chips and cards up.

"You could say that. The dog has been leery of me since me and you started playing."

"I finished this today," Mike said putting the last full yellow legal tab into his small backpack.

"Can I ask what it is?"

"I wrote a story."

"Well, it sure wasn't a short one."

"No, it wasn't."

"You going to let me read it?"

"Hell no. No one is reading it."

"What did you write it for then?"

"I wrote it for me."

"Well, what's the title at least?"

"I've been going back and forth, but I'm thinking about calling it *The Hanging Tree*."

"Romance then?" Jed asked with a straight face.

"Yup, right up your alley."

"Come on, let's go home, I've got to apologize to Bailey."

"Who?"

"My dog. Aren't you paying attention?"

"Not usually."

"At least you're honest."

Mike walked into his apartment and placed the last pad with the rest of the filled tablets located in the back of the cabinet by the crock pot Jandilyn had to have that was still unused in its box. *They're safe here*, he thought.

He quickly stripped off his uniform and climbed into bed with her, content for seemingly the first time since his friends had died. On some level he knew it had to do with the completion of his story but he hadn't put the pieces together.

***

Freshman year for Jandilyn thankfully ended without further incident, sometime around mid-June she was again able to take a shower without Mike present or the door open in case she had to make a hasty retreat. In late June unbeknownst to either of them, Jandilyn's parents sent her an airline ticket to come home on the Fourth of July weekend, Mike's invitation was suspiciously missing.

"I'm not going!" Jandilyn cried indignantly as she shook the envelope under Mike's nose. "The nerve of her. Of them both!"

"It's first class," Mike said, trying to get a clearer picture of the ticket as she shook it violently back and forth.

"I don't care, Mike, how could they be so rude?"

Mike grabbed Jandilyn's hand and took the

accompanying message from her. He paused to read it for a minute. "It says they're having a family reunion. I'm not family, Jandilyn. I really hate to not side with you on this one, especially since the other side has your mother on their team, but I think it's pretty nice of them. It's first class and at least it's round trip. I'd be more concerned if it wasn't."

"That's not the point, Mike. They know we live together, we should go on trips together."

"Jandilyn, you know I don't get any vacation time for another few months, I couldn't go, even if they had invited me."

"I know you're just being understanding, Mike, and I love you for it, but I'm not going."

"They give you free cookies in first class."

"Oatmeal?" she asked sniffing.

"I would imagine. Probably even white chocolate macadamia nut."

"Really?" she asked, her mascara now starting to run.

"Jandilyn, go. Go see your folks, you know you miss them. If you stayed here, they would blame me for it. Your mom already has enough stacked up against me. Don't give her any more ammunition."

"Will you be alright without me?" Jandilyn asked sincerely.

Mike was going to say, "What could possibly go wrong?" but he didn't want to mess with that kind of wording even if it was only rooted in superstition. "It's only four days…most likely I'll go to Jed's, watch some fireworks, and eat some barbecue. I'll be fine."

Three weeks later Jandilyn said a special goodbye. Mike made sure to get a good left-eyed look at her as she left. He was still smiling with the remembrance of her heat on his body as she closed the door and drove herself to the airport.

It was a few hours later and the sun was beginning to set. An approaching siren awoke Mike with a start from his slumber.

"Jandilyn?" he asked, sitting upright. Then he remembered she was heading home.

Mike thought about calling his home, he hadn't talked to anyone there in close to a year, but he was afraid they would think he was someone making a cruel crank call and he couldn't handle that right now. When Jandilyn walked out the door she took the best part of him with her. What was left was merely a shell that she filled when she was around.

A knock on his front door got his attention. For a momentary pang he thought it might be the cops coming to tell him Jandilyn had been in an accident.

"Kid, get your ass up!"

"Jed?" Mike asked softly from the hallway he had been dreading to head down.

"Open the damn door. I knew you'd be in here all crying and stuff because your girl was gone."

Mike opened the damn door.

"Get dressed, big card game at my house. I'm getting some of my money back. And don't even think about saying 'no' I can see it in on your lips."

"Fine, I needed some new sneakers anyway, the money will come in handy," Mike said as he let Jed in while he got dressed.

Mike quickly threw on some pants and a shirt and headed into the kitchen to grab his apartment key.

"I thought you said Jandilyn was leaving today?" Jed asked, looking over at Mike.

"She did," Mike answered absently.

"Are you stepping out on her? Because if you are…" Jed said hotly.

"What are you talking about, Jed? I'd no sooner cheat on Jandilyn than I would walk across hot coals!"

"Yet you see those dumb shits do that just about every day, Mike."

"Jed, what's the matter?"

"I just saw someone in your room, Mike."

Mike froze. "Did you actually see them, Jed?"

"Well, no, just the shadow of someone passing by. Who is she, Mike? You can't do this to that girl, she loves you."

"Jed, there's no one else here."

Jed looked at him dubiously.

"Go look, Jed, I won't stop you."

"Is this some kind of reverse psychology shit? You tell me I can go look so I feel guilty about it and don't go?"

"Nailed me, Jed, I've secretly been studying the works of Freud and Jung. Come on," Mike said grabbing Jed's arm.

A couple of minutes later, Jed scratched his head. "I'm sorry, Mike, I would have sworn I saw something. I…I guess maybe Gracie was right and I need to get a new prescription for my glasses."

Mike wanted to tell him his eyesight was more than likely fine but he didn't think Jed would believe the alternative.

Six hours later as Jed was dropping Mike—now thirty-eight dollars and fifty-seven cents richer—off at the curb to his building he asked the question that had been bothering him all night.

"What was it, Mike?" Jed asked.

"Well, you see, it's superior gamesmanship mixed in with the ability to bluff."

"We'll get back to that and, oh, by the way, my friends don't want to play with you anymore."

"Don't blame them," Mike said, fanning his face with a fistful of ones.

"You know what I'm talking about. In the apartment, you seemed confused at first and then it looked like something dawned in you."

"You believe in ghosts?" Mike asked.

"No."

"Then we're probably done here."

"I'll be by tomorrow at three to pick you up for the barbecue and the fireworks."

"You didn't even ask," Mike said.

"Asking would imply I was giving you a choice."

"Did Jandilyn put you up to this?"

Jed hesitated. "Sort of, but I wanted you over the house anyway."

"I'm not sure how I feel about this."

"How much money you have in your hand?"

"Almost forty bucks."

"Then shut the hell up and enjoy yourself."

"Thanks, Jed."

"It's a pleasure, my friend," Jed said honestly.

Mike tapped the hood of Jed's car as he took off for home. Mike was thankful that from his angle he couldn't see his apartment window because he would have bet thirty-eight dollars and fifty-seven cents that something was looking down at him.

Mike was sitting in his darkened apartment, the television was on but he wasn't watching it. He was drifting off to sleep and thought that he had when he heard someone speak.

"How long do you think you can hide from me?"

"What?" Mike asked shaking his head. He got up and shut the TV off. The apartment was only illuminated by a street lamp outside. It wasn't much and it did little to penetrate the dark corners.

"I've been watching you for a while, I'm not sure how you have eluded me this long."

"Who are you?" Mike asked, wishing he had left the set on for the added light.

"I am nothingness, I am the void."

Mike wanted to comment on the presence's banality, but this wasn't some open-mic-at-a-coffee-shop, I'm-more-important-than-you poet spewing forth his manic ravings.

"I don't know what you want with me," was the only

thing Mike could think to say.

"I want only one thing from you," it said, and then was gone.

It took another thirty minutes before Mike stopped seeing his breath and thirty more to stop shivering.

"Well, it only wanted one thing. Maybe it's an overdue library book." He was half right, although he didn't know it, something *was* indeed overdue.

***

Mike was like a little kid waiting for Santa on the day Jandilyn was to come home. He was hopping back and forth and finally had to go wait on the sidewalk even though Southern California was in the midst of its rainy season. Jandilyn jerked the car to a halt as she slammed it into park before it had come to a complete stop. She jumped out of the car and into Mike's arms, rapidly kissing him until he had to force her away.

"Miss me, I take it?" he asked.

"Oh, don't you go getting all aloof on me, you know you missed me, too."

Mike grabbed her bags and they headed upstairs. "Did you have a good time?"

"I did, but it didn't seem right without you there. Is everything alright here?" she asked, searching for something.

"Yeah, I ended up taking almost seventy-five bucks from Jed and his friends."

"Mike! You can't be a guest at someone's house and take all their money!"

"Shit, Jandilyn, they were almost throwing it at me. What was I supposed to do?"

"Lose some of it back."

Mike looked at her like she had two noses. "Why would I do that?"

"It's not always about winning."

"Sure it is."

"Forget it, I'll send them a 'thank you' note and try to smooth over your uncouthness."

"I told you what I think about those big words."

"Mike, be serious for a second. Is everything alright here?"

"I think so, Jandilyn."

"I had a strange dream about you. You were in a field and you were looking for something, but you weren't alone. I couldn't see who was with you but you both were looking for the same thing and if it found you first, it was going to kill you, Mike."

Mike shuddered, thankful Jandilyn was still ahead of him on the stairs and couldn't see it.

She stopped and turned. "It felt so real, Mike. I couldn't stop crying, my mother thought it was because I had to come back here." She laughed a short burst.

"Well, you can see I'm fine and from this angle I can tell you're fine too," Mike said as he was staring directly at Jandilyn's backside.

They spent the next two days secluded in their apartment reacquainting themselves with each other, taking momentary breaks to only fuel up for the next exploration.

"I'm almost frightened, Mike, how close we are," Jandilyn said at one point with Mike looking down on her. Tears had formed in the corners of her eyes.

"It would be tough to get any closer than we are right now, Jandilyn," Mike said with a wicked grin.

She smacked his arm. "You know what I mean. There's so much more than the physical, there's a connection between us. I can't imagine how I walked through my life before you. I can't even think how I could move forward without you."

"I'm not going anywhere, Jandilyn."

"I need to believe you, Michael Talbot."

Mike leaned down and kissed a tear. Jandilyn

shivered. They moved slowly in perfect unison, the tension winding through their bodies. When the end did come they lay exhausted and spent. Mike closed his eyes and was breathing huskily. Jandilyn rolled over and propped herself on her elbow and stared intently at Mike. He looked so peaceful, an irrational fear raced through her as she thought he might be dead. She reached out and stroked his cheek. She was relieved when she was rewarded with a smile.

"I'm not a damn machine, Jandilyn, I need a break," he said with a laugh.

"I'll allow it for now," she kidded. She had nothing left to give at the moment herself.

***

"Jandilyn must be home," Jed said as he reached over and unlocked the passenger door.

"That obvious?" Mike answered.

"How the hell can you wear your emotions on your sleeve like this and be such a good poker player? By the way, my friends said you're not invited back."

"That's alright, I can buy new friends now."

"Ouch. Jandilyn's good?"

"Jandilyn's great."

"Let's go. The wonderful world of coffee bean protection awaits."

"Actually sounds good, I could use a break."

"I don't even want to know. I'm married, Gracie and my idea of a good time is staying up late enough to watch Johnny Carson."

"Who?"

"Shut up, kid. Let's go."

***

Mike would dwell long and hard on the next couple

of years of his life. He could not imagine anything more idyllic than this time. His friendship with Jed, his chance to write, and heads and shoulders above it all was his relationship with Jandilyn. Every time when he thought they could not love each other anymore or that it could not get any more intense, they would reach a new threshold within themselves and each other propelling their relationship to new heights. They had transcended anything either one could have achieved on their own. Two more times over that period the Hollows had sent airline tickets for Jandilyn, she had refused them both.

Finally, Drew Hollow visited alone. He gave a lame excuse about Gina being afraid to fly. Mike was happy to have Jandilyn's dad visit as was Jandilyn. But Mike could tell she was silently seething about her mother. Jandilyn blazed through school but was still somehow unable to grasp the concept of how to cook a grilled cheese, much to Mike's delight.

"Just can't have everything from a girl, I guess," he said sadly, shaking his head when he came into the kitchen through a dense cloud of smoke.

"And what exactly does that mean, Mr. Talbot?" Jandilyn asked, her tongue in her cheek as she tried in vain to flip over the burnt remains of whatever had been in the nonstick pan and now was most likely an integral part of the cookware.

"I'm just saying, you have beauty and brains but I don't think you could boil water."

"Oh, you're a funny one, aren't you? I was making you lunch!"

"Is that what that was? I figured you were trying to create a new life form."

"You're going to eat this."

"You can't make me, Jandilyn, that's attempted murder."

Just then the smoke alarm went off. "Son, of a bitch!"

she said, stomping her foot in a small temper tantrum. "What is so damn hard about browning butter on a slice of bread?"

Mike came over and turned the stove top off. He moved the pan away from the heat and fanned the alarm until it quit. "Get dressed, I won a few bucks from Jed. Let's go out to eat."

"I could make you a peanut butter and jelly?"

"We should go out until the smoke clears up a bit."

She looked up at him, thankful for his rescue. And it was that image of Jandilyn that Mike usually went back to in his mind. Her beautiful, slightly upturned face, eyes wide with unspoken thanks, and a light of love burning fiercely.

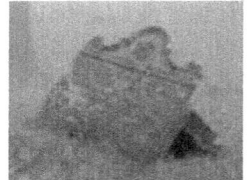

CHAPTER NINE – End of School

"One more final, Mike, and I'm done!" Jandilyn said, looking up from their small kitchen table. Her hair was mostly pulled back, but a bunch of strands had wiggled free and were framing her face.

"Did you know you just about glow?" Mike asked leaning up against the doorframe leading into the kitchen.

"I recognize that smile—I can't right now, I have to finish studying!"

"That's not it at all. I got you something."

"Does it rhyme with schmocolate?"

"Not quite." Mike pulled out a small box from his pocket.

Jandilyn's eyes grew, Mike couldn't tell if she was excited or surprised—in a bad way.

"What is that, Mike?" Jandilyn asked pushing her chair away from the table. Mike thought she was going to bolt out into the street.

"Umm, maybe nothing," Mike said, thinking that maybe putting the thing back in his pocket might be the right move.

"Is that what I think it is?" She had finally stood completely up and had backed up even farther.

"Jandilyn, I'm sorry, we could just call it a future promise or something."

"It is!" she squealed, she hadn't been backing up to get away she had been backing up so she could gain more speed as she flew into his arms. Mike grabbed her in mid-flight after she launched herself at him. "Yes, yes, yes!" she said over and over, punctuating each word with a kiss.

"I mean, if you're hesitant at all, we can talk about this," Mike said sarcastically between lips smacks.

"What took you so long? We've been living together for four years. My mother said why would he want to fertilize the lawn when all he needs to do is mow it."

"What does that even mean?" Mike asked. "Forget it, I don't even want to know. I wanted to wait until you were done with school."

"Oh, my God, it's beautiful!" Jandilyn yelled, holding the small-stoned ring up to the light.

"How did you get that out of my hand?" Mike asked, putting her down and looking at the now empty open purple jewelry box in his right hand.

"Are you going to get down on one knee now?" she asked excitedly.

"You already said yes, I don't see why I should go through the trouble."

"Because I command it." She laughed.

"Nice, we're off to a stellar beginning." Mike snatched the ring from her hand.

"Hey."

"If we're going to do this we're going to do it right."

"Fine," she pouted.

Mike made a great show of getting down on one knee. "Here ye, here ye. I, Michael Talbot of sound mind and more than sound body, doth bequest thy hand, Jandilyn Hollow, in holy matrimony. What say thee?" Mike asked as he opened the box back up.

"A thousand yeses," she said softly, a tear rolling down her face.

"That went well," Mike said as he put the ring on Jandilyn's finger.

***

Three hours later, Jandilyn had called everyone,

including her parents, in her phonebook. "Well, that's seven congratulations, five, 'oh, that's nices,' twelve 'aren't you a little youngs?' three 'who is thises?' and one 'you're going to marry that puissant?'. I'm sorry, Mike, but the general consensus doesn't really seem to be on our side—we'll have to call it all off."

"I figured as much, the ring is only a loaner anyway. By the way, was the last one your mother?"

Jandilyn's stare had 'what do you think?' written all over it.

"How did you afford this, Mike?" she asked, holding it up to the light.

"Well, it's not exactly the crown jewels, but you might want to be especially nice to Jed when you see him next."

"Cards?"

"Every last nickel, I've saved everything I've won from him."

"Oh, that poor man, maybe I should marry him since he bought me the ring."

"I'm sure he'd be flattered but he's married."

"It's always the good ones." She sighed. "I've got something for you, too."

"Really?"

"Now don't get mad."

"I hate it when you preface stuff that way, Jandilyn. Last time you did that we ended up with a cat. I don't like cats."

"Winter loves you," she said, defending their coal black cat.

"She's alright, but as a whole, cats are the gatekeepers to the underworld, Jandilyn, and as such…they cannot be trusted."

"Do you want to see what I got you or not?"

"Sorry, I forgot."

Jandilyn ran down the hallway, Mike could hear her

rummaging around in their bedroom, she came out a moment later holding a spiral bound book with *The Hanging Tree by Michael Talbot* written on the front in large calligraphy.

Mike at first didn't understand what was going on.

"About four months ago I was going to make a roast," Jandilyn started. Mike began to fidget. "When I pulled the crock pot out, a legal pad fell out too, so I tried to see where it came from and I saw the whole stack of them."

"Jandilyn, those were private."

"Well, I figured they were the way you had them locked up in a safety deposit box. Anyway, I started to read it, Mike, and then I can't explain it, I fell into the story. I felt like I was a part of everything going on in it. I couldn't read it fast enough, I stayed awake just about three nights straight trying to finish it. It was amazing, Mike! Luckily, I'm well-versed in chicken scratch or I wouldn't have been able to decipher it, but other people need to see this story, so I typed it out for you and then the local copier store did this binding."

"First off, I'm a little embarrassed, I honestly didn't mean for anyone but me to read it, but you really liked it? I mean you're not just saying that?"

"Mike, I thought maybe perhaps I was a little biased, so I showed the first three chapters to my English professor."

"What?" Mike rose out of his seat.

"Mike, he loved it maybe even more than I did, if that's even possible. He did some editing but said it was almost impossible because he was having such a difficult time separating himself from what was happening. He has some friends in the literary world who he wants you to send that to."

"You mean so it can be published?"

"No, so it can be used at a book burning event in Utah."

"I don't know, Jandilyn, this is a lot to take in."

"Mike, you have a gift, I don't care if you are a

security guard for the rest of your life, it makes absolutely no difference to me, but you owe it to yourself to put this book out there."

"Jandilyn."

"I thought you might have some indecision."

"What did you do?"

"What do you think I did?"

"How long ago?"

"About a week. Are you mad?"

"At you? When's the last time I've been mad at you? I just wish you had asked me first."

"You should be happy I asked at all, even if it is after the fact."

***

Three months passed by. Mike alternated between extreme excitement at the potential of having his book published and the abject fear of a rejection letter. Jandilyn, on the other hand, was walking around as if she possessed hover sneakers; her feet barely touched the floor as she thought about their upcoming wedding. Out of necessity it would be a very small affair, the Hollows (or at least Mrs. Hollow) had made it abundantly clear they in no way would sponsor the event.

Jed seemed to be purposefully playing worse poker if that were even possible.

"Jed, you're making this way too easy," Mike said as he scooped up another pot.

"I'm just thrilled for you two kids," Jed said as he shuffled the cards.

"Yeah, but you don't need to pay for my retirement fund. I liked it better when I was taking your money and you were trying."

"Kid, I'm just setting you up."

"Oh, is this the five year hustle plan?"

"Something like that. Go do a round, I'm going to take a bathroom break."

Mike was in good spirits as he headed out to check the building. There had not been so much as a rat turd in the last four years, so Mike had no apprehension as he headed down the hallway to the sign-in sheet. He had been so lost in his thoughts he barely registered the large door at the end of the hallway finally coming to a rest as if someone had just pushed it open.

A feeling of cold as if he had fallen into icy water washed over him. He stood there holding the clipboard. "Jed?" He knew it wasn't him, Jed wasn't a practical joker and he would have had to sprint to get down here before Mike.

Mike pushed through the double-hinged door. The warehouse was at least twenty degrees cooler than the hallway. The smell of coffee was strangely absent again. The lack of heat seemed to have Mike frozen in indecision.

"Are you the thing I saw at our apartment?" Mike asked.

"Mike," he heard his name faintly. If he had had a change of clothes handy, he might have soiled the ones he was wearing just out of principle or sheer terror. He heard his name again, only this time it was behind him.

"Jed?" He said as he pushed back through the warehouse door. Jed was leaning against the wall at the far end of the hallway. He was clutching his chest. "Jed!" Mike said louder, running toward his friend.

Mike watched as Jed's form went rigid and then he collapsed to the floor. By the time the ambulance and fire department got there Jed had turned the hue of a violent winter morning sky.

"He didn't suffer," the EMT said as he witnessed Mike's distress. "He died before he hit the floor."

Only he hadn't, Mike thought. Oh sure, Jed's heart had stopped and he was no longer taking breaths, but when

Mike skidded to a stop by his fallen friend's head, Jed's eyes had still been open and were focused on him. "You're a good kid, Mike—who's that with you?" he asked, looking over Mike's shoulder, and then he was still.

"No!" Mike had said defiantly, stepping between Jed and whatever harbinger had come. It had been far too late. Mike thought he heard the echo of laughter on the cold breeze passing through him.

Mike and Jandilyn sat in the front row along with Grace for Jed's memorial service. The church was three-quarters packed. Mike knew Jed was a great guy, but had no idea he had so many friends and family. He considered it an honor to be counted among them. Mike was in a daze throughout most of the service, he could feel eyes upon him but every time he would do a quick scan of his surroundings he never saw anyone focused on him; most were wiping tears from their faces.

"If anyone would like to say a few words?" the priest asked.

Mike rose woodenly and walked to the pulpit. He tried to clear the knot in his throat. "Jed was a lot of things to a great many people—husband, father, grandfather, crappy card player (that elicited some laughs and a couple of 'ain't that the truths' from the crowd), but he was also my friend. He took on a kid that life had kind of twisted into knots and gave him a chance. My fiancée, Jandilyn, and myself loved Jed and his wife Grace who invited us into their house dozens of times over the last few years for dinners and barbecues, mostly I think because they knew we hadn't eaten anything better than Ramen noodles for the last week (more small laughs). I cared so much for the man, I had asked him to be my best man at our upcoming wedding." Mike broke down, he turned away as tears free fell from his face. Grace, Jed's wife, came up and wrapped her arms around a now sobbing Mike.

"He loved you, we love you both so much. We

consider you family."

"I'm supposed to be consoling you, Grace," Mike said haltingly.

The gray skies finally let go their yield as Jed's casket was lowered into the ground. "Fitting," Mike said as he put his hands out to collect some of the cold water to rub on his face. "I'll miss you, dear friend," Mike said as he tossed a flower onto the casket. He was empty inside. Mike and Jandilyn left the cemetery hand in hand.

CHAPTER TEN – The Wedding

Jandilyn's parents had come around somewhat on the urging from Mr. Hollow that Mrs. Hollow should make things right with her daughter no matter what she thought of the man who was marrying her.

"For God's sake, Drew, he's a goddamn security guard. He must bring home a whopping three hundred dollars a week. What kind of life is that asswipe going to give our little girl?"

"Our 'little girl' is twenty-two and that 'asswipe' as you call him saved our daughter's life."

She waved his response away. "So what! This isn't colonial Japan, she doesn't owe him the rest of her life in return."

"For Chrissakes, Gina that isn't what this is about. She loves him."

"Love? How pathetic—marriage is about creating a stronger union among individuals, a collecting of wealth."

"Yes, look how well that's worked for us," Drew said sarcastically. Gina sneered at him.

"With or without your blessing, I'm helping them out."

"Throw them some welfare money. They'll be just like the coloreds in the Bronx, waiting for the mailman to bring them their crack money."

"What in the hell are you talking about? I'm going to help them have a small ceremony and a little seed money to start their new life together. Crack? Coloreds? When did you become a cynical racist?" Drew began to walk out of the room. He didn't want to be anywhere near this stranger. He turned back before he was completely out the door. "The ceremony is next month, I bought you a ticket on the flight but I suspect I'll be traveling alone."

"I wouldn't go if it were to save my very soul."

"That would imply that you had one," he said as he walked out of the room, wondering why he had wasted the last twenty-two years of his life with her.

***

The ceremony was beautiful in its simplicity. Jed and Grace had previously discussed renting out a small function room for Jandilyn and Mike. Grace had seen no reason to not follow through, the day was a beautiful seventy degrees, the grounds were on a small hillside looking out onto the Pacific. The wedding was held outdoors.

"Thank you, Grace," Mike had said, giving her a huge hug.

"Mike, that's at least the seventeenth time you've said that, I get it," Grace said as she stood by his shoulder.

"This isn't weird for you being my best man?" Mike asked, stooping down to her ear so he wouldn't be heard by the fair number of Jandilyn's friends and family that had showed.

"I'm honored you thought highly enough of me enough to ask." She beamed.

"Thank you, Grace."

The organist started up the wedding song and Mike thought his heart might have stopped for a few beats as he caught site of Jandilyn coming down the aisle. Mike bent over slightly as his contact slid. As he came back up, his heart almost stopped beating for the second time that day, black flecks that looked like a cloud of flies were at the periphery of Jandilyn's aura, but even that could not hold a candle to the sight of the thin black clad man that stood next to the organ player, its features were blurry as if being viewed from underwater. One thing Mike could tell was that whatever the creature used as eyes, they were fixated on Jandilyn.

"*No!*" Michael screamed, the thin man whipped around to look at Mike and when it realized it was visible it dissipated much like the apparition in their apartment.

"You alright?" Grace asked. "My God, you have no color!"

Mike rocked on his heels and if not for the steadfastness of Grace he would have pitched over face first.

The organist who had stopped at Michael's scream resumed. When Grace was certain Mike wouldn't topple she had urged the player on. Jandilyn was looking up at Mike, confusion clearly across her features.

Color was flushing into Mike's cheeks as he now became the focus of the wedding guests.

"I'm sorry…I—"

"It's my fault," Grace said slyly. "I told him an inappropriate joke." The crowd seemed to titter and then relax.

"Thank you, Grace," Mike said softly as Jandilyn resumed her march down the aisle.

"You alright?"

"I saw something, that's all," Mike said, vaguely not wanting to elaborate—ever.

The rest of the wedding went off without a hitch Mike's earlier outburst all but forgotten. Mike swore when they got back from their honeymoon he was going to see about having his contact super glued in place.

"You saw something again, didn't you?" Jandilyn asked as they lay in their bedroom that night before heading out on their honeymoon.

He thought about lying, but they were married now, that transgression seemed to carry more weight. "I did."

"The same thing that was here?" she asked.

Mike could feel the ripples of goose bumps form on

her skin. "Yes, I think. I don't know," Mike said, trying to avoid finding an answer.

"Is there more you're not telling me?"

Vows or not, he would not voice his fears. To do so would bring validity to them. "No."

***

As beautiful as Hawaii was, courtesy of Jandilyn's dad, Mike could not relax. He imagined every possible bad outcome, from the flight plunging into the deep blue sea, to attacks by hammerhead sharks every time Jandilyn even looked at the ocean.

"Mike, don't get me wrong," Jandilyn said after a particularly long marathon session. "Being in bed with you is phenomenal. But how often are we going to get to Hawaii? I want to go exploring."

"What if the volcano takes this inopportune time to go all volcanoey?" Mike asked, raising his hands as if they were hot magma.

"Volcanoey? Mike this is Oahu, only the big island has an active volcano."

"Oh."

"Let's go for a drive, I'd like to see the North Shore where they do all the surfing competitions."

"Are there sharks?"

Jandilyn just looked at him with her head tilted. "You're acting strange. I mean even stranger than normal."

"Fine, let's go look at the big waves. If I see a killer whale, we're coming back."

"Fair enough." She laughed.

"I'm serious," Mike said earnestly.

"I got that. Come on, you're being a wet shirt."

"Better than wet pants."

Jandilyn drove their rental Ford up the Likelike Highway, then went on to Highway 91 which was something of a misnomer unless two lane roadways not much wider than what a rickshaw would feel comfortable on, now qualified as such.

"Jandilyn, wait-wait," Mike said as he peered out of his window. "It's the Dole plantation. This is where they grow pineapples!" Mike said excitedly. "I fucking love pineapples, but wait," he said with confusion, "it's empty. All the fields are empty—where the hell are the trees?"

"You're kidding, right?" Jandilyn asked, pulling over so she could safely look at the same fields Mike was with the huge Dole sign.

"I don't see a tree for days," Mike said, stepping out of the car. "Did they have a fire or something? Oh, man, there's going to be a huge shortage of them now, I bet they'll cost like ten bucks a pound if you can even get them."

"Mike," Jandilyn said, tapping him on the shoulder after she also had got out of the car. Mike was pacing up and down the roadway, contemplating how he was going to stock up on his favorite fruit before he couldn't afford it anymore.

"Yeah, Hon?" Mike said, wiping his hand over his face.

"Pineapples don't grow on trees."

"What? You're shitting me, right? Are you just trying to make me feel better?"

"Mike, look at the ground. Closer," she instructed while his eyes were still dancing around.

Mike looked from where he expected trees to be blooming to the ground where spiky green leaves where poking out of the dirt.

"Holy shit, Jandilyn, I'm looking at it and I still don't believe it. I really thought they grew from trees."

"Convinced yet?"

"Not yet, but we can get going. This still might be a conspiracy."

"Yeah, they uprooted the trees and buried a few of the pineapples just to fool you."

"It could drive the prices up too," Mike said, failing miserably to defend his position.

***

The North Shore of Oahu is what most folks who travel to the island expect it to be. Laid back Islanders with ponytails, locals surfing in the huge breaking waves, whales within sight of the coast. Deep blue waters, dotted with sailboats. Local eateries with reasonable prices offering a variety of local cuisine heavy on the spam. What the vast majority encounter instead is Waikiki beach where the sand is so packed with tourists it is impossible to make it to the water without stepping over the quilted patchwork of oversized beach towels as thousands of tourists try to parcel out an eight foot square segment of beach. Traffic rivals downtown LA, fine dining establishments can set someone back two hundred dollars for appetizers and the tourist trap is in full-on money-squeezing mode.

It was quiet on the North Shore except for the occasional seagull. The sun was shining, it was a beautiful seventy-five degrees with a cooling breeze coming off the ocean and still Mike could not relax.

"Maybe we should move a few more feet up the beach," Mike said as he watched a whale breach a half mile away from their location.

"This place is perfect, Mike," Jandilyn said, looking up from her book. "Are you going to tell me what's going on in that head of yours? And don't give me that 'I don't know what you're talking about' crap."

"How well do you know me?" Mike asked, clearly confused that his new wife could see so easily through him. "Will I ever be able to have a secret again?"

"Probably not, so out with it—what's going on?"

Mike took a heavy breath. To have fears was one thing, to voice them was another. It gave them life or so the superstition goes. "I saw something…" he started. She prodded him on. "The day of our wedding, my contact slipped."

"You saw more than the ghost?"

Mike wasn't convinced that what he was seeing was a ghost, but that seemed like the least benign of all the possibilities, so he went with that.

"I did."

"And?"

"Are you kidding me? Are there messages flashing on my forehead or something?"

"Your transparency is one of the things I love about you."

"Great, I'm the glass man."

"Mike."

"Sorry. Jandilyn, there was something around you, too."

Now she sat up. The last time Mike had seen something around her, Roger had meant her a great deal of bodily harm. "Like the time at the library?" she asked.

"No, it was different. There were all your colors like normal, but right on the edges were these little flecks of black, almost like ash from a fire."

"Do you know what it means?"

"I don't, Jandilyn, and that's why I'm so afraid. If something were to happen to you, I would cease to exist."

"Don't say that. Don't ever say that. Besides, I'm fine."

"And what would you have said the morning you left to go to the library?"

"Michael!" she shouted. "We cannot live our lives like that. Always looking over our shoulders."

"Are you sorry you married me?"

"Are you insane?"

"According to the US Government."

"What?" she asked, completely stopped in her tracks.

"If you've tripped more than ten times the government considers you clinically insane."

"What?" she asked again, shaking her head, trying to make the cobwebs Mike was throwing at her go away.

"It's true."

"Fine. Whatever, but it was more of a rhetorical question. I think I've been in love with you since that time on the football field and it has done nothing except grow each and every day, you bonehead."

"Bonehead? Does that mean today we've had a slight downturn in our love growth?" Mike asked smiling.

"What do you see now?"

"I see the most beautiful woman I could ever imagine, smiling back at me and her eyes say she's really horny and wants to go back to our hotel room and ruin the bed springs."

"You see all that, huh? Now how about without your contact."

"Jandilyn?"

"Mike, are you precognitive?"

"I don't think so."

"Then you don't really know what you're seeing, do you," she said more as a statement.

"No, just feelings."

"Take your contact out."

"I'd rather get a root canal."

"I think I'm going to go for a swim," Jandilyn said, getting up and heading for the surf where ten foot high waves crested over the shoreline.

"Fine-fine, hold on," Mike said as he placed his finger into his left eye. He slowly eased the contact out of position and then grasped it between his thumb and forefinger. The light that flooded in overwhelmed his senses. For a brief second his eyeball seared in the Pacific Isle sun.

Jandilyn was looking down on him. "Well?"

"You're still gorgeous," he said, blinking rapidly, hoping his eye would adjust to the blinding light soon.

She placed her hands on her hips.

Inexplicably, the light brightened even more, a burst occurred deep in Mike's head. His eyes rolled back as he fought to stay conscious.

"Mike?" Jandilyn screamed from across the universe.

"Jandilyn, I'm dead!" Mike screamed as his head slumped down to the towel covered sand.

***

Mike awoke seven hours later, although he didn't know how much time had passed. The bed he was laying in was cool, the sheets itchy, and the monitor next to his head beeped quietly. Jandilyn was sitting in a chair barely designed for human use, it looked entirely too stiff and uncomfortable. Her back was ramrod straight her head to the side as she tried to sleep.

"How you doing?" she asked, her eyes twinkling by the glow of the monitors.

"What's going on?"

"The Dole consortium decided you knew too much and tried to take you out."

"This is bad," Mike said, agreeing with her. If she was trying to cover it with humor it had to be bad.

"Mike, the doctor's say you're blind in your left eye," she said taking his hand.

"I think I'd rather have it that way," he told her, but the loss of function of any part of him, no matter how suspect its actually workings, disturbed him.

"There's more."

"I hate 'more', Jandilyn."

"They said you've been blind probably since the accident."

"What?"

"That's good news, right? They said that anything you saw out of there were residual images probably—ghost imagery, they said."

That makes more sense, Mike thought. *The ghost imagery, not the blindness.*

"So anything you thought you had seen surrounding me wasn't really there," she said.

Mike thought she was trying to be convincing but was falling flat.

"I know what I saw, Jandilyn."

Mike spent the remainder of the night in the hospital, Jandilyn crawled into the small bed with him. It was not the most comfortable set up, but it beat the torture chair by a mile.

"I think the police use that thing to interrogate terrorists," she said, pointing over to the salmon-colored misery device that somewhat resembled a chair.

"I'd like to get a Dole representative or two in that thing. I'd find out what was going on with the world's supply of pineapple."

Jandilyn snuggled up close, resting her head on Mike's chest. She took comfort in the strong beat of his heart. Mike absently stroked her hair as she fell asleep. His left eye itched under the patch the hospital had applied, even without 'seeing it' he knew they were not alone in the room.

"I know you're here," he said softly so as not to disturb his wife. "I don't know what you are or what you want, but I'm going to find out. When I do…you'll be sorry." He hoped the visitor could see the truth in his words as easily as his wife.

Jandilyn listened to Mike's soft words, his hammering heart had awoken her, she shivered as he spoke. Even the tropical air could not keep her warm, she didn't know if it was the power of suggestion but she felt a presence as well.

***

"Hello, Michael," a thin-lipped Japanese man said as he peered down at Mike's chart attempting to see through his glasses. "Damn bifocals, I've had them for six months and I still haven't got used to them. Piece of advice, son, don't grow old," he said smiling, his eyes nearly vanishing as he did so. Mike instantly liked the man.

"Can we leave today?" Mike asked.

"Well, she can leave whenever she likes," the doctor said, pointing to Jandilyn. The smile returned. "And yes, I just need to sign your discharge papers."

"What happened to me?"

"We think it was sunstroke, it happens to a lot of vacationers. They don't realize how intense the sun is out here, especially when they lay in it all day."

"Did the Dole consortium send you?"

"What? Are you still having residual effects?" The doctor took out a small penlight from his breast pocket and focused it into Mike's right eye. The pupil contracted. The doctor lifted the patch and Mike shied away as the intense beam seemed to scrape against the back of his head.

"You do realize there is no activity in that eye, yes?" the doctor asked. "Your pupil does not dilate and the loss of pigmentation most likely is associated with the loss of blood to the eye."

"Doc, I'm telling you I can see that light."

Mike said it with such conviction the doctor peered into the eye again. "Mike, I think you should see a specialist, possibly get an MRI—that should come up with conclusive evidence to the devastation the accident you were in caused, then possibly a therapist so that you can deal with the loss of vision on this side."

"Doc, I'm not making this up."

"Oh, I never thought that, Michael. I just believe that your brain is overcompensating for the loss, I believe that you are seeing echoes of things you remember seeing."

Don't ever recall seeing a smoke clad thin man

before the accident, Mike thought sourly.

"What time is it?" Jandilyn asked, stretching.

"About time to go," Mike said, smiling at her.

"You're alright?"

"Heat stroke apparently brought on by evil Dole hit men—how bad off could I be?"

"Doctor, is there any chance you can give him something for this?" Jandilyn asked jokingly.

The doctor shrugged his shoulders. "A nurse will be right back with your discharge papers. I hope you two enjoy the rest of your stay in our fair state."

"Thank you," Jandilyn said.

Mike was staring out the window.

"Did you 'see' anything yesterday before you screamed?"

"I screamed?"

She nodded.

"Was it girlie?"

"No, honey, it was one of the manliest screams I've ever heard," she said, stroking his cheek.

"Did I just scream or did I say something?"

"You told me that you were dead, Mike. But the doctors say people with heat stroke say crazy stuff all the time, something about their thoughts getting fried."

"I don't have heat stroke, Jandilyn."

"I know, baby."

"And no, I didn't see anything except the sun. It was so intensely bright I couldn't make anything else out."

'Right back' for the nurse was forty-five minutes. Mike was seconds from walking out the door. "What's the worst they could do, extradite us back from the mainland?" Mike quipped with Jandilyn urging him to stay for just a few minutes longer.

Mike was glad he had stayed the extra time. The doctor advised that he spend the majority of his time in his hotel room, limiting his exposure to the Hawaiian sun. It was something Mike had been advocating all along with Jandilyn. The downside was that Jandilyn decided that if they couldn't go out during the day they would have to check out the nightlife. And who knew what ghouls that would bring out of the wood work.

Except for some minor speed bumps the vacation had been more than either one could have imagined, so Mike figured the plane was going to go down on their way home.

He turned to Jandilyn. "Would you rather the plane crash during takeoff or landing?" he asked.

"You tell me. You've obviously been thinking about it." She put her book down to look at him.

"Take off. Definitely take off."

"I'm waiting."

"For what?" Mike asked.

"Your explanation of why."

"That's easy. Nobody likes plane travel so I'd rather go down at the beginning than have to sit in this damn tube for six hours and then crash and burn."

"You're scaring my children," a scarecrow thin woman said, covering her three-year-old son's ears with her claw-like hands.

"I don't even think he heard me because he seems to be minding his own business," he told Mrs. Strawman. She got the point.

She turned her child's head as he was still smiling his gap-toothed grin at Mike.

"Michael!" Jandilyn said as she smacked him. "You need to be nice to people."

He didn't think he hadn't been.

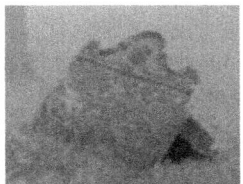

CHAPTER ELEVEN – Life Changes

Mike went back to the coffee warehouse, the security firm he worked for had decided to not replace Jed. From this point forward, all shifts would be manned by one individual. It meant he was on call seven days a week in the event of a person calling in sick. He didn't mind, it meant he had more time to write. He did miss the additional income he had made playing cards with Jed, but life rolled on.

"I miss you, old man," he said as every shift started. He even took the cards out of the pack and would lay two hands out, 'just in case'.

For two more months the world traveled in this fashion, but if there is one thing the planet abhors, it is stagnation. The world thrives on change; it is the agent upon which all life revolves, for good or bad.

"You sitting, Mike?" Jandilyn asked as he walked in the door.

"Do I look like I am?" he asked her, clearly confused.

"You should then."

There was something clearly wrong, Mike thought. Her brow was beaded in sweat and she looked flushed, like she sometimes did after a go around on the treadmill at the gym.

"Jandilyn?"

"Relax you baby, I've got some news."

"I hate the news, I never watch it. It's always about missing people, murder, and drugs—"

"Shush, I've got good news and good news. Which do you want first?"

"Jandilyn, my heart is going to come out of my

throat—could you just tell me?"

"Which one?" she said, almost dancing back and forth from foot to foot.

"The good news," he said, half rising.

She pushed him back down. "Touch my belly, do you feel anything?"

"Didn't I tell you to stay away from that Mexican restaurant? You always feel like crap when you go there for lunch with your work mates? Maybe *el gato* doesn't agree with you."

"It is not cat! And the food there is delicious, but yes it does tend to hurt my belly afterwards."

"And then I'm the recipient. I bet you don't let go of those stinkers while you're at work. No, you save them all up for me and I've been meaning to tell you, you're burning out my olfactory—"

"I'm pregnant, you shit!" She laughed.

"Is it mine?" Mike asked, standing up. "Sorry, knee-jerk reaction. That's awesome." His grin matched hers.

He twirled her a couple of times around their tiny kitchen.

"You'd better put me down or you are going to see what I had for breakfast."

Mike gently placed her down.

"This is more than I could have ever hoped for, Jandilyn!"

"Are you sure?" she asked, biting her bottom lip.

"What the hell do you think all that practice was for?" he asked, pointing to their bedroom.

"I guess practice makes perfect."

"I'll ask for some more shifts at the warehouse. With Lou on vacation and Jeff always calling in sick it shouldn't be a problem and then there's holiday pay..." Mike was going on calculating all the different ways he could earn more money.

"Mike, stop for a sec. Now don't get mad."

"Mad at you? For what? Does this go back to the whole 'is it mine' thing? Do I need to get a DNA test?"

"Stop, will you? I opened your mail."

"What!" Mike bellowed. "That is a federal offense!" he said, stomping around. "You know I like to open up all my bill notices when I'm on the john, it relaxes me."

"Don't worry, I didn't open up anything that might take away from your man time. I needed to open this up."

Mike was intrigued. "Well, go ahead woman, your flare for the dramatic is killing me. Do I have a long lost uncle who just died and left me untold fortunes?"

"Sort of. It's from Random."

"Who's Random?"

"The book publishing house."

"What about them?" Mike asked, still not putting the whole equation together yet.

"Mike, they loved your book. They want the rights to it. They offered a two hundred and fifty thousand dollar advance."

Mike sat down so hard, he thought he might have broken his butt. "This is a joke, right? And it's not really funny, Jandilyn…not even a little bit. You know how many years I'd have to work at the warehouse to get that kind of money."

"Mike, I like a good practical joke from time to time, but I'm not cruel."

"Devious, maybe," Mike said, looking up at her. "But no, definitely not cruel."

"Look," she said excitedly, pushing the papers almost into his nose.

"And this is real, not one of your friends pulling a prank and sending this to us?" Mike asked as he quickly looked over the acceptance letter and the contract.

"I didn't tell anyone except you that I sent it."

"What do I tell—" he almost said Jed. If the old man were still there he thought he'd stay, but with his friend gone he saw no reason to. "Do I give two weeks' notice?"

"It's the right thing to do. They've treated us fairly."

"Holy shit, Jandilyn, I'm an author! And you're pregnant, I think I need to go have some man time, I'm so happy I could—"

"Don't you dare say it."

***

"Everything looks great," the doctor said with a smile as she showed Mike and Jandilyn the ultrasound monitor. "There's the heart and the hands. Do you want to know the sex?"

Mike absolutely did and did not.

"Mike?" Jandilyn asked, looking over at him.

"Up to you," he said grinning like the village idiot.

"Okay," Jandilyn said.

The doctor began to move her ultrasound device around. "And there."

"I'm going to get a sandwich—anyone want anything?" Mike said, standing quickly and rapidly heading for the door.

"Chicken," Jandilyn called to his retreating back.

"With mayo?" Mike yelled back, trying his best to get out of earshot from the doctor.

Her minor insult now sounded like good eats. "With pickles!"

Mike threw his hand up over his shoulder in acknowledgement of getting her order.

"So do you want to know?" Jandilyn asked him that night as they sat on their new couch in their new apartment.

"If it's mine, you mean?" Mike asked back.

"You're lucky I'm as big as a house or I'd waddle after you and squish you under my bulk.

"I've been worried about you rolling over at night and doing me some bodily harm."

"Don't make my mom be right about you!"

"Wow, you play dirty," Mike said with a shocked face.

"Come here," she said.

"You look beautiful, Jandilyn," Mike said as he approached.

"That's not going to make it all better. Now get closer." Mike leaned down so Jandilyn could brush her lips against his. "I love you, Mr. Talbot, now if you could make me a grilled cheese and peanut butter sandwich I might forget we had this entire conversation."

"Jandilyn, that sounds disgusting. I'd rather keep having this talk."

The smell of cooking peanut butter dominated the kitchen area a moment later.

"Throw some jalapeños in there!" Jandilyn yelled from the living room.

Mike gagged a little as he opened the sandwich up and tossed some peppers in the mix. "I wouldn't give this to your mother," he said softly.

"What about my mother?"

"I'm looking forward to seeing her," he said through gritted teeth.

"Mike, you really should look into some acting classes before she gets out here so you can at least pretend to be civil."

"I will act as nice to her as she does to me."

"Oh, that oughtta be fun. Is my sandwich ready?"

"Jandilyn, she asked me what drugs I got you hooked on that were making you stay with me."

"Yeah, and if I remember correctly you told her, manmeatadone."

Mike snorted. "Hey, that was some pretty funny shit."

Jandilyn laughed too. "I wonder if she ever figured that out."

"I kind of hope so and I don't, but your dad had to

walk out of the room before he lost it."

"She'll only be out for a week once the baby is born."

"How impressionistic are newborns?"

"Don't worry, the baby won't catch anything from her."

"Now I am." Mike walked in holding the sandwich away from his face, the heated peanut butter mixed with the heat of the pepper and brine of the vinegar were not doing his stomach any favors. "You can barely eat saltines in the morning and you eat this thing at night?"

"How's the new book going, Mr. Talbot?"

"I was thinking about writing a zombie book with your mom as the lead character."

"You know she'll read it, right?"

"I think she'd be a perfect zombie, she's already got the groans down to a tee."

"You're horrible," she said around a mouthful of dripping cheese.

"I'll get over it," Mike said, going back to the kitchen to get some paper towels. Mike smiled. Since Jandilyn's pregnancy had started, she had forgotten all of her table manners and Mike found that to be completely endearing, especially since he was sure that Mrs. Hollow was going to be horrified by her daughter's newest manners, or lack thereof.

"Are you eating?" Jandilyn asked as cheese dripped from her face.

"Not hungry," Mike said, watching her.

"Did you make two sandwiches?" she asked hopefully.

"Yup," Mike said heading back into the kitchen and grabbing all the ingredients.

"It would be great if the second sandwich had marshmallow fluff on it."

"Come on, Jandilyn, are you just making this stuff up?" Mike asked, digging through the cabinet.

"You should try it."

"I'd rather go cross country with your mother in a small car, backwards." His hand came across the half empty jar of fluff. He was not surprised to see a handful of jalapeños sitting on top of the marshmallow as he cracked the lid. She had fallen in love with the spicy pepper since her pregnancy started and added it to nearly everything. Mike never thought it would get worse than the time she sprinkled them over her bowl of Cheerios, but she kept pushing the envelope.

***

"Damn good to see you, son," Mr. Hollow said, pumping Mike's hand up and down vigorously. There had been a slight change in plans, the Hollows had decided to come out before the birth and stay a little while after also. Mike hoped Jandilyn went into labor that night, just as long as it wasn't while he was at the airport picking up her parents.

"Michael," Mrs. Hollow said as she handed him her carry-on.

"Always a pleasure," Mike said, putting the strap over his shoulder. "What do you have in here, rocks?"

"Jandilyn's old boyfriend, Durgan, now he was a strong one, wasn't he?" she asked her husband.

"Gina, he was an asshole," Mr. Hollow told his wife while he winked at Mike.

Mike loved him for that small gesture.

Mrs. Hollow strode ahead of them. Mr. Hollow clapped his hand around Mike's shoulder. "I've been telling all my friends my daughter's husband is a famous author now." He beamed.

"I don't know about famous, Mr. Hollow."

"Call me Drew."

"Drew."

"Nonsense. How's my baby girl?"

"She's the best thing that's ever happened to me, Mr.…Drew. She's doing great except for her jalapeño addiction, I almost ran out about a week ago, it was the closest thing to a national disaster I'd ever encountered."

Mr. Hollow laughed.

"Jalapeños?" Mrs. Hollow asked. "And you give them to her? How very working class of you."

"I seem to remember you having a love affair with a very pedestrian food while you were pregnant with Jandilyn."

"Don't be silly. And should we be talking about this in front of strangers?" she asked, pulling ahead again.

"Cherry Pop-Tarts," he whispered to Mike. "She couldn't eat enough of them. One day, I was exhausted and I picked up strawberry ones, she damn near took off the top of my head when she threw them back at me. Another time we were on a tight budget and I bought the store brand, I at least had the foresight to stick them in a used Pop-Tart box. She knew the ruse for what it was, told me that she could tell by the foil packaging."

"Cherry Pop-Tarts are the root of all evil," Mike returned softly.

"Maybe that's her problem." Mr. Hollow laughed.

"I'll go get the car," Mike said as they exited the airport. He pulled up a few moments later in his brand new-to-him fire engine red Jeep Wrangler. He hopped out and opened the passenger door, moved the passenger seat so Mrs. Hollow could climb in the back.

"When did you start driving, Mike?" Mr. Hollow asked as he looked the Jeep over.

"I got a provisional license on Jandilyn's urging. She wanted to make sure she could get to the hospital when the time came. I'm not supposed to drive at night, but I'm not sure what I'm supposed to tell the baby if he or she decides they want out at midnight."

"I don't think so." Gina looked into the car. "You drive my daughter around in this thing?" she asked, looking at it as if it were covered in used diapers.

"You used to be fun, Gina," Mr. Hollow said as he threw his bags in the back and hopped in.

Mike pushed the seat back, slamming the bags into Drew's knees. "Oh, shit. Sorry, sir," Mike said, sucking air in through his teeth. "That looked like it hurt."

"I'll be fine." Drew winced, shifting his legs to the side so he would have more room.

Mrs. Hollow looked up and down the concourse.

"Get in, Gina, I don't think there are any limos here," her husband said from the backseat.

The ride back was, for the most part, quiet…except for some attempts at conversation from Drew, but Gina was having none of it.

"How quaint," Mrs. Hollow said snidely as they pulled up to the apartment. "You would think a 'famous' author, as my husband so eloquently put it, would be able to afford something a little better."

"That's enough!" Drew said as he extracted himself from the clutches of the Jeep's backseat. "This kid has done nothing but right by our daughter and yet any chance you get, you cut him down. I'm sick of it, either act civilly, which might be a stretch for you, or go home. I plan on enjoying my time out here. and if you can't manage the same…I would rather you were gone.

Holy shit, Mike thought as he grabbed the bags and was heading out of Dodge. He had no desire to be anywhere nearby once the bullets started to fly. Mike could feel the venomous looks Mrs. Hollow was giving him and her husband, but gave her some small measure of credit, she didn't say anything, at least not with her mouth.

"Hi, Dad!" Jandilyn said excitedly as she pinioned her way off the couch.

"Stay there, honey," her father said as he rushed over

to give her a hug. "Are you having twins?" he asked before even thinking.

"Oooh, wrong question," Mike said, but no one in the apartment heard him and that was just fine with him.

"Am I fat?" Tears started to roll down her face. "I'm like a weeble!" she wailed.

"No, nothing like that, honey. I was just playing," Mr. Hollow said, now in full backpedal mode.

"Honey, I got you something," Mike said, trying to intervene.

"Mike, how do you stand being with me?" she fairly wailed.

Mike held up a Toblerone candy bar.

"Oh!" Her expression quickly changed. "Could you put some jalapeños on it!"

"Thank you so much," Drew whispered in Mike's ear as he went by him into the kitchen.

"Oh, I've been to this rodeo a few times now," Mike said conspiratorially.

"What is that smell?" Mrs. Hollow asked as she reluctantly stepped farther into the apartment.

"That would be *eau de* peanut butter," Mike told her from the kitchen door.

"Hi, Mom!" Jandilyn said, trying to shift herself around until she could maneuver off the couch.

"Don't, you'll—" Mrs. Hollow started.

Mike ran in with the whole jar of peppers before she could say anything that would upset her daughter. "Hi, honey, here you go," Mike said, a little out of breath.

"I don't need the whole jar, silly." Yet she eyed the large candy bar and the oversized container of peppers greedily.

Crisis averted, Mike directed Mr. Hollow to the spare bedroom.

"Someday she'll come around," Mr. Hollow said to Mike.

"Drew, we dated for four years and have been married for one. I think you're a lot more optimistic than I am."

"The baby will soften her up."

"If I thought that I would have made sure we were having triplets."

"That's funny, you should use that in your new book. How's that going, by the way?"

"I mostly write at night because Jandilyn goes to bed at like seven so there's not much to do while she's sleeping."

"You love her, don't you?"

"A little late in the game if I didn't." Mike smiled. "She's everything to me, Drew. You know my family and I had a falling out after the accident I was in, so she's really all I've got."

"I'm here for you two—well, three soon. Always, Mike. I don't want you to think I wouldn't help out in any way that I could. No matter what Gina thinks."

"Thank you, sir, that means a lot."

"Anytime, kid, now let's get back before my wife says something she shouldn't."

Mike thought it was probably too late, but he agreed.

***

Mike was grateful at least one of Jandilyn's parents was staying with them when his wife's water broke. He would not have felt confident calling a cab and he was far too jittery to contemplate driving, plus it was nighttime and his lack of depth perception might get them to the hospital alright but for far different reasons than a child birth.

"Oh, Mike, this hurts," Jandilyn said through gritted teeth as she reached her hand into the backseat where he was seated next to Mrs. Hollow. He wanted to tell her it couldn't hurt as much as what he was going through right then, but he kept his thoughts to himself. Mike could feel the bones in his right hand shift around as Jandilyn squeezed with every contraction.

"How far apart, Mike?" Mr. Hollow asked. To Mike, he didn't appear to be holding it together much better than he was himself.

"I'd say about a minute, just enough time for the bones in my hand to resettle into their proper position," Mike answered.

"I'm sorry, honey, am I hurting you? This is me getting even."

"Fair enough," Mike answered as she again tried to squeeze juice out of his fingers.

The fifteen minute ride to the hospital was punctuated by twenty-two bone bending squeezes. "Their getting closer!" Mike said excitedly as they pulled up to the emergency doors.

"That's what they generally do," Mrs. Hollow said. Mike didn't hear her and Mr. Hollow shot her a glance through the rearview mirror, imploring her to just ease up, at least for today.

***

Jandilyn was sitting up in her hospital bed, sweat pouring off her forehead. Mrs. Hollow was giving her daughter ice chips, Mike was pacing back and forth, trying to figure out how long it would take to wear a groove in the floor.

"It'll be alright, son," a clearly flustered Mr. Hollow said, trying his best to calm Mike down. It might have had more effect if the magazine he was pretending to read was not jittering around like Jell-O in an earthquake.

Mike and Jandilyn's pediatrician came in, put on some Latex gloves, and positioned herself so she could check Jandilyn's dilation. "Five centimeters, you're doing great, Jandilyn."

Mike shrugged at Mr. Hollow. Neither one of them had a clue what that meant.

The doctor turned to Mike. "Michael there are scrubs in the closet, I suggest you get them on."

Mike's knees almost buckled. He walked woodenly to the closet, surreal wasn't even beginning to cover what he was feeling.

"Where are mine?" Mrs. Hollow asked.

"Only one family member is allowed in the delivery room, Mrs. Hollow," the doctor said kindly.

"Then why is it *him*?" She pointed vehemently.

"I...I just assumed," the doctor said, now trying to extricate herself from the conflict.

"Mom!" Jandilyn said between huffs. "What is your problem!"

Had Mrs. Hollow asked with some semblance of sincerity and respect, Mike felt he would have willingly and gratefully given up his spot in the delivery room. Now he'd put the scrubs on just so he could shove it up her ass.

"I'm a blood relative, they are merely related by a piece of paper that could burn by a single match."

"That's it, Gina," Mr. Hollow stood up, "let's go get some coffee," he said as he physically removed her from the chair she was sitting next to the bed in. "I love you, honey," he said as he leaned over and kissed Jandilyn's glistening forehead.

"You sure do have a way with women," the doctor said to Mike once Jandilyn's parents were out of the room.

"It's a gift, really," he told her.

The doctor laughed. "You ready?" she turned and asked Jandilyn.

"No."

"It doesn't work like that," the doctor said as she disengaged the brakes on the bed and began to wheel Jandilyn out of the room and down the corridor. An orderly came up and relieved the doctor from her chauffeur duties.

Mike struggled to keep pace by the side of the bed as Jandilyn held his hand. "You look beautiful," he said to her. "A little pale, but beautiful."

"You switch places with me and see how much color you retain."

"I'm good," Mike said.

"One, two, three," the lead nurse said as they moved Jandilyn from her gurney to the birthing bed.

"Blood pressure is one twenty over seventy-five," one of the technicians said aloud.

"That's a little low," the doctor said.

"Sounds about perfect," Mike said, throwing in his minimal medical knowledge, not really meaning to voice his opinion, but the doctor answered him.

"Sure, for you or me," she said, "not for someone in a great deal of pain having a baby."

"Oh." Mike still didn't have a clue if he should be concerned or not.

"One fifteen over seventy," the technician said again.

"Jandilyn," the doctor said loudly. "How you feeling?"

Mike hadn't noticed, but Jandilyn's eyelids were nearly closed.

"Fine," Jandilyn mumbled. "Mike, take care of her."

"What?" Mike asked, alarm bells began to go off in his head and on the myriad of monitors around him.

"She's bleeding out!" the doctor said. "Get the crash cart! Get surgical down here now. I need three units of A-positive!"

"Jandilyn?" Mike said by her side.

"It really is beautiful," she said, looking over at him.

A big boned nurse physically removed Mike from his bedside position. He stood against the wall wishing he could be anywhere but there.

Jandilyn's color drained as if she'd been washed in bleach.

He knew what he had to do no matter how distasteful. He placed his hand up to his left eye and jerked the contact out, the room tilted on its axis. Deep crimson intermingled with light shearing blackness. A thin man that had not been there previously occupied the space against the far wall; his attention rapt on Jandilyn and the baby. When it looked over to Mike, its mouth opened wide enough to swallow him whole.

Mike slid down the wall and grabbed his knees. Tears blotted his scrubs as he rocked back and forth.

Machines, nurses and doctors flooded around him as they did everything humanly possible to keep Jandilyn from leaving this plane of existence. Used medical supplies rained down on the floor like B-movie props.

"This isn't happening. I'm having a nightmare." Mike squeezed his eyes shut as he banged his head against the wall.

"What's he doing here?" one of the surgical team asked, looking at Mike. Mike thought the doctor was referring to the thin man and he knew why *he* was there.

A nurse was coming to escort Mike out when the monitor screamed its flat-lined tone, she rushed back to the bed to charge the cardiac paddles.

"Wait! We've got to get the baby out, the shock will kill her!"

"No time, we'll lose the mother for sure."

"Jandilyn," Mike whispered. "Her name is Jandilyn." No one heard him over the din of death.

"Clear," came the doctor's warning.

Mike looked up. Whatever energy constituted life was no longer present in his wife or unborn child. To their credit the team worked an additional thirty futile minutes trying to drag her back.

"Time of death three thirty-three PM," the lead doctor told his nurse.

"And the baby?" she asked.

"Same."

Mike sat there until everyone had cleared out. He then got up to be beside her body. He stroked her hair and kissed her gently on the lips.

"Get away from her!" Mrs. Hollow screamed. "You did this to her! You're a cancer! You injected her with your poison and it killed her."

"Please," Michael cried.

"Gina! What is wrong with you?" Tears flowed freely down Mr. Hollow's face, in contrast his wife wore a mask of hate and venom. "I'm so sorry, Mike," Mr. Hollow said in consolation.

"How dare you apologize to your daughter's killer!" Gina screamed. She was charging at Mike and would have succeeded in bowling him over had she not slipped on a blooded up ball of cotton on the floor.

Mike's mind was reeling, he couldn't even comprehend the vitriol that Mrs. Hollow was hurling at him from the floor as she clawed her way toward him. He looked over to Mr. Hollow, the cascading tears made it nearly impossible to distinguish much beside his general shape. But he didn't miss the fine filaments of black that seemed to wave back and forth like seaweed caught in a gentle current above Drew's head.

Mike felt tugging on the cuff of his pants as Mrs. Hollow pulled her now blood-soaked self up, using him as her crutch.

"I should have killed you when I had the opportunity!" she yelled as she was halfway up.

"What?" Mike asked trying to wrap his thoughts around her words. "When did you have an opportunity?"

"I own a gun, I could have done it at any time, and don't think I didn't fantasize about it!" she was still yelling.

Mr. Hollow was grappling with his wife who was swiping at Mike with her hands shaped into claws. Mike didn't move as she opened up wounds on his forehead and cheeks. She dug her fingers into his top lip and would have succeeded in ripping it off if Drew hadn't manhandled her out of the room.

Nurses had come running when they heard the commotion. Mike and Jandilyn's primary care doctor had a syringe of sedative and plunged it into Mrs. Hollow's left arm.

"I hope you die!" she yelled one last time before the drug took effect.

"Too late," Mike answered her. "I already did."

After the hospital had Gina admitted and secure in her room, Drew came and stood next to Mike. They stood there for hours both lost in their grief, immersed too deeply to even look to each other for support.

"My little princess is gone," Drew finally said. He brushed a lock of hair away from her face, gave her a kiss on the forehead, and went back to his wife's room.

CHAPTER TWELVE – The Aftermath Part Two

Mike stayed long after the cleanup crew swabbed up the remains of a life bled dry and would have stayed longer if the people from the hospital mortuary hadn't come to collect their pound of flesh. He wandered the hospital hallways aimlessly, not knowing what he should do or where he should go, he was numb. No, that wasn't quite right, numb would have been welcome. Numb would have meant he wasn't feeling anything. He was feeling *everything*. Every part of his being ached from the loss, he would have felt more whole if he had just lost a leg.

Mike eventually found himself at the doors to the hospital morgue. The attendant felt for Mike, but hospital rules were hospital rules, he was not allowed in, and that maybe he should go home and get some rest.

Mike could not reconcile the fact that Jandilyn was dead, he did not want to leave her alone in that cold, clinical room; she would get scared. Mike tried to plead his case to the young intern, even telling him his wife always slept with dozens of pillows and if she didn't have them she would have a hard time falling asleep.

"This will get better," the young man told Mike.

Mike looked deeply at the man, his eyes completely red rimmed from crying. "The world without Jandilyn Talbot is a much colder place."

The intern shivered as Mike turned and went back down the hallway from where he had come. Something about the stranger's eyes had unnerved him, and he worked with the dead, so that was not an easy feat.

Mike walked out into the night; a light mist coated his

face as he walked toward the parking garage. Mike had never driven at night, he more than hoped his lack of experience and depth perception would have him plow head-on into a tree and erase the stain of the day upon the folds of his brain. He weaved all over the road until a patrolman spotted him and thinking he was drunk, pulled him over.

"License, registration…you alright, partner?" the cop asked him when Mike turned to face him.

"My wife and child died today," Mike said, never letting go of the steering wheel.

Corporal Gibson had been on the force long enough and had heard just about every excuse. This was not one of them. "Should you be driving?"

"No, I have a restricted permit, only supposed to drive during day time. I should be at the hospital right now cradling my baby daughter while my beautiful wife smiles at me. They're both dead and the man at the hospital wouldn't let me sleep with them in the morgue. They're going to be so scared there in the dark, and they'll be so cold without their blankets and pillows."

"How far away is your home?"

"I have no home anymore," Mike said as he rested his head on the steering wheel.

Officer Gibson had compassion, he hadn't had that emotion completely burned out of him yet. Even still, he wished he had not pulled this car over. He was not equipped to deal with this type of encounter.

"You married, officer?" Mike asked, now looking at the cop.

Officer Gibson stepped back as he gazed into Mike's white eye. "I am."

"You should get your head checked."

The cop had thought the distressed guy he had pulled over was telling him he was crazy for tying the knot, something he'd thought on more than one occasion. It was two months later when he had his first seizure that he put two and two together. The crazy driver with the white eye had given him a warning. Of course by then it was too late, the aggressive tumor had spread tendrils throughout the majority of his brain and was choking the life out of him.

"I'm not going to give you a warning, just get yourself home, maybe pour yourself a stiff two or three drinks. I'm sorry, I truly am."

Mike pulled away without saying another word. His right tires squealed as he rode the curb for fifteen feet before getting out onto the roadway.

Officer Gibson stood there long after the Jeep's taillights vanished over a rise in the road. When he got back into his cruiser he made sure to make a U-turn and see what was happening on the other side of town. It had to be better than what he had just been party to. He made sure to stop and call his wife first.

Mike opened up the door to his apartment, the kitchen light was on and he noticed a piece of paper on the table. A hastily scrawled note lay there as if the person who had penned it wanted to make sure they were long gone before he came home:

> Mike,
>
> They let Gina leave after an hour. I got Jandilyn's key from her personal belongings and we took a cab here. Gina was still ranting so I thought it would be better if we got a hotel room, I will call tomorrow with funeral arrangements. Drew.
>
> P.S. Gina grabbed the cat and I could not convince her to leave it, she said it was the only thing living in the apartment now and she couldn't bear to leave it alone. I will return it once she calms down.

The paper was littered with crinkled spots where

Drew's tears had struck and dried, a fair portion of the letters had smeared but the message was clear. Gina still blamed him for her daughter's death. Everything in the apartment was a testament to the life of Jandilyn. Her smiling picture as they stood at the lip of the Grand Canyon adorned the refrigerator. Her bonsai tree she had named Mimoto was on the window sill. Her obsession with throw pillows.

"Where are you now, you thin fuck!" Michael screamed. "I'll fucking kill you!"

Mike thought he heard a rustling down the hallway in the bedroom. He sprinted, hoping to catch the intruder and make them pay. The bedroom window was open, the billowing sheer curtain was rubbing up against Jandilyn's nightstand.

"Are you here, Jandilyn?" Mike asked as the atmosphere in the room seemed to shift. The curtain which had almost been horizontal to the floor stilled suddenly, the air got heavy, Mike had difficulty catching his breath. As soon as it happened it passed, the curtain began to billow again and the cloistered feeling left. It wasn't his Jandilyn, what he felt had been malevolent.

Mike grabbed every article that belonged to Jandilyn and placed them on the bed, he pushed out just enough room so that he could fit himself on the mattress with her possessions. As much as he had hoped for solace, perhaps hoping for a shred of her being infused with the article, he was dismayed to discover that when she had died the inanimate objects she had loved reverted to their original forms of cold metal, plastic, or wood. Any life she had breathed in them had died when she had.

Mike slept until Drew called the following morning.

"The service is Tuesday, Our Lady of Christ, nine-thirty." Then he hung up.

Mike held the phone to his ear a while longer, when he realized that it wasn't a practical joke, he placed it back down on the receiver.

Occasionally, Mike would venture forth from his chair and rummage in the fridge to eat something but only when crippling hunger cramps threatened to overtake the pain he felt for Jandilyn. His heart nearly broke as he looked for sustenance and ended up shattering the jar of jalapeños on the floor. He dropped to the floor, his knees becoming imbedded with glass as he scooped up the pickled peppers and began to place them in the bowl he had been holding. He wept as his fingers bled, he was certain if he could save even some of them Jandilyn would have to come back and claim them. And how mad would she be if there were none left?

Two days later Mike sat under a shower of cold water, hoping he would start to feel something besides bitter misery. The stinging bite of the water droplets only reminded him he was still alive. He put on a suit Jandilyn had tailored for him for when he started on his book signing tour, something he had not yet done. The suit seemed to hang on him, he had diminished both physically and spiritually. He drove to the church where he had planned on having his child baptized; the parking lot was packed as he knew it would be. He walked into the church, most of the pews were occupied, as more and more people realized he had entered they turned to watch his progression up to the front. Some mouthed, 'I'm sorry', others just shook their heads, still others seemed to have that same scornful look of reproach on their faces as if it should be him lying in that casket and not her.

Mike's steps faltered when he saw the second much smaller casket, he had not been expecting that and had nearly pitched over. A hand reached out to help him, Mike couldn't remember the guy's name but thought it might be Brian— one of Jandilyn's coworkers.

"I hate you, you killed her," Brian had said as he steadied Mike.

Mike looked into the man's eyes, trying to figure out what he had heard and if quite possibly he had misunderstood the words. Even if that had been the case, though, Brian's eyes told the whole story, they burned with the hatred. Mike pulled back quickly and staggered his way up the center aisle. Gina Hollow sat at the very edge of the pew on the front right, she never turned to look at Mike and made it clear she would not move even if he had wanted her to. Mike quickly sat at the pew on the front left which was completely devoid of any others.

Mike sat quietly with his head bowed as the priest delivered his service. A few of Jandilyn's friends went up and gave tearful eulogies. Mike never even realized when the mass was over until Drew came and put his hand on his shoulder.

"My promise still holds." Drew told him. "I'll be here for you."

Mike couldn't bring himself to look up. The weight of his crashing world seemed to have him permanently bowed.

"It was good knowing you, Drew," Mike said as he stared down at his clasped hands.

"I won't see you again then?" It was asked as a question, but sat on the fence as a statement also.

"Tell Gina, if she'll listen, that I'm sorry."

"Son…" Mike winced at the word, he was no one's son, he was driftwood in the sea of humanity. "This wasn't your fault."

"I think maybe your wife was right, I'm poisonous. Everyone I have loved who lets me into their lives dies."

"Mike, that's crazy."

"I'm moving, Drew, I've got everything I want in my Jeep. Go take whatever you want of Jandilyn's that will give you some comfort in the cold nights to come." Mike rose and walked out of the church. He passed Gina who had regained a smoking habit she had dropped twenty years previous when Jandilyn was a toddler. She said nothing as he passed.

Mike walked through the billow of her exhaust and strode purposefully to his car, throwing his tie and jacket to the side of the road.

Mike drove up the coast for a few miles, wondering where he might like to finish off the remainder of his life. He toyed briefly with the thought of going east, back to his childhood home, but he hadn't been welcome there in over half a decade. He didn't even know if his parents still lived in the same house or had moved and failed to send him a forwarding address. He really didn't care.

Alaska seemed as good an idea as any and he most likely would have made it if not for a torrential downpour in Seattle that exactly matched his mood.

"This'll work," he told himself as he took shelter within the Cleverly named Baits (and Lures) Motel. 'Rooms with a view and no crazy relatives' the in-house brochure proclaimed. It seemed like a welcome promise to Mike.

Mike spent two days lying on top of sheets that felt like burlap bags. If not for the infrequent need to purge himself he would not have moved. His thoughts swirled around his disbelief that Jandilyn was gone and the gut-punching reality of that fact.

Mike knew Jandilyn would be pissed if she saw him in the state he was in.

"Feeling sorry for yourself, are you?" she asked.

"I am, Jandilyn. I miss you so much."

"You know I'm still here. Now I'm just inside of you. That doesn't mean you can just crawl inside of yourself and exclude the rest of the world, though."

"How did you know I was thinking that?" Mike exclaimed.

"Mike, sometimes I didn't know where I ended and you began. This is just an extension of that."

"I liked it better when we could touch."

"We can again."

Mike sat up fast. "How, Jandilyn?" he begged.

CHAPTER THIRTEEN – 7 Cefalo Road

Two hours later, Mike was sitting in Real Estate Agent Kylie Milligan's heated Toyota Camry as they wound their way through tree-lined roads.

"This is really off the beaten trek," the young woman said to Mike.

Her stomach was telling her that something was just not quite right about her new client. Just last month she had attended a seminar on realtor safety, stressing that realtors and brokers should get all the pertinent information regarding their client's personal and financial lives *before* taking them out to show houses. Foremost was for safety, last year one of Seattle's most prominent realtors had been beaten, raped, and killed in a foreclosed home and the police still had no leads. Secondly, was for valuable time; on more occasions than Kylie would like to remember she had shown couples multitudes of homes to only discover they were merely window shopping. She wondered how many lost weekends that she could never get back had been wasted that way. She would have told Mike no way, but her mortgage on her modest ranch home was already ten days overdue and he was the first potential buyer she had seen in a month.

Mike had not said more than two words to her since they had got in the car. The further they traveled from the city the more unsettled she became.

"We really should go back to my office and do some paperwork. I mean, check out how much financing you have. You know, so you can figure out what you can afford."

Mike leaned forward. "Right here," he said pointing to an opening in some brush along the road.

Oh, God, there's nothing there, Kylie thought, *he's going to kill me here.*

"You're going to pass it," Mike said, turning toward her.

The eye patch was something she could not get over, she'd read enough Dean Koontz novels to know that killers always had some sort of disfigurement.

"You're scared?" Mike asked her. "Of me?"

Kylie merely nodded.

Mike reached into his pocket. Kylie flinched. He pulled out his wallet and showed her his license. Why that should calm her down, she didn't know, dead women told no tales.

"I noticed you're a reader," Mike told her.

"Uh-huh." She nodded.

"What do you think of that book you've got on your backseat?"

"I don't really know what that has to do with anything?" she asked, her alert flags really flapping in the breeze.

"Please, humor me."

"It was alright, the character development could have gone into a little more depth. The author seemed slightly sexist and some of the humor was on the lowbrow side, but all in all I'd say a three, maybe two-and-a-half out of five."

"That's harsh." Mike smiled.

Kylie noticed the smile but it was strained as if there were some deep sadness keeping it from becoming a full-fledged grin.

Kylie looked down at the driver's license that Mike held in front of her. The car had come to a complete stop on the deserted roadway right before the turn Kylie was reluctant to take.

She did a double take, first on the driver's license, then the book in the back. She grabbed the book and then turned it over to match up the dust jacket picture. "It's you, oh it's you! I'm sorry!"

"Don't be. You're far from my first critic."

"Do you mind if I ask what happened to your eye since this picture was taken?"

"I'm wearing a contact in the picture. This," he said pointing to his eye patch covered eye. "Is courtesy of a car accident some years ago. Now if you don't mind there is a house for sale up this drive that I am very interested in purchasing."

"Have you seen it before?" Kylie asked as she took the turn.

"No." He offered no further clarification.

The dirt path was not much wider than Kylie's car and on occasion even less so as branches reached out and clawed against the glass. After a quarter mile, Kylie was about to ask him if he was sure about the location when a large clapboard sided wooden structure arose out of the shallow mist.

"That's it!" Mike said excitedly, getting out before the car had even stopped.

Kylie opened her oversize workbag slash purse and grabbed the paperwork that went with the house and just for good measure a contract.

"It sits on forty-two acres, has three-and-a-half..."

"I'll take it," Mike said, coming back to her.

"You haven't even seen the inside."

"How much is it?"

Kylie flipped back to the front sheet that had the list price. "One sixty-nine, nine."

"Offer one seventy with a closing next week and let's be done."

"Wait, are you sure? You haven't seen the inside, you should really get a home inspector up here. In good conscience, I strongly urge you to at least get the ground water tested, this house uses well water."

Mike was going to argue with her to just get it done,

that she sort of looked like she needed the sale as badly as he did or she wouldn't have come out with him on such short notice, but looking at her, he could tell she wanted to do right by him and wasn't in it *just* for the money.

"Okay, let's go look inside. If you could please set up the home inspection including the well I would make it worth your time. Unless the house is going to fall in on itself within the next year, I would like to close on this place by the end of the month."

"That's only two weeks—can you secure the financing that fast?"

"I'm paying cash."

"Well, that helps. Let's go look at your new home." She smiled, feeling much better about her day, no matter how hard the drizzle tried to dampen her spirits.

The front door opened up, noiselessly. In contrast to the dreary weather outside, the house was full of light. Off to their left was a great room with a thirty-five foot high cathedral ceiling. An over-sized stairway was to their front and down a narrow tiled corridor led to a large kitchen dominated by an island. Mike immediately headed upstairs, Kylie had a moment of hesitation as a cold chill spread across her shoulders and then followed him up. Large bay windows in the great room looked out toward a lake about a half mile away.

"What a spectacular view," Kylie said, stopping to admire.

"What's up there?" Mike asked, his back to the view. They were on a landing and he was pointing toward an opening a level up from them with no discernible way to get there.

Kylie started rifling through her paperwork. "I'm not sure, there's a picture of the opening from down in the great room but it doesn't list it as usable footage. Probably just a crawl space." Mike looked at her funny. Kylie shivered as she tried to peer into the pitch blackness of the 'crawl space'.

"Maybe there's a way to get in from the bedroom," Kylie said, pointing down the hallway to the master bedroom. A small bedroom was off to their right. "You could use this as an office to write." Kylie said trying to bring her thoughts away from the room above them.

Mike had already left her and was standing in the middle of the master bedroom looking around. "No way up there from here."

"Wow, the bathroom is even bigger than the pictures show," Kylie said. "The Jacuzzi bathtub comes with the house."

"How old is this place?" Mike asked, completely ignoring her statements.

"You really don't know? How did you know about this place?" she asked off-handedly as she again looked through her sheets. He again did not answer her as he kept looking for a way upstairs. "Four years."

"Certainly not old enough for a haunting," he said ambiguously.

Kylie was not so certain as she thought about that gaping wound in the wall above the landing.

"There's more to the house," Kylie said, wishing to get a little farther away from the sinister feeling settling at the back of her skull.

"You know I want the house—is the rest necessary?"

"I've just never had someone so sure about a property, especially without ever having seen it. And this is a very secluded region. You seem too young to bury yourself away back here." As soon as the words came out, she wished she had the ability to pull them back in like a bad fishing cast.

There was an awkward moment of silence as Mike eyed her. "Listen, I've never been great with people. My wife, who meant everything to me, is gone, I no longer have any desire to be around…" he almost said the living and was not sure why, "…large communities. For some reason, people like my book enough to make me able to afford to live out in the sticks. I need the peace and quiet this place affords so I can continue to write." He was not sure where or why the lies were coming with such ease or even why he felt the need to tell her all this. But if it got everything done quicker, then it was worth it.

"Okay, I brought a contract. Let's go down to the kitchen and we can use the-island to fill it out." *And we can get away from here*, she thought as she took a cursory glance out to the placid pristine lake and headed downstairs.

Within ten minutes, Mike had signed and initialed the appropriate lines and they were heading back to her car, something made her look back to the house. All color drained from her face as she saw something she could not identify pass across the large bay windows where she had been looking out earlier. "You alright?" Mike asked as he stopped his egress into the car. He watched her face as she stared at the house. He turned quickly and thought he might have caught a shadow, but it just as easily could have been a trick of the light.

"Mike, are you sure about this place?" she asked with unusual candor as she quickly hopped into the driver's side. "I…I just think it's too far away from everything. I can set up at least a dozen or so houses closer to the city and still within your price range."

"You don't even know my range," he quipped. "Don't worry, this is exactly the place I want to be."

"The customer's always right," she said with a sideways smile that belied the queasiness she was feeling in the pit of her stomach.

"Don't worry, I don't plan on inviting you to the housewarming party."

Kylie was relieved. *It's his funeral, and I need the money.*

Mike didn't say much all the way back to the motel, but Kylie thought he had seemed relieved.

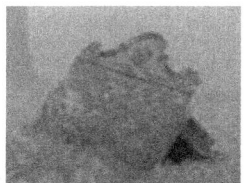

CHAPTER FOURTEEN – The Walkthrough

"I thought Kylie would be here for the final walkthrough?" Mike asked the older gentleman who was now exiting his sleek Audi.

"I'm Bob Lambert, her business partner. She had a family emergency," the white haired and bearded man said.

"My name is Mike Talbot," Mike said, extending his hand. "I hope everything's alright." They shook.

"Between you and me I think she didn't want to come all the way out here. If it wasn't such a nice day, I might have passed this on to someone else my damned self."

"Is she going to be at the closing?"

"Well, that would mean she would have to reveal that her 'emergency'," he added with air quotes. "Wasn't quite the disaster she led on for it to be."

"Understood."

"Shall we?" Bob asked, sweeping his arm toward the house.

The sun was out and the birds were chirping, but unlike the last time he was here, the house was now darker than the outside world. Mike couldn't put his finger on it, but he felt it was expectant. Waiting for something—if he had to give a quick answer it would have to be him, yes the house was waiting for him. *Jandilyn is waiting for me*, he thought. Happiness at that thought stripped some of the lead sheathing from around his heart.

"This is a beautiful home," Bob said as he stepped into the great room. "And a view." He walked over to the large set of french doors that led out to a deck. "This deck is huge, you and the missus can have your morning coffee out here."

"There's a deck?" Mike asked hollowly.

"We should check out the basement and make sure there isn't a swimming pool down there."

"There's a basement? And why would someone put a pool there?" Mike asked.

"Son, is this the same house you looked at with Kylie?"

"It was raining," Mike said in defense.

"Inside?" Bob asked dubiously.

"I'm an author. I need seclusion," Mike offered, hoping that would be enough to quell any further questioning.

It did, but more so because Bob was a salesman and the customer was always right as long as they were putting money in his pocket. The kid had some secrets he wasn't saying, and it was curious for sure, but he wasn't going to push him on it.

Just as they were about to head downstairs both men looked up as the sound of footsteps was heard above them on the landing.

"Is someone here?" Bob asked.

"Maybe it's the home inspector," Mike said.

"No, he was out here last week."

"Hello?" Bob asked, moving back toward the great room so he could see onto the balcony above.

As Bob moved away from him, Mike heard soft footsteps running back toward the master bedroom.

"I don't see anyone," Bob said. "Damn, I've got the chills."

"Someone's up there."

"How do you know?" Bob looked somewhere in the middle of running for his life and determined to charge upstairs and confront the trespasser.

"I heard them running away."

"Come out here!" Bob yelled up, looking over toward

the door. He felt confident he could make it out quicker than someone could make it down the staircase. "I'm going to call the cops!"

"It sounded like a kid," Mike said.

"It could be a vagrant or a squatter. We need to get them out before you sign any papers, Mike. It could be a legal nightmare for you if they decide not to leave. Sometimes, they come way out here into the sticks and think nobody is ever going to live out here." Bob spoke into his phone, "Yes, hello, my name is Bob Lambert, I'm a real estate agent with Liberty Realty of Spokane and I'm at a house with a client. The address is 7 Cefalo Road. Yes, I'll hold. Glad I'm not getting murdered," he said, smiling toward Mike.

"That would be unfortunate."

Mike's deadpan delivery caught Bob off guard. He seemed unsure in which direction his biggest threat now came. *No wonder Kylie didn't want to come out here. This house is off*, was the best way he could describe it, if he was being honest with himself, so was the new owner.

"Hi," Bob started back on his phone. "I'm at a house with a client and I believe we have a vagrant squatting in the residence…an hour!" Bob exclaimed into his phone. "Yes, I realize how far from the city limits it is and no, right now it technically isn't an emergency. If he has a knife I'll make sure to call you back immediately," Bob said gruffly. "Well, it seems we're on our own for a bit. I'm not sure about you, but I'd feel more comfortable if we waited outside. That whole cornered animal thing makes me nervous."

"Us or him?" Mike asked, pointing upstairs.

"Both."

"Fair enough."

Mike was leaning up against Bob's car, staring back at the house, trying to see any movement when he kept catching glaring looks from the realtor.

"Something wrong?" Mike asked.

"That's a sixty thousand dollar car you're leaning against."

"Sorry," Mike said, standing up quickly.

A loud rustling came twenty yards away in the tree line.

"That sounded big," Bob said, inching toward his door.

"Mountain lion?" Mike asked.

"It's not out of the realm of possibilities out here. I'd be more inclined to think deer, but who knows?" Bob said, grasping his door handle. *This is the last time I let Kylie talk me into this shit*, Bob thought as he got in his car, making sure to lock the door.

Bob rolled down his window to ask, "What are you doing?" as he watched the young man head toward the tree line.

"Just trying to figure out what it is," Mike answered.

"We should just wait for the cops. They'll be here in another fifty-five minutes," Bob said scornfully.

Mike reluctantly turned back toward the car and got in, both men fidgeted around unendingly. Neither vocalized it, but they both felt they were being watched. It wasn't the kind of thing strangers told each other—they waited another hour and a half under a blanket of silence until a sheriff's deputy showed up.

He was tall, at least six foot four and looked like he benched VWs. Bob and Mike got out to greet him. The deputy was all business as he put his hat on and strode toward the door. Even this giant of a man seemed to hesitate as he crossed the threshold, much more willing to call out than to rush into anything.

"This is Sheriff's Deputy Caldwell, you are trespassing on private property. If you come out now I will let you go on your way. If I have to come and find you, I'll be bringing you back to the station for processing. Your call," he added and waited for a reply. When there was none forthcoming he moved farther into the house. "The hard way it is," he said, heading up the stairs. Deputy Caldwell rushed up the stairs when the small group heard a loud thump followed by the rapid retreat of footfalls.

"What the fuck?" Bob said uncharacteristically. "Sorry." He turned to Mike.

"It's alright. I've heard it before."

"Usually the worst thing we find on a walkthrough is missing garage door remotes."

"Does this place have a garage?" Mike asked.

Bob looked over at Mike and was about to answer when they heard some commotion from the deputy. "Is someone coming your way?" the deputy asked.

"No, should they be?" Bob yelled, looking like he was getting ready to bolt out the door. He was not making enough commission for this to be worth his while.

The deputy came out to the landing and looked down at Mike and Bob, scratching his head. "I thought I had him cornered in the bathroom, but they must have been hiding behind the door. As soon as I got in, something pushed me from behind and then shut the door on me and wedged it shut. It had to have come this way, where else could she have gone?" he said, turning a complete three sixty and then looking up at the loft above his head. "Is there any access to there?" The deputy asked.

"None that I've found," Mike answered. He was wondering if anybody but him had noted the various descriptors the deputy had used to describe whatever was in the house. It ranged, from 'he,' 'she,' 'it,' 'they' and 'something'. *Well, it's got to be one of those things*, Mike mused sourly. The churning in his stomach was giving him second thoughts about this purchase, how could Jandilyn be so wrong?

Bob was a salesman first and foremost and had a nose for when deals were heading south. He could tell by the expression on Mike's face his partner's client was starting to have second thoughts and with good reason, but his gambling addiction needed a booster shot and he was not about to let his fix off the hook.

"Probably just a squirrel," Bob said to Mike, flashing entirely too many teeth.

"That wasn't any squirrel," the deputy said, still staring up at the loft. "Why in the hell would anyone build a loft you can't get up to?" the deputy asked no one in particular.

"Maybe to house their pet squirrels," Mike said as he looked at Bob.

"Doubtful," the deputy answered, thinking Mike was serious.

Bob's grin left his face.

"Nothing came by, huh?" the deputy asked.

"It's quite possible, we were busy discussing the finer points of knitting," Bob said snidely.

The deputy looked down at Bob. "There's no need to be rude."

"How could we have missed someone running down the stairs? We're standing right here!" Bob said. They were at the foot of the steps.

"Is there a ladder? Because it's up there."

"Maybe the garage, I'll check," Mike said.

Bob looked like he wanted to be the one to run the errand if only to get out of the house, then seemed to think better of it when he remembered there might be something in the woods.

Mike headed outside and immediately was confronted with the feeling he was being watched again. He ignored it as he headed off to the garage he just realized was on the property. "How the hell did I miss that thing?" he asked himself. "Damn, thing's almost a small barn."

He walked into the side door and almost tripped on two bags of cement. Dust lazily sifted in the air as light flooded in behind him. He heard scurrying in the corner but was more convinced it was a field mouse than a mountain lion or a vagrant. There was an old rickety-looking wooden ladder, in the opposite corner he heard the noise from.

"I wouldn't climb a curb with this thing," he said aloud as he picked it up.

It appeared to have been made poorly from scrap two-by-fours. Mike walked across the yard with the ten foot climbing apparatus—he was reluctant to describe it as a ladder.

"What the hell is that thing?" the deputy asked, looking down at Mike.

"This is all that was in there."

"Bring it up, I'll at least try it," the deputy said.

"Are you sure?" Bob asked. "That thing doesn't look like it would hold a small child and you have to be pushing two fifty."

"Two twenty-five, but thanks for noticing," the deputy said as he took the ladder from Mike.

"You want me to go up?" Mike asked reluctantly.

"No, I've got it, but I'd appreciate you holding it in place."

Mike propped his foot up against the leg until Deputy Caldwell got to the third rung and then Mike moved so that his hands were on each side and his legs were braced out behind him. The ladder was swaying like a suspension bridge in high winds and the deputy was still a good three more rungs from cresting over the floor of the crawl space.

The ladder swayed and Mike held on for dear life…then it was still. Mike could hear the deputy exhale loudly. He looked up to see what was going on, but his view was dominated by the large man's posterior. The deputy was coming down noticeably faster than his ascent.

Mike hastily moved out of his way before the man stepped on him. The deputy was halfway down the stairs before he spoke. "Nothing there, I've got another call." And he was out the door, the cruiser started up and spit rocks from its rear as the police car took off for its 'emergency'.

"I wonder if it has anything to do with Kylie?" Mike asked wryly.

"Anything else you need to check out?" Bob asked, not really waiting for a response as he also headed for the door.

"What about the swimming pool in the basement?" Mike asked, but the storm door was already closing. Mike quickly turned back around when the wooden ladder fell to the ground. "What the hell did that?" Mike asked. But he didn't go up to investigate, instead he followed Bob outside.

"Are you still set on this house or should I set up some new showings?" Bob asked, his hands fidgeting for a pack of smokes he had dropped more than fifteen years ago.

"Why wouldn't I want this one?" Mike asked.

Why would you? Bob thought, but he let the greedy side of himself take over. "Well, it is a good price. We should get going or we're going to be even later to the closing."

***

Mike spent the first evening in his new house in the great room on an air mattress he had picked up at a local sporting goods store. It was about as comfortable as the floor and had the added bonus of making a particularly loud squelching noise whenever he moved, up to and including breathing. At first he was positioned so he could stare out the french doors and to the lake beyond, but even with a three-quarter moon shining bright, he couldn't make out much past the tree line about fifty yards in that direction. He repositioned so he was looking at the staircase and subsequently the dark black maw of the loft opening. Somehow the hole the deputy had looked through a few hours earlier was even darker than the surrounding area.

Mike didn't sense anything sinister or evil, but he

sure wasn't getting any warm and fuzzies either as he stared at the opening, confident something was staring back. Mike finally drifted off, his sleep troubled. He kept having the feeling someone was standing over him and he would start awake, compounded with his sudden movements, causing increased noise from his mattress. He rested some that night but not nearly the quantity or quality he had hoped for before morning reared its ugly head.

"Well, that sucked," Mike said as he sat up. Light from the french doors streamed in, warming his exposed feet. Mike rechecked his orientation, confident in his memory that he had been positioned with the top of his head to the back of the doors. "How the hell did that happen?" he asked as he got up quickly. He thought he heard the remnants of laughter, but it just as easily could have been the house settling.

Mike went to the front door, deciding today he was going to buy real furniture, this Spartan shit was for the birds. He had no sooner walked out the door when he heard heavy rustling in the exact same spot as yesterday. His apprehension grew, a deer was one thing, but if it was a moose or a bear, or even a mountain lion he was as defenseless as a cow in a slaughterhouse.

Trees, not necessarily saplings, either, were thrashing violently about. Mike had his hand on the door handle and was a moment away from barricading himself in the house. He began to figure what his options might be from that point. He had no phone service yet and he wasn't planning on having any visitors pretty much ever. He could scramble up to the loft and push the ladder over so whatever came in couldn't get to him and then what?

Would the animal get sick of waiting for its meal? Mike thought it might be better to hop in his car and go get some back up of the .30-06 variety. He was frozen in indecision when a black and white mottled feline bolted out from underneath the brush. Mike had one foot back in his house by the time his mind had a name from the intruder on his land.

"A fucking cat. Are you kidding me? There is no way that thing did that." He had no time to dwell on it, though, as the cat made a beeline for him. *Rabies?* Mike thought. *Fleas at the very minimum.* The cat paid Mike absolutely no heed as it brushed past him and in through the open door. Mike followed as the cat stopped at the bottom of the stairs. It had seemed prepared to scale the wooden steps and then thought better of it. The animal headed toward Mike's rumpled blankets and slipped beneath them so that all that was visible were two ears, one of which was thoroughly chewed up.

"Make yourself at home, fleabag," Mike said as he walked back into the house. The still slightly swaying trees were now forgotten.

Mike rooted around until he found an old piece of Tupperware. He turned the faucet on, waiting until the brown-red rust water turned a more civilized brackish gray and then to something almost potable.

He filled the container halfway and walked over to the cat. The animal finally pulled its gaze from the loft and looked at Mike like it finally realized there was someone else with him.

"Want some water?" Mike asked.

The cat got lower, the hair on its back bristled. It showed all of its teeth and hissed. Mike stopped his forward progress, he wasn't excessively concerned that the cat was going to attack, but if the thing had rabies he would be forced to undergo a series of painful injections and that did concern him.

Mike put the container down where he stood and backed away slowly. The cat stopped hissing, its fur laid down a little as it stood and looked over the edge of the bed to see the container. The cat stood up on the bed to get a better look.

"Just put your claws away, okay?" Mike asked. Almost immediately following was a heavy whooshing of escaping air from his mattress. "You suck, cat," Mike said as the cat ran away from the new noise. The cat ran to the kitchen. Mike went to see if there was anything he could do with his now ventilated bedding. He picked up the rapidly emptying bed and found at least three perforations. At some point the cat had realized Mike wasn't a threat or its thirst needed to be slaked, but either way it had come back to the water bowl and was contentedly lapping away as Mike walked past with his now useless pile of plastic. He saw no need to replace the thing.

"Well, I guess a bed rises to the top cf the list," Mike said. The cat looked at him as he spoke but kept drinking. Mike threw the thing onto his porch and was about to head out when he wondered what he should do with his uninvited guest. He did not need to worry as the cat again brushed past and went outside.

"So you pretty much came in just to destroy some of my shit then?" Mike asked. The cat sat and began to lick its right paw. "Fuckin' cats, you know you're basically just a rat with a 'c' at the front of your name, right?" The cat paid him no attention as it moved on to its left paw.

Mike headed toward his Jeep, the cat watched his every movement. As Mike hopped in the cat began to mewl loudly on the porch.

"What? I'll get you some food, you mooch," Mike said as he placed the key in the ignition. The cat ran off the porch and was now at his door, meowing incessantly. "What do you want?" Mike asked loudly, opening his door so he could see the cat directly. The animal lunged, its claws finding purchase in his thighs as it hopped onto him and then deftly onto the passenger seat. "Motherfucker!" Mike yelled from the razor barbs that had been injected into him. "You did that on purpose, you vermin." The cat was again licking its paws, Mike figured it was cleaning his blood off them.

"I wonder how far the shelter is from here. I'd drop you off in the woods, but I'm afraid you'd just come back."

The cat was fast asleep and purred heavily, he couldn't help but pet the top of its head. Even in sleep the cat hissed at him.

"I can see this is going to be a one way relationship, I'll basically give you everything you need and you'll ignore the living shit out of me. Perfect. You know I've dated girls like you." Even as he said it, Mike smiled. Even the small bit of companionship the animal offered was welcome and his first stop when he got into town was not a furniture store but rather a pet one, he spent roughly equivalent to what he thought he would on furniture that day in the pet store.

The cat had remained asleep in a pool of sunlight on the passenger seat and had not been able to be roused until it reluctantly accepted a liver flavored snack from Mike which it ate contemptuously.

"Whatever made early man decide you would be something worth having around I'll never know," Mike said as he pulled away from the store, the owner of Pets Are People Too now confident he could get his son those braces he'd been needing.

Mike spent half the time and half the amount of money in the furniture store as he had in the pet store, but he had paid a premium for a rush delivery to such a distant location. Mike grabbed some food and was heading back to his house when he got a sudden inspiration to just keep going, to put as many miles as he could from this place. He quickly dismissed the notion, but the idea did not leave him for many more miles, well until the point where he was turning into his long and winding driveway.

The cat finally began to perk up as the house came into view. Mike pulled up and opened his door, but before he could swing his legs out, the cat walked over his lap, somehow finding the exact pathway it had used before. Welts of blood began to seep into his jeans. The cat jumped down, took a cursory glance at the woods from which it had emerged and sprang up onto the porch. It seemed to be telling him to hurry up, that it wanted to get back in the house.

Mike noted the trees were slightly swaying, but did not notice there was no breeze with which to stir them. He grabbed a bunch of bags from the rear of his vehicle. "At least you'll have somewhere comfortable to sleep tonight," Mike said, hefting the large cat bed inside. Mike almost stepped on the cat that had stopped, hesitant to go in and now so was Mike. His sheet and blankets were halfway upstairs, like he had interrupted a sleepy robber.

"Hello?" Mike's voice rang out. "Tell me again why I didn't stop at the sporting goods store?" he seemed to ask the cat.

He wondered if his real estate agent Kylie had possibly stopped by, but couldn't imagine in what scenario she would let herself in and move his meager bedding supplies.

"Hello?" he asked again.

He thought he heard scampering and even the cat's head swiveled toward the sound and then all was quiet. The cat waited a moment longer and then strode in as if it owned the place. Mike followed suit.

Mike would have pondered on the problem longer if the cat hadn't made it known vociferously that it was hungry. He pulled out the set of bowls, found some salmon and kidney chunks and poured it in. The cat sniffed at it as if it couldn't believe it had been reduced to eating this swill that had cost Mike two-fifty a can and was probably of better quality than the fast food hamburger he had gotten for himself at ninety-nine cents. It was all for show though as the furry critter ate ravenously.

"I'm going to have to call you something besides cat," Mike said as he leaned against the counter, watching the cat eat. "Are you a male or a female?" he asked as he approached. The cat stiffened, stopped eating and hissed loudly at him. "Whoa, no need to thank me for the food, asshole. Maybe that's what I should name you."

The cat was still eyeing him warily. "No, that

probably won't work because I've got to sleep at some point. Well, since I'm not sure if you have little kitty balls or not I'll have to go with something unisex. Wait, let me just check." Mike tried to circle around to check the cat from the rear but the cat kept pace. "Fine, have it your way. Okay, let's figure this out, you look like a quilt made out of discarded rags. How about that? I'll call you Rags." The cat hissed. "Scratch that one, not literally," he said, involuntarily reaching for his thighs. "Patches? How about Patches? That sounds good."

The cat may have purred momentarily or it could have been a burp, but it didn't hiss, so Mike took that as a positive. "Patches it is, you cantankerous fuck."

Mike walked out of the kitchen and back out the door to grab the rest of the stuff he had bought in town. He dropped a bag on his way in when he noticed the red blanket was now all the way at the top of the stairs.

"What is going on?" Patches was again at his side. "This is bullshit," he said without much conviction, but he was trying to psyche himself up for a potential encounter with a trickster. "I'm coming up, and I have a vicious animal with me!" Mike yelled up the stairs. "He or she is not afraid to attack on command!"

Patches looked up at him as if to ask, 'Who me? Don't get me involved in this'. Patches started toward the door.

"Are you kidding me?" Mike asked Patches. "Fair-weather friend," Mike said as he climbed the first couple of risers.

Mike was three-quarters of the way up when he was able to grab the trailing edge of the blanket. He quickly ascended, balled the covers up and tossed it on the landing, wanting to make sure his hands were free for whatever might come his way. He quickly climbed the rest of the way up the stairs, looking to his right and checking his office. It was empty. *Here goes nothing*, he thought as he headed down the hallway into the master bedroom.

He put his arms up, fearful whoever was there would have a weapon and would try to club him with it. As he walked into the bedroom he couldn't help but notice as the hair on his arms began to rise. *Great, now I'm freaking myself out.* He quickly scanned the room, looking for a perceived threat. There was nothing and nowhere to hide, the two closet doors were open and unless they had false backs that led to Narnia they were empty as well. *I guess that leaves the bathroom.*

"I'm coming in!" Mike told his intruder. *Maybe I shouldn't have warned them.* A direct conflict was unavoidable now, Mike had half hoped that, by leaving the front door open and going into the kitchen, whomever or whatever—*Where did that thought come from?*—would find its way out without any guidance from him. Mike stepped into the bathroom, the once opaque shower curtain now covered with a thick coat of mildew, stirred slightly.

"This sucks," Mike said out loud, not meaning to.

His heart was thudding in his chest, threatening to crack a rib. His hand reached out slowly, he felt detached from the whole event as if he were a voyeur. His hand had just brushed up against the plastic when someone shrieked. He was chagrined when he realized it was himself and that he had betrayed the code of man.

"Fuck, cat, you scared the shit out of me," he said to Patches who had brushed up against his lower leg.

The cat continued past and rubbed up against the curtain, Mike reached out and pulled it back quickly, the small shower stall empty. A breeze from the window across the bathroom was most likely the culprit of the earlier movement. *Too bad the window is closed*, Mike thought. He took the overused, under-cleaned curtain and rusted out shower rod down.

"What is going on here?"

Mike would have pondered longer if he hadn't heard

the rumble of a large diesel engine. "Sounds like we have company, cat," Mike said, heading back downstairs. As if in confirmation, a blat from a large horn sounded. "Yeah, like I couldn't hear the damn truck, you idiot," Mike walked outside.

"Yo!" a burly barrel-chested man yelled as he came down off the passenger side of the truck. "You Michael Tolbot?" He scanned the order sheet in front of him.

Mike was under the impression the man did this to fool others into believing he could actually read, but in reality he had heard Mike's name earlier and was merely reciting it like a parrot.

"Talbot, Mike Talbot. Not *Tol*bot."

"Yeah, that's what I said," the man said, squinting at the piece of paper as if this would make it yield the truth.

"I wasn't expecting you until tomorrow," Mike said, realizing this was the furniture store truck.

"Wells…we're here today," Burly said as if he were a mobster coming to collect his points early. "Unless yous want us to come back tomorrow."

"You'll have to excuse my partner," the driver said as he gingerly climbed down off the truck. The man was stooped over a bit, holding his lower back, he had a hernia girdle on. Mike didn't think the man could move anything bigger than a lamp without hurting himself. "He gets cranky without lunch."

"I was just sayin' that we could have stopped and at least got a sandwich, Lenny."

"Dana, I don't like driving this truck at night, you know that. And we're out in the sticks."

Barrel-chest had the unfortunate moniker of Dana. That was a lot to bear during the 'mean kid' years. Mike decided he would ease up on his opinion of the brute. "Yeah, whys you want to live out here—yous a hermit or somethin'?"

"Dana, you're from Spokane why do you insist on

talking like you're from Jersey?" the driver asked. But Dana was already opening the rear of the truck and operating the lift gate.

"Do you want some help with that?" Mike asked Dana as he grabbed the sofa. The driver had asked Mike if he could use his bathroom and hadn't returned as of yet. Dana didn't look like he cared as he grunted non-committally.

Mike grabbed one end of the couch as they headed in, the driver was kind enough to hold the door open for them. "Thanks," Mike said sarcastically.

The driver warmly welcomed him.

"Where's you want this?" Dana asked.

Mike was about to tell him he thought the upstairs bathroom would be a great place for it, but he thought Dana would believe him and he wasn't quite ready to revisit it.

"The great room," he answered instead.

"Where's that?" Dana asked.

"Probably the room with the huge picture windows and thirty-five foot high cathedral ceilings," the driver said, making sure the screen door shut once Dana was in.

Dana didn't realize he had been slighted as he put his end down the moment he entered the great room.

"I guess that'll do," Mike said, putting his end down. The driver gave him a 'what can you do?' shrug.

Mike had a gesture for the driver too...but kept it to himself.

Dana was headed back out to get the bed.

The driver was busy wiping his brow with a rag he had produced from his back pocket.

"Tough work, huh?" Mike asked.

"You have no idea. You got any tea or something cold to drink?"

Mike thought the man was fishing for a beer without coming out and saying. "I think I've got some Tab—you want some?"

"No, that's alright, just a glass of water then. Thanks.

I didn't even know they still made Tab."

I'm not sure either, Mike thought.

Dana came in with a mattress in his arms. "Where's you want this?"

Mike thought the great room was a fine place for that also, he just wasn't ready for upstairs yet, but he didn't want to have to wrestle the king-size mattress up there when he *was* ready.

"Upstairs. End of the hall," he answered instead.

Within half an hour, the few things Mike had bought to transform his accommodations into something remotely homelike were now inside. Dana was sweating profusely, though it was the truck driver who kept wiping his forehead almost in sympathy of his partner.

Mike did want to give Dana a beer. The guy might be a little brusque, but he was a hard worker. But if he gave one to Dana his diet Tab ruse would be exposed.

"Well, I guess we're gonna get going," the driver said as Mike signed off on the delivery form. The driver was lingering ever so slightly waiting for something; *possibly a tip*, Mike thought.

"Well, I appreciate you coming out here so quickly," was all he offered.

The driver scowled. "I hope ragged strips of meat are ripped from your live, thrashing body," the man said with a smile.

"What?" Mike said taking a step back, color draining from his face.

"He says that whatever time you have left on this earth he hopes is punctuated with great pain and misery," Dana said.

"Get the fuck out!" Mike yelled throwing the papers he had signed at the driver's chest.

"What the hell's your problem, man?" the driver asked. "I just said that I hope your experience with Perry's furniture was a good one." A downward turn of the lips let

Mike know this for the lie it was.

Menace oozed from Dana. Whatever had been thrashing in the woods had nothing on the behemoth now inside his house. Mike wanted to shrink and hide in the smallest hole he could. Instead he stood tall. If he was to die it would be fighting, not cowering.

"I asked you to leave," he said with as much force as he could muster. He felt he fell extremely short.

"He axed us to leave," Dana laughed, brown rotting teeth glowed dully from his smile.

Patches stood on the top of the staircase staring down, she meowed loudly and in an instant the moment passed.

"You have a nice day," the driver said, clapping his partner across the shoulder and then they left.

It was all Mike could do to lock the door behind them and sit on the couch. Thankful that Dana had not gone any further than he had or Mike would have found himself on the floor as a permanent fixture.

"I think you just saved my life," Mike told Patches as the cat hopped onto the couch with him. "Probably should have gotten a darker color." Mike watched the trail of fur the cat was leaving behind.

"Jandilyn, I'm not sure I like this place," Mike said as he finally stood up. Patches watched him but did not follow as Mike headed upstairs, twilight taking full hold of the region, the house now cast in long shadows.

Mike turned on the bedroom light and was mildly surprised to find the bed was made. He thanked Dana even though he was fairly certain the man hadn't done it.

Mike wandered around the house for what remained of the day, notating a growing list of things he was going to need if he was going to make his time here... what? he asked himself—tolerable? Maybe. Enjoyable? Never. He didn't think he would ever enjoy life again, not without Jandilyn— but wasn't that why he was here now? He wondered how desperate he had to be to start hearing voices directing him.

Patches was sitting at the door, pretending not to take notice of the new guardian of the house.

"You and me against the world, cat." Patches walked away. "I'll make sure to get you vegetarian cat food going forward, you little ingrate," Mike said.

Mike debated about a shower, but he had neither a curtain to stop the flow of water nor a towel to dry off with. His contact with the movers had left him unnerved and it had also left an oily dirty residue upon his skin.

"How much water do those things really stop?" he asked as he stripped down. Mike enjoyed the openness of the shower, he also figured he would be able to see whatever was coming at him, although he wouldn't be able to defend himself with much more than a travel size container of shampoo. And then the next unsettling thought came to the fore—what the hell did he have to defend himself against?

"I really should have kept driving to Alaska, I'm still too close to Cali," he said as he shut the water off and stepped out into a burgeoning puddle of cold water pooled on the tile floor. He threw his dirty clothes on it in an attempt to soak up the majority of the spill. "I guess they stop more water than I thought." He wrote, 'shower curtain' in bold letters on his list, but underlined the word 'CLEAR' three times as if he would need reminding.

"Well, it's either laundry day tomorrow or clothes shopping," he said as he put on an old pair of paint-stained shorts and a hole-riddled Ozzy Osbourne t-shirt Jandilyn had wanted to get rid of when they had moved in together. He had saved it from the trash twice, more so for the reaction she would give him when she saw him wearing it again.

"Oh, gross!" she had said. "I put that thing under the moldy potato salad from last week's picnic—how did you find it? Did you even wash it, it smells like dirty diapers."

"It does smell a little like dirty diapers," Mike had laughed as he pulled the bottom of the shirt to his nose. "And if I get hungry I can even lick some of the old potato salad off the sleeve," he'd said as he licked his left side.

"Come on, Mike! You kiss me with that mouth!" She had run away as Mike chased her. He had finally pinned her on the couch making sure to mash her face with the front of his shirt.

"Mike, I can't breathe!" she had squealed as he tickled her.

He'd stopped and removed the shirt, replacing it with his lips. They had laughed as they kissed. She needn't have worried about any smell emanating from Mike's shirt as it was shorn quickly and the scene quickly dissolved into a sweet and tender love-making session.

Today's Michael sat on the couch weeping, tears dropped heavily as he remembered the tenderness they had shared. "I can't go on without you, Jandilyn!" he wailed.

A loud thumping upstairs pulled his thoughts from the past. His first thought was the cat, but he/she was sitting next to him. The knocking grew from a small child's hand on an oak door to a hammer-wielding carpenter on a two-by-four. As soon as Mike stood to go see if his pipes were bursting, the sound ceased.

Mike went into the kitchen and checked the flow of water—it seemed fine. "Must be what happens when the water cools." He doubted it, but what else could he say?

He spent the next few minutes going through the freezer to select which box of frozen grossness he wanted to eat for dinner. The Salisbury steak wannabe with hard-as-nails peas won out. Mike thought Patches' beef and chicken medley looked much more appetizing than his steaming pile of food-like substance. The smell wafting up from his dinner was worse than his unwashed t-shirt had ever been.

Dark came fast in the middle of nowhere. With no television, Mike crawled into bed with a book he'd been trying to read for a month, but he kept forgetting where he had left off and found himself rereading the same paragraphs over and over.

"Wow, seven on a Friday, I sure am a party animal," Mike said as he slid between the cool sheets. Patches hopped up onto the bed and looked at Mike as if to say 'What took you so long?'

"Sorry, not all of us like to sleep eighteen hours a day," he told her. "So you are a she," he said as she turned her back to him. "I should have known with how fickle you are. I should have named you Mrs. Hollow, no, I'm sorry, I take it back. I kind of like you."

Mike hadn't got more than ten pages through what he was pretty sure he had already read when his head started to nod. He jerked awake when he felt something brush against his arm. "Fuck off, Patches," he said sleepily. His head bolted up when he realized the cat was as far from him as she could be while staying on the bed and had not moved since she turned her tail on him.

"Jandilyn, is that you?" he pleaded. Nothing answered in return. Patches had turned her head and was eyeing Mike, but not quite. She was looking at something over his shoulder. She hissed once and leapt off the bed. Mike heard her rapidly descending the steps. "Was it something I said?" A cold breath of death kissed his ear.

He jumped out of bed, his skin goose-fleshed to the size of chicken eggs. If the mattress hadn't been a king size he would have pulled it to the landing and thrown it over the balcony so he could sleep in the great room. As it was, he was exhausted and had to drive back into town and do a bunch of shopping the next day. He lay back down after a few moments, making sure to stay closer to the center of the bed, cat be damned. She would have to get over her aversion to him or she could stay on the couch downstairs, although he hoped she wouldn't. She wasn't much company but she was infinitely better than the alternative.

Mike tried to read, but again he did not know his place and really he didn't care all that much. He tossed the book across the room and shut the light off next to his bed.

The light from the bathroom was still on and it splayed into the bedroom, but he was fine with it at least tonight. At some point during the evening Mike awoke when something passed across the path of light that led from the bathroom to his face. His mind not fully engaged figured it was the cat, although she was pooled by his feet.

That morning Mike awoke with Patches less than an inch from his face and she was peering at him as if he were bathed in *Eau de Mouse*. "Not cool, cat," Mike said, pulling back so he could focus on the feline. She hopped down and walked into the bathroom where, Mike had set up one of the two litter boxes, the other being next to the kitchen leading down a small hallway that led to a dining room he hadn't done more than place some empty boxes in.

"That sounds like a good idea," Mike said. "My bladder is gonna burst, you'd better hurry." He rose out of bed. He was halfway across the room when he noticed the book he had discarded, his need for elimination all but forgotten. Three claw marks had been dragged down the front of it, shredding at least a quarter of the book all the way through. He desperately wanted to blame Patches, but unless she turned into a werecat in the middle of the night, she didn't have the size or the strength to do that kind of damage.

"Couldn't get into it anyway," Mike said to himself. He picked the book up, it felt preternaturally warm in his hand and he quickly deposited it in an empty box he was temporarily using as a trash bin. "I probably could have talked them down on the price," Mike said to Patches as she hissed at him. "Sorry, I should know better than to bother you, especially when you're busy."

Mike gnawed on a piece of bread, staring out his kitchen window, not really taking in any sights, but it beat looking at the wall. He hadn't realized what he was waiting for until Patches padded down the stairs. "You ready to go?" he asked as he put his sneakers on.

Patches hopped up into the Jeep and immediately

curled up to sleep. "Rough day, cat?" Mike asked her. "I know you need a nap from your night of sleeping. Oh, to be a cat and not worry about anything." His words couldn't have been any more wrong, there was just no way he could have known that.

Mike needed a few more pieces of furniture, but he figured he'd make due for now. He had no desire to have his moving buddies come back, not unless he was armed. *Speaking of which*, he thought as he swung into a local sporting goods store.

"What is the best home defense weapon?" Mike asked the elderly clerk. The man could have called Jed 'son' and that thought brought another pang of longing.

"Having some problems out there at the old Granger homestead?" the man asked.

"What?" Mike stated and then he remembered seeing that name somewhere on the small encyclopedia of forms he had to sign when he bought the house. "How do you know?"

"Not much happens in this town I don't know about. Name is Fred," the clerk said, but he didn't offer his hand which Mike found strange. "Did you know the previous owner went insane? Kept ranting and raving that something lived upstairs."

"Did—" Mike gulped. "Did he kill his family in some gruesome way and then himself?"

Fred looked at him strangely. "Where you from? They might do that there, but this is a nice community, he just picked up his stuff and left."

"Oh. Well, that's a much better ending."

"So you're a writer," Fred said more as a statement than a question.

"Some think so, but I've got enough critics who would argue the point."

"That's funny. You have a Washington driver's license yet?"

Mike shook his head.

"I suggest a Walther P5, got a nice used one over here. But I can't sell you any firearms without a valid in-state id. You could always get a Taser."

"Would that stop a bear?"

"Why would you want to be close enough to a bear to use a Taser?" Fred asked. "Are you daft? Besides, you would have to go a lot deeper into the woods even more than you already are to come across one. You aren't one of those Bigfoot kooks, are you? They're always coming in here looking for supplies and nets as if a stupid butterfly net was going to snag him all up." Fred mimicked an ensnared animal. "That is if there even was such an animal."

"I haven't thought about Bigfoot since I was ten, but now I guess I'll be wondering if he's going to venture into my yard, so thank you for that."

"You want a net to catch him with? Got a whole wall full of them."

"I'll pass."

"I can sell you a bow or a crossbow if you want—if that'll make you feel a little better."

Mike thought only a priest would be able to make him feel more secure, but yes, the crossbow did offer some piece of mind if only in his head. Mike bought the bow, a bunch of arrows a few other supplies and checked out.

Fred walked from around the cash register. "I'll walk you out—about time for my smoke."

Mike was going to inquire about the other patrons, but then he realized he was the only one in the store.

"My wife stops by from time to time. I used to smoke in the store but she said it made the merchandise stink like Camels and that paying customers didn't want the added smell. I was going to argue with her and then I realized I hadn't won a fight with her since Kennedy was in office and that was more because she passed out from the liquor than a win on my part."

Mike laughed. He crossed the sidewalk and opened

the passenger door to put his stuff in. "Thanks for the help," Mike said after placing his stuff in the backseat. He turned to offer Fred a final wave, but Fred was fully fixated on Patches. The Camel he had been wanting to smoke was now rolling down the walkway.

"Where…where'd you get that cat?" His cigarette-less hand was pointing and shaking violently.

"She came out of the woods, she's just a stray. You alright, Fred? Do you need an ambulance?" Mike approached the old man, fairly certain he was going to need to catch him.

Fred backed up into the store. "Get the fuck outta here," he said, looking up at Mike. "You and that fucking cat get out of here!"

"Fred, what's the matter?" Mike asked confused and not moving

"That cat's dead!" Fred shrieked. "I ran it over fifteen fucking years ago!"

"Fred, she just looks the same, it can't possibly be the same cat."

"If she's dead then that means you must be dead too! I'm not going to tell you again—get the fuck out of here!" Fred exclaimed, this time punctuating his point with the barrel of some heavy gauge weapon he had been wearing on his hip but was now alternating between pointing it at Mike's head and Patches' body.

Patches couldn't have been any less concerned as she stretched her front paws on Mike's seat, catching her claws on the material for good measure.

"Okay, Fred, I'm leaving put the damn cannon away."

"If you get your license, don't come back here," Fred said as he stepped back into his shop and threw the lock. Still backing up, he fell into a canoe he had displayed.

Mike was shaking when he pulled away. "That went well, don't you think?" Mike asked, his voice quavering.

Patches didn't acknowledge him. She was busy

looking back the way they had come. Mike tried for the rest of the day to forget the incident with the sporting goods store owner but it just kept nagging him. He was on the long lonely road to his house before it began to slip away from his thoughts.

"Home sweet home," Mike said sourly.

He carried all the bags into the house. Patches didn't help.

"Suppose you want some food now for all the hard work you've been doing today," Mike said, bending down to pick up her bowl. As he rose he saw what had to be a practical joke. Written on the refrigerator door in what he had first assumed to be blood but turned out to be ketchup were the words 'YOU SHOULD LEAVE.'

"I would have expected 'GET OUT', that seems like a much more forceful statement. Obviously, someone has a key to this place and is really trying to mess with my head, but for what reason? I don't know anyone here. This isn't going to end well!" Mike shouted, just in case whoever had let themselves in was still within ear shot. "I'm armed now. And I need that damn ketchup—have you seen what I'm eating?" Mike tried for levity he did not truly feel. And the words on the fridge felt more like a warning than a threat, but from whom and for what reason?

Mike unwrapped the new coffee maker he had purchased and brewed a large pot. He was enjoying sleep less and less even though it was an escape from the constant reminder of Jandilyn's absence. He knew heartache, he thought his heart was going to strangle itself at the loss of his friends but the pain he felt now went deeper. His heart labored merely to beat, each pounding a confirmation, no an accusation, that he was alive and she was dead.

The cat had jumped up on the counter and was watching the strange brew percolate as if it contained the hidden meaning to life. When it was done, Mike dumped a fair measure of sugar and enough cream to turn the amber brown liquid to a soft shade of Irish white. He took the whole pot and a cup and headed for the front porch. He sat in an antique rocker old man Granger had left behind in his haste to get away from a bank debt or bad demon, both of which shared the same initials.

Mike figured the latter was the true reason, the debt may have been part of it, but the underlying reason was housed in the loft area. "Yeah, it's a nice day out. I'd much rather be out here," Mike told Patches. The only problem was now he was looking directly at the patch of trees that inexplicably liked to move. He quickly ran into the house, grabbed the crossbow, and began to assemble it.

"Wouldn't that suck if I got mauled by something while I was trying to put this stuff together?" he asked Patches, but she was lying on the top step, fully immersed in the rays of the sun. "You look good for being years dead," he told her. She flicked her tail in response.

Mike was three-quarters through the pot of coffee as the sun began to set over a distant mount when a chill wind coursed through him. He grabbed his now functional weapon and headed inside.

"You coming in?" he asked Patches.

She looked up at him and then into the house before bounding down the remainder of the steps and into the woods from where she had first emerged. Mike thought about following her, but it was rapidly darkening and he didn't think he'd be able to even see her or get through the brush for that matter.

"I'm going to eat your food!" he yelled, hoping to entice his companion back. She didn't listen.

Mike went in and subconsciously flipped every switch he passed that was attached to something that lit up. He refilled Patches' already overflowing bowl and stood up. The warning on the fridge was gone, the words maybe, but not the medium in which they were written. The ketchup was smeared across the whole front of the appliance as if a petulant three-year-old had been let loose.

"Why?" he asked, an involuntary sob escaping his lips.

He knew he was going insane and he had no family, no friends, and no Jandilyn to help him. He began to ponder if it would be possible to put a crossbow bolt through his head.

"Maybe I could buy that Taser and off myself in the tub—would that kill me if I dropped it in there?" He laughed at the insanity of the words, but not the message. *That* he took seriously as the heart attack he hoped it would incite.

Mike was crying, his head resting against the cool marble countertop when he felt something brush up against his leg. Through blurred vision he made out the form of Patches who had made her way in and was now eating. He couldn't remember if he had left the screen door open for her to get back in or she was just Houdini. It was far removed from the strangest thing that had happened that day and he soon forgot about it.

Mike cleaned the fridge off and dug around in the freezer, grabbing something he hoped would take the edge off the gnawing in his stomach. He wished he had the foresight to pick up another bottle of ketchup; it was the only thing that made the frozen meals somewhat palatable. He opened the door, the condiment was just about where he had put it the last time but, he couldn't be completely sure. Who takes note of that kind of thing anyway?

He stopped mid-reach, wondering if he wanted to touch something that was last in possession of what? A ghost? An entity? A sort-of-mad squatter? What exactly was going on here? He thought Jandilyn had led him here, but now he wasn't sure and even if she had, for what purpose? So that he would rapidly descend into madness culminating in suicide? He had enough Catholic in him to know he would never see his love again if he took that road. An eternity of damnation was all he could expect at the end of a rope, bullet, arrow or insert-deadly-instrument-here.

He could deal with what *felt* like an eternity to meet back up with his love and his baby, he thought, as long as each second wasn't drawn agonizingly out and the pain he felt would at some point ebb. The exact opposite had been happening, though, instead of dropping off it had actually been building like a giant wave off the coast of some Southern Pacific Island that was now going to be threatened by a wall of murderous water some hundred feet high, nothing and nobody would be able to survive and that was how he felt.

"Kind of dramatic don't you think, Patches?" he asked as he leaned on his elbows on the countertop. He yawned and his jaw popped. "What the hell—I should be until next Thursday," he said as he eyed his nearly empty pot of coffee. "Fuck me," he said softly when he looked at the bag of coffee grounds. "Decaf. Son of a bitch." He yawned again.

He grabbed one of the bags off the counter and headed up, he left the lights blazing. Patches took one long look around the kitchen and followed. "This oughtta help me sleep," Mike said as he opened up the sound maker he had purchased at the local Radio Shack. He plugged the small machine in and placed it on his milk crate nightstand.

He pressed the first button without checking what it was and instantly regretted his decision as a beating heart amplified throughout his room, the remembrance of their first sonogram and the beating heart of his unborn child slammed into him with all the force of a gale fueled wind. He started button mashing until something—anything different came through the speakers. Ocean waves breaking on a beach came next, but since that hit a little too close to home in actual feelings he moved on.

The chirp of crickets came next, but he didn't think he'd be able to sleep with insects in his room. "Last choice or into the trash with you," Mike said as he pressed the button labeled 'White Noise'. Static filled the room, much like late night television from its early era when, after the National Anthem, all broadcasting stopped. The noise made his teeth chatter at high decibels but was somewhat soothing on the lowest setting.

"I guess that's the point," he said. "To remind us of when we were kids and we would fall asleep with the tube on." He set the device down.

Patches didn't seem to mind what noise came out of the thing, she was already curled up and purring contentedly. "I know it's early, cat, but I'm wiped out. Do you mind?"

He shut the light off. Mike was having dreams of Jandilyn and the baby, a boy he figured by the blue pajamas he was wearing. Jandilyn was laughing, her eyes twinkling as Mike swung the baby gently around their old apartment. The baby was squealing with delight, issuing small gurgling sounds and grinning toothlessly.

The baby's smile started to droop as color began to vanish, pink turned to blue, Jandilyn was screaming at him to stop swinging the baby, but his feet wouldn't listen, in fact they started speeding up so that the room was violently spinning. Jandilyn was reaching out, but he kept moving farther away, the baby went slack in his hands. The blue terry cloth pajamas began to sprout a patchwork quilt of fur, within moments the baby's lifeless face turned into the intense watchful gaze of Patches. Mike tried to push the cat away, but the faster he twirled the closer the centrifugal force pulled them together almost in unification.

Just as Patches' nose was about to touch his own he woke with a start, not realizing where the nightmare ended and reality began. Patches was within inches of his face staring intently.

"Fuck, cat!" he yelled, scooting back, his head slamming into the headboard.

Mike was rubbing the back of his head, Patches was alternating looks between Mike and the white noise generator. Chills began to spread down Mike's arms as his heavy breathing became visible, a wisp of breath drifted up like a fine filament of smoke.

Through the static Mike could hear something trying to make itself known, his first initial fear was that it would be the gurgling of a dying baby. "Michael," came through, hardly louder than a whisper.

"Jed?" Mike asked. The voice was male. That was the only thing he could be certain of.

"Michael…" again hardly above a whisper. "THE CLEARING!" Blared through the machine, ripping a hole through the speaker.

Mike had enough adrenaline splashing through his veins that two pots of coffee and a pound of sugar wouldn't have been able to match. The white noise now sounded like ripped paper blowing in a stiff breeze. Mike made sure to tear the plug out of the wall, he'd seen enough horror movies to realize it would without a doubt turn itself back on sometime in the middle of the night. Although he'd also seen enough to where it didn't matter if it was plugged in or not.

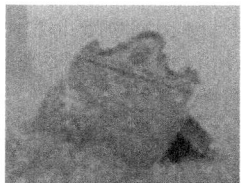

CHAPTER FIFTEEN – The Clearing

"I'm in a horror movie now—when did this happen?" But he knew the answer, it was the very second Jandilyn's heart stopped beating. Everything since was merely filler. Mike sat there waiting for the surge of endorphins to wind their way through his body. He got up and took the sound machine out of the room and downstairs to throw it into the trash barrel in the kitchen. He was not surprised in the least to see the words 'THE CLEARING' on the fridge, what put ice into his veins was that whatever had done those letters had used something sharp enough to engrave them permanently into the stainless steel.

"That was a nice fridge!" Mike shouted, pulling the fridge out of its little cubby against the wall.

He unhooked the plug and pulled it clear from the kitchen and down the hallway. He opened the front door and then propped open the screen door. He only became concerned for a moment when the fridge caught on the small riser but he still had enough reserves in the adrenaline tank to get the large machine over the hump, so to speak. It tottered for a second then crashed to the porch. A flock of something lifted off from the woods nearby and gave a loud protest at the disturbance.

"And fuck you too!" Mike yelled to the retreating fowl.

Mike pushed the fridge far enough so that he could again shut the screen door. "Write something on that, you asshole!" Somewhere deep down Mike knew he was losing his grasp on reality, at the moment, though, he was just really thankful he didn't have any neighbors to watch him.

Patches was sitting on top of the stairs, watching the whole scene seemingly unconcerned. What did she care? Her food was in the pantry.

"Jandilyn, help me!" Mike shrieked to the heavens. A ghostly, imagined voice sang out and Mike knew what he had to do.

"Do I even own a flashlight?" he asked himself as he sat down and put his boots on. Patches came down and watched him intently. "What, cat? Are you hungry? Go eat, your bowl is overflowing with food."

Mike got up and walked toward the door and out, almost falling over his newly discarded appliance in his haste to get to where he was going. Patches was at the bottom of the porch steps. "Holy shit, you're fast," Mike said, avoiding stepping on her by the minutest fraction. She hissed violently at him. "Oh, shut up, I didn't even touch you."

Mike headed to the brush line where he had seen Patches emerge some years ago. *Days*, he corrected. *What made me think that?* he wondered. Thorns caught on his bed clothes, most punctured and ripped at his skin, the pain did little to deter him, if anything it spurred him on. Mike was bloody with effort by the time he came out to a small moss laden clearing roughly six feet in diameter. Moonlight flooded the small space and illuminated just how much damage he had sustained.

Blood welled up from over a dozen wounds, some considerably worse than others, his bed clothes were in tatters, getting the blood out was of no concern at this point, by the end of the night he figured he would toss them on top of the discarded fridge. A small hand axe was imbedded in a tree a few feet from where he had entered the opening. With some effort he pulled it free, remarking how warm the handle was, as if the last lumberjack had just clocked out and now it was Mike's shift. The blade glinted in the moonlight; it appeared as if it had just received its factory edge yesterday. Mike's arms vibrated as he buried the blade deep into a tree.

Patches howled loudly, Mike paid her absolutely no heed as he swung repeatedly.

Mike barely stopped to watch as the forty foot behemoth crashed to the ground before he began swinging at the next tree. The woods had become deathly quiet except for the hammering blows of Mike's axe on the trees. Any animals that had not completely vacated the area waited expectantly. The sun was burning high overhead by the time Mike's shoulders could not rise much more than an inch or two from the sides of his body and still he tried to wield the axe by turning quickly hoping centrifugal force would plant the head of the axe where it needed to be.

He might have had a modicum of success if not for the blood pouring from his hands, making his grasp tenuous at best. He lay down on the ground, blessedly thankful for how cool the moss was. Patches was a cat with a vengeance, she kept meowing at him, completely walking around the clearing, protesting loudly, always staying out of reach of his half-hearted attempts to shut her up. She was in absolutely no danger as Mike could do little more than point a finger at her and tell her to hush up.

The sun was past its peak but, it was not yet twilight when Mike poked his head up. "I need to get to town!" he said, sitting up, his arms still twitching violently from overexertion. Patches was at the outer edge of the expanding clearing. She led the way as Mike effortlessly walked back through the brush. The thorns were angled to keep intruders out, not in, he noted. Mike stepped back onto the grass, he was not in the least amazed to see that his fridge was no longer on his porch, in all reality he didn't even care.

That it was back in its original cubby and plugged in made him pause, but not for long as he grabbed his keys off the counter.

"Must have dreamed that whole fridge thing," he told Patches who was sitting in the passenger seat. "How did you get there?" Mike asked as he pulled out of his long drive.

He was mildly surprised to see small rivulets of blood rolling down his steering wheel from his damaged hands and falling on to the floor mat below, an ant might not drown in the growing puddle but it would have to swim across. Mike jerkily stopped at the front of the hardware store, effectively cutting off the strategically placed fire hydrant, and quickly walked in.

He took no notice of the people staring at him as he went around the store grabbing the supplies he would need. A brownish mixture of blood and dirt covered the majority of his bed clothes. Welted flesh oozed out of every torn hole in them.

"You alright?" the clerk asked, wishing it was his break time now so that he wouldn't have to be close to this person who smelled of sweat and insanity which, if the latter had a scent, then the man before him was bathed in it.

Mike grunted a potential affirmative as he gingerly pulled the items out of the shopping cart.

"Leave the big ones in. I'll scan them," the clerk said. "In fact, leave them all in, I'll get them." The clerk was wondering how he was going to touch any of the items without touching this man's blood, they were coated in it like they were factory shipped that way. "I'll be right back."

Mike didn't acknowledge him as the clerk walked over to the register at customer service.

"What's his story?" Becky, the owner's daughter, asked Darvin, the clerk who had the unfortunate luck of the draw to be checking Mike out instead of manning the plumbing section like he usually did.

"Hell if I know, but this is the last time I cover for Lacy when she goes on break. The freak has blood on everything."

"Blood? Are you sure?"

"Yeah, I'm sure. It's fucking disgusting. Do you have gloves?"

Becky handed him the whole box of surgical gloves.

"Should I call the cops?"

"He probably did murder someone. He's got an axe and a shovel and what's left of his clothes look like something you'd wear to bed. Maybe you should call Sheriff Wamsley."

"Don't think we're going to need to," Becky said, pointing to the front door, where the town's only other deputy besides Caldwell was walking in.

"Okay, who's the brain child parked right outside? Now I realize from your plates you're from out of state. But I can't imagine that even California, with its strange set of values, allows cars to park in front of fire hydrants. Now, if someone here were to say, maybe get in that car while I was all distracted, looking at some new lawn mowers they probably could get out of here before I find my way back to my squad car and grabbed my ticket book. Sound like a fair enough deal, Mister or Missus California?" True to his word the deputy began to stroll over toward the new line of John Deere lawn mowers that he'd been trying to persuade his wife to no avail, that they needed desperately. He was at the first row of grass cutters when his gaze fell upon Mike. A ticket he could afford to avoid…this he could not.

"Sir?" the deputy asked with concern. "Are you alright?" He didn't know whether to pull his sidearm or radio for a medic—both seemed like valid responses. Darvin was making his way back to the register before Deputy Baker waved him away. Darvin didn't need to be told twice as he retreated back to Becky's station.

Mike looked up and staggered. His contact which he had been long neglecting had shifted slightly throwing his world askew. Light and dark flooded into the far reaches of his mind, he gripped the counter to keep from succumbing to the vertigo. He fell backward as his blood soaked hands could not seek purchase. He was looking up at the very large barrel of a Colt .45 when the spinning subsided.

"Stay down, sir. An ambulance is on the way."

"I need to get back to her," Mike croaked.

"Is she hurt?" the deputy asked, trying to pull information from the man on the ground.

Mike looked at the deputy strangely. "She's dead," he answered.

"Sir, you have the right to remain silent, anything you…"

Mike passed out, he awoke a few hours later in a hospital bed. His clothes gone, replaced by a less-than-modest hospital gown, his cuts and scrapes covered in a thick goo that could only be Bacitracin and a soap opera was playing on the television across the room.

The deputy, upon seeing Mike come awake, immediately turned the television off. "I was looking for some sports," the deputy said guiltily.

"I won't tell anyone," Mike promised. "What's going on?"

"You tell us. You look like you were on the losing end of a fight with a floral shop owner. The sheriff went out to your house, he said the front door was wide open and your fridge looks like you went to town on it with a sledgehammer"

"Damn thing's been acting up," Mike said, his voice raw.

"We ran your plates. We know who you are."

"Deputy, you say that like I'm a known fugitive on the FBI's most wanted list."

"Are you doing research for another novel?" the deputy asked in all seriousness.

"I'd really be taking my craft to another level if that were the case. No, I hate to disappoint you, but I'm just doing some much needed yard work. There's a cat in my Jeep, deputy, she's more of a pain in the ass than any company, but is she okay?"

"Didn't see a cat in your car and I looked pretty good. Thought maybe you had a weapon in there before we knew who you were."

"Are you sure she didn't get by you?"

"Mr. Talbot, I can assure you there was no cat in that car when I opened the door. More than likely she crawled out your window."

"How's she going to find her way home? It's got to be twenty miles to my house."

"You don't concern yourself with that right now. I'll keep an eye out for her. She'll get hungry soon enough…"

"Is there something else?" Mike asked.

The deputy was wringing the back of his neck with a heavily callused hand. "Mr. Talbot, was there ever a cat?"

"What are you talking about?"

"Well, besides the mangled fridge, the sheriff said you had a small mountain of cat food on the kitchen floor and the litter box upstairs is clean as the day you bought it, which according to your receipts was three days ago. Seems to me that a cat eating as much as the one you're saying you have would be taking care of business a lot if you get my meaning."

"I think I'd know if I had a damn cat or not, most times she won't even let me touch her. She's about as fickle a woman as I'd ever met, but she's as real as me and you!" Mike said heatedly.

"I'm sorry to get you riled. I'll keep an eye out for her," the deputy said as he dipped his head slightly and put his hat back on. "You have a good day, sir, I hope you're feeling better."

"Am I under any type of house arrest?" Mike asked before the deputy left.

"No, but the sheriff would like to talk to you at some point."

"Where's my Jeep now?"

"In the parking lot, we had it towed here."

Mike got up and almost beat the deputy out of the room.

"You're going out like that?"

"These are in better shape than the ones I came in with, I consider it an improvement."

"Fair enough, but you might want to get a better grip on the back side or I'm going to have to haul you in for indecent exposure."

Mike had a brief stop at the nurse's station, grabbed some discharge papers which he promised to fill out and bring back in at some point.

He walked across the small parking lot, one bandaged hand wrapped tightly with the draw strings on his gown and the other holding his boots. Patches had her paws against the window and was watching his approach. Mike thought she looked almost happy to see him. That's when he figured that must not really be his cat.

"I knew that deputy was full of shit. Miss me?" Mike asked as he hopped in.

Patches licked a paw and did her best to pretend he wasn't there.

"Gotta love small towns," Mike said, looking in the backseat where all his hardware purchases rested. A receipt needing his signature was taped to one of the bags. "They could have just cancelled the whole order, but I'm glad they didn't."

Mike pulled into his long drive, happy to realize the sheriff wasn't waiting for him and more importantly that his fridge wasn't back on the porch. He was actually hungry and the frozen dinners might taste like cardboard, but he still needed the fuel for what he desired to do.

"Wow, the sheriff was right," Mike said, running his hand along one of the many dents on the face of the fridge. "I don't know about a sledgehammer, though, looks more like a fist did this, a hammer would be deeper." He fit his hand perfectly into the crevice."

Mike ate his meal hurriedly, strapped his boots on, and headed to grab some of his new expenditures out of the

Jeep. He cut a small path through the growth to the clearing with his machete, even so, he was still rewarded with a few new wounds. The thorns seemed to grow almost as rapidly as he cut them, like tossing water out of the ocean. The sight of the green floored clearing both quickened his heart and calmed his soul.

"I can feel you here, Jandilyn," he said, reaching down and rubbing his palm against the moss.

Mike went back to the car and grabbed his brand new prize possession, the chainsaw ripped through the cedar, pine and oak trees like a steak knife through tenderized veal. The clearing was some twelve feet in diameter when he felt that was the appropriate size, for what, he didn't quite know yet. Just that it was.

Patches circled around the entire area, never stepping onto the moss and mewling loudly in protest of the work Mike was doing. He was cutting the trees up into manageable two foot lengths and hauling them out into his backyard. It was the fortieth or fiftieth trip when he emerged from the brush. The sheriff was leaning up against the side of his car, drinking what appeared to be an iced tea.

Mike placed the log on the growing pile.

"The door was open. I hope you don't mind?" the sheriff asked, holding the glass up.

"I had iced tea?"

"It's iced coffee. I don't like cream…was going to make a sandwich but you don't really have much of anything."

"Well, if I'd known you were coming I would have stocked up."

"Can I ask you what you're doing?"

"Gardening."

"That's some heavy duty gardening—you always work in a hospital gown?"

"It's all the rage in Paris," Mike answered. "I'd thought about just going buck naked, but if I ended up with a tick on my crotch, well you can understand the embarrassment."

"I don't really like you," the sheriff said, taking a long sip of coffee as he waited for a response from Mike.

Mike got the feeling if he answered wrong, the sheriff might shoot him a couple of times for good measure and deposit him in his new project.

"I wish I could say I care," Mike told him.

"Jandilyn's not in there," the sheriff said, pointing back to the path.

"Excuse me?" Mike said, his heart firing on cylinders he wasn't even aware he had.

"Coffee could use a little more sugar."

"Who sent you?" Mike said, backing up, wanting to put as much distance between himself and the bullet he felt had his name on it.

"You take care," the sheriff said as he tipped his hat. He dropped the glass onto the ground where it shattered. "Don't cut yourself on that." He got into his car and drove off.

Patches came over and sniffed at the liquid which was rapidly soaking into the soil and then headed into the house.

"I could have used a little back-up!" Mike yelled to her retreating form.

He was shaken up from his encounter with the law and wasn't quite certain he had heard the man correctly. How could he possibly know? Mike himself didn't really know what he was doing, it was more of an awareness of something that needed to be done.

By the time the sun set, Mike had convinced himself that the buzz of the chainsaw and the lack of hearing protection had made him miss some crucial part of the conversation with the sheriff and that was probably why the man had become so hostile so quickly. But no matter how much he tried to rationalize the whole thing away 'Jandilyn's not in there' kept ringing out clear as a bell on a Sunday morning.

"You ready for bed, cat? It's got to be at least eight thirty." Mike skipped past a shower, dirt clung greedily to the pockets of salve the hospital had applied liberally to his body. Blood, puss and blisters oozed onto his sheets. It looked like a crime scene in the making.

Mike was dead asleep when he felt something wasn't quite right. He was on his side and should have been facing the cat, but with the small sliver of moonlight illuminating his room he knew she wasn't on the bed with him, at least not in her usual spot. A heaviness had descended upon his chest and breathing was becoming difficult. He rolled onto his back to see if that would alleviate the pressure. It was then he took notice of the dark figure at the foot of his bed. Mike scrambled toward the headboard, attempting to put as much distance as possible between him and the dark outline of a man that seemed to repel any light that dared approach.

"Am I imagining you?" Mike asked, hoping that insanity had finally claimed him, because that was a far better option than what he was presented with now.

"Hello, Michael," issued from an even blacker fissure in the being's face. "It seems like only hours ago we met."

"I think I would have remembered that." Mike said, his bladder urging for release. It was concentrating on holding onto that small piece of dignity that kept him from being swept over the edge into the abyss of madness.

"Oh, I think you do. Paul and Dennis most certainly did."

"What are you?"

"I am the completion of the circle."

"Why is everyone so vague?"

"You died over five years ago, Michael."

"Is that why I haven't been able to get quality healthcare?" Mike knew it was over for him. The sheriff would come back tomorrow to find a drooling Mike, his head hanging over the lip of the bathtub as he watched mold grow.

"Someone has interfered with the natural order of things, Michael. I have my ideas of who it may be, and eventually she will have to pay for her transgression, but in the mean time we have some unfinished business."

"Will I be with Jandilyn?" Mike dared to ask. If that were the case, he would go willingly.

"It is not for me to decide the fate of the souls I collect."

"That's not good enough."

"This is not something you have a choice in. We will talk further." With that the apparition was gone.

The pressure eased off Mike, Patches jumped onto the bed, startling him all over again. "You really suck for support," Mike said to the cat. Patches was still on edge with the residual presence, the light took its time filling in the void left by the departure of the being.

"That couldn't have been real, could it? I was sleeping or the meatloaf-like frozen dinner is messing my gut up and I'm having one hell of a vivid dream." Dream or not, Mike found his bladder needed urgent attention and he left a one hundred watt illuminated trail to find the bathroom.

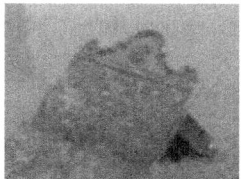

CHAPTER SIXTEEN – The Past Returns

As the sun came up, it was much easier to dismiss the notion that anything amiss had happened the previous night. That did little to ease how he felt when he entered his clearing today. The moss had already traveled halfway up the newly hewn tree trunks and now he couldn't truly remember if they had been there at all. He ran his hands along the moss, it was moist and cool and felt exactly like the rest of the space he was in.

His thoughts were abruptly changed as he heard the distinctive sound of tires on gravel. "The sheriff back for round two?" Mike asked. "Aw shit, I have got to expand my wardrobe." He looked down at the front of his blue hospital nightie. "It really is difficult to strike an imposing figure in this thing."

Mike made sure to grab his axe. If things got out of hand he wanted to make sure he would at least be able to have an opportunity to defend himself, but unless the sheriff would be so kind as to shoot him from less than five feet away it was going to be difficult. He was wholly unprepared for what he witnessed.

"Hello, Mike."

Mike racked his memory for that night so many years ago on the Hill. "Durgan?"

"Wasn't sure you'd remember me."

"You tend to make an impression," Mike said, circling behind the wood pile.

"I'm sorry about that."

"You'll forgive me my doubts," Mike said as Durgan stood, he wasn't nearly as large as the memory of him Mike had made. *He looks smaller, diminished perhaps*, Mike thought.

"I understand."

"Are you real?" Mike asked, pointing the axe his way.

"What?"

"Things are tending to get a little blurry lately. I think it might have something to do with my head injury, but then how would I know? My brain is going to tell me whatever it wants."

"I'm sorry about Jandilyn."

Mike almost doubled over from the mere mention of her name.

"I called Mrs. Hollow. I was trying to track you two down. I've had a life altering event and I'm going back to all of those who I've been 'difficult' to," he said with a pained expression.

"Is that how you classify it? Difficult? Does that let you sleep at night?"

"I'm dying, Mike. I have stage-two lymph node cancer. I've got two months at the most."

"Why are you here, Durgan? It seems like you should be spending this time with your friends and family?"

"Mike, there were very few people in life who I treated with anything less than contempt. I have no one."

"What were you expecting here? Pity?"

Mike thought Durgan was on the verge of tears.

"I came to make all the wrongs in my life right."

"How's that going for you?"

"About as well as this conversation. Seems the adage forgive and forget has been forgotten."

"Fine, I accept your apology. You can go now."

"I come with another message, Mike."

"Don't!" Mike said with force.

"She says you should leave here, no good can come from this."

"Don't you dare!" Mike screamed, coming out from his makeshift blockade, axe held high.

Durgan stood his ground; a quick axe to the head seemed like a blissful ending compared to the withering, lingering death by internal decay.

"Who the fuck are you to come onto my property and tell me anything?" Mike screamed, he had raised the axe and threatened to bring its full weight to bear on Durgan.

"I'm a lot closer to the other side now, Mike. I see things."

"Yeah, welcome to my fucking world. Great place, isn't it?" Mike asked sarcastically.

Durgan was left to look at Mike with a confused glaze. "I saw her in a dream, Mike, but it wasn't a dream. She wanted me to tell you she loved you." Mike dropped the axe. "And that they're waiting for you on the other side." This time Mike dropped next to his axe, his face buried in his hands. "She says you're doing things here that are better left undone."

"I don't believe you," Mike said without much conviction.

"You're right, Mike, I came cross country to deliver one final cruel prank."

Mike searched Durgan's face, hoping maybe *that* was the truth.

"Come on," Durgan said, extending a hand, "I'm pretty thirsty and I could use a seat."

"Don't you have someplace you should be?" Mike asked.

"Not much into entertaining?" Durgan asked.

"I'm pretty selective on my company and the few I've had lately have been anything but model citizens."

"One drink and a small rest and I'll leave, I promise," Durgan said as Mike grabbed his proffered hand. There was still power behind the grip, but Mike was fairly certain at this point they might be an even match if it came down to it.

"Fine, but I don't have much. The fridge has been acting up."

"Water will be fine," Durgan said as he began to approach the house.

Mike thought about racing ahead and grabbing a chair to put on the porch but thought better of it.

"Mrs. Hollow is no fan of yours." Durgan laughed as he took another giant swig of his glass of water.

"You want another glass?" Mike said from the sink as Durgan sat at the table across the room.

"She said the first time she laid eyes on you, she wanted to stick a knitting needle in your eye." Durgan laughed. "Who says that shit?"

"If I hadn't loved Jandilyn as much as I did, I would have left her because of her mother."

Durgan harrumphed. He eyed his empty glass. "Got anything stronger?"

"You said one drink and then you were going to leave."

"I came across the damn country to see you."

"I don't remember asking you to," Mike said, standing up straight, figuring this conversation was going downhill fast. He wished he had brought in the axe with him.

"I should have called first," Durgan said, dipping his head.

"I wouldn't have picked up even if I had a phone. I can't believe I'm doing this," Mike said as he stooped down below the sink and grabbed a brown bottle. I've got some Jeff Daniels."

"Some what?"

"Jeff."

"Is that like a generic brand? Or his less famous brother trying to cash in on the family name?"

"What in the hell are you talking about?"

"It's Jack Daniels."

"That's what I said."

"Just pour me some."

Mike grabbed a couple of mason jars he had found in the cabinet and poured them both a couple of fingers worth of the bitter liquor.

"That's about as smooth as sandpaper," Durgan said as he took in a sharp intake of air.

"I think I'd rather get in a fist fight with you than finish the rest of this crap," Mike said as he gulped the remainder of the firewater down. He poured them some more when Durgan matched him.

"Why here, Mike?" Durgan asked as he took another small sip.

Mike felt a small fuzziness begin to build behind his eyes, the first sign of an oncoming buzz. "No people," he answered. That was at least partly the truth. He downed the contents of his glass and poured another. "You know Mrs. Hollow really liked you." Mike added.

"That battleaxe?" Durgan said, arching an eyebrow. "Doubtful. Pour me another, would you?" He raised a glass. Mike complied. "She couldn't stand anyone, least of all me."

"She always told me how much she wished that Jandilyn had married you."

"That's rich," he said smiling. "Me over you. I think she would have learned the error of her ways right quick." He tipped his glass to Mike before he took a significant swallow.

The bottle was a third gone when Mike asked his next question. "You're not really intending on leaving, are you?"

"I thought you'd never ask."

"I didn't."

"Where am I going to sleep?" Durgan asked, looking around.

"Motel 6?" Mike asked.

"You wouldn't want me to drive like this, would you?"

"We're not buddies, you and me, Durgan."

"I think right now, Mike, we might not be friends, but

we need each other."

"I was—am doing fine."

"Me too," Durgan lied. "Well, let's do this again tomorrow night." Durgan stood and staggered over to the couch. He face-planted into the cushion, his legs raising up and draping over the arm of the lounger.

"Good night to you, too." Mike headed upstairs. He came back down with a spare pillow and blanket. He placed them next to the softly snoring Durgan, but then fanned the blanket out across his body. "I ain't tucking your ass in, though," he said as he headed back upstairs.

"What a weird ass day," Mike said as he stared at the ceiling. He thought sleep might be elusive even with all the alcohol pumping through his system, but he was out within minutes. Somehow having his previous mortal enemy asleep in his house made him feel safer. He hadn't even had a chance to really dwell on it before he was fast asleep.

***

Mike awoke the next morning, a splash of light across his eye, blistering into a plume of pain. He jolted awake when he realized he wasn't alone. He scrambled out of the bed and slammed onto the floor, the percussion of the contact sending waves of nausea through his stomach.

"Hey there," Durgan said, squinting his eyes.

"What are you doing in my bed?" Mike asked from the floor.

"Your couch sucks, it's not very comfortable."

"I don't give a shit if it has spikes for cushions—what the hell are you doing in my bed?"

"There's nothing wrong with two men sharing a bed." Durgan stretched.

"No, there isn't, but it is for us. Get out of my damn bed."

Durgan groaned, he looked worse than Mike felt.

"You got any food?" Durgan stood, stretched, and scratched his nether regions.

"Oh, man, this day is going from bad to horrible, really quick," Mike said, pointing to the doorway, hoping Durgan would get the hint.

"Want me to make you some breakfast?" he asked.

"Not after where your hands have been," Mike told him.

"I make a mean omelet."

"Eggs?" Mike turned a little green. "Any chance I could be sick without an audience?"

Mike was praying to the porcelain gods when he heard Durgan's car start up and drive away. He uttered the words 'thank God' and then found himself a little perturbed that Durgan hadn't even said goodbye.

He stayed there another half hour, confident the dry retching had come to a conclusion and he could start back up on the Clearing. The sun and the work would do him some good.

A lone bird watched as he descended the path to his work site. He knew if he looked hard enough it would be a raven and probably even the one with one white eye. He refused to let anything delay him today and if he stopped to wonder about the bird and its significance he would lose even more time. The chainsaw was out of gas and Mike had no desire to go back into town.

"Just like in the good 'ole days." He grimaced.

The axe bit deep as he swung it, the first hundred or so swipes were pure torture on his head. The vibration rattled his teeth which set off seismic explosions in his skull. He debated more than once the validity of the day's work. As the first tree fell over he began to hit his stride. He had planted his axe into the second tree when he saw the ghostly figure of a man staring back at him. He jumped back quickly, letting go of his only weapon.

"Fuck, man. You scared the shit out of me. I thought

you were a ghost."

Durgan said nothing for long seconds until Mike thought perhaps he was. Maybe he had still been drunk and plowed his car into a tree or the stage two cancer had caught up with him a little early.

"This doesn't feel right, Mike," Durgan said, finally speaking as he looked around.

"Why are you back?" Mike groaned. "You apologized, we drank—hell, we even slept together. Everything should be hunky dory. You can go meet your maker in peace." Mike paused for a second. "I'm sorry, that was a crappy thing to say."

Durgan plowed on as if Mike had never spoke. "You had no food and I'm not drinking any Daniels—Jeff or Jack—ever again. I bought some good stuff." Durgan smiled wickedly, pulling out a bottle of Tequila.

Mike could feel his stomach lurching just thinking of drinking the caustic liquid. Yet he still walked over to where Durgan was, grabbed the bottle, spun the top off, and took a swallow.

"Tastes like ass," Mike said, wiping his mouth.

"What are you doing, Mike? I mean really," Durgan said, swiping the bottle from Mike's hand.

Mike stopped for a moment to think about it. "I guess I don't really know," Mike answered.

"Fair enough. I'm going to make breakfast, come up in a half hour."

"You know this whole little set up we have going is pretty weird, right?" Mike asked.

"What? We slept together last night, the least I owe you is a decent breakfast."

"If you say anything about how you 'can't quit me' I'm going to use my axe on you."

"You like sausage in your omelets?" Durgan asked, smiling.

Mike was about to answer when the ground under his

feet began to sway, although it wasn't quite that pronounced, it was more like a ripple, like a stone in a pond.

"Mike?" Durgan asked with concern.

"Yeah-yeah, bacon is fine," Mike answered and then more quietly. "I'm close."

Mike came into the house an hour-and-a-half later and only because the blade of his axe had skipped off the side of a tree and cut into his leg.

"The eggs are colder than my mom's tits." Durgan laughed as Mike came in the door. He noticed the free-flowing blood. "Holy shit, Mike."

"Feeling a little woozy," Mike said as his eyes rolled up and he went down.

***

"Jandilyn!" Mike said sitting up.

"Not quite," Durgan said from his chair. Mike was on the couch and Durgan was sitting at the kitchen table doing his best to single-handedly take care of the tequila.

"You know I saved your life today, don't you?" Durgan asked.

Mike looked over at him; the tone did in no way convey the same meaning as the message. "You alright?" Mike asked, wincing as he tried to move his leg.

"There you were, bleeding like a stuck pig, and all I could think was that maybe I should just…" He paused. "Do nothing. I mean, you went down, man. I'm thinking you really would have just bled out and I'd be rid of you."

"Rid of me? What are you talking about?" Mike asked as he looked around for something, anything that could be used as a weapon. A small broom looked like his best option, might as well get some bandages so he could sop up the remainder of his blood after the beat down.

"Jandilyn, was mine," Durgan said as he swung his gaze over, his head was lowered and his stare was through menacing eyes.

"I thought we'd already been through this," Mike said, stalling, trying his best to sit up and get moving. The pain in his leg and the dizziness in his head were huge hindrances to that.

"I wanted to kill you that night on the hill."

"Why didn't you?" Mike asked. "You would have saved all of us a lot of trouble."

Durgan stood up.

Here we go, Mike thought as he stood. Between the vertigo and the searing pain in his leg, his moment of gravity defying standing was short-lived.

Durgan laughed, a small cruel sound issued forth.

Mike did the only thing he could think of, he removed his contact and spun around, not at all expecting to be witness to what he saw. Durgan looked to be immersed in a being double his size, a perfect black outline that mimicked all the moves and hatred portrayed on his face.

"I almost forgot about that," Durgan said, pointing at Mike's eye. "Mrs. Hollow says that's where the devil marked you. He stuck his finger in your eye and drained your soul through it."

Mike thought that almost sounded rational. He was convinced he'd have an easier time choking out a bear than fighting Durgan.

"What happened to the kinder, gentler Durgan?" Mike asked.

"He was an asshole," Durgan said, coming across the room slowly, taking another swig off the tequila bottle.

Mike was finally able to get his legs to support his body and it seemed that his head would cooperate for the moment, although it was an uneasy alliance.

"It'd be easier for both of us if you stayed seated."

"Do you mean me and you, or you and the thing controlling you?"

Durgan hesitated. "There isn't shit controlling me."

"Well, I'd beg to differ, but I'm thinking debate time is over," Mike said as he took a few tentative steps toward the broom. "Why are you doing this now? Seems you could have done it at any point last night or even while I was bleeding all over the place."

Durgan hesitated again. "It just seems funner this way—you all injured and barely able to move. Like a cat playing with a mouse, you know?" Durgan said, the glint coming back in his eye.

"So all that apology stuff?

"A bunch of bullshit to get in the door. I had put some drugs in your eggs, poison really, it wouldn't have killed you, just immobilized you and then I had planned a hugely entertaining night revolving around some serious torture culminating in your death."

Mike shivered. "What the fuck is wrong with you?"

"The doctors had a lot of names—dissociative disorder came up a lot, though." Durgan was inching closer, taking his time. He seemed to be savoring the moment. "What do you really think you're going to be able to do with that broom?"

"A little light cleaning, when I'm nervous it really helps to calm my nerves."

"You're a funny little fuck," Durgan said, pointing at Mike with the hand that was holding the bottle. "I'm curious to see how much you're laughing when I'm through with you."

"Killing me won't bring Jandilyn back."

"That's not the point!" Durgan screamed. "You took something that was mine and now you have to pay!"

Mike had finally wrapped his hands around the broom handle and it felt pathetic. A fully extended swing would do little more than bring up a welt and that would be if the wood could even handle the contact without snapping.

Mike looked over Durgan's shoulder, which was no easy feat considering the entity that had him encased. The kitchen was bathed in an ethereal light. "Can you see that?" Mike asked.

"How stupid do I look?"

"Oh, you'd be amazed," Mike told him. "If there is such a thing as honor among adversaries, I promise you I don't have any tricks up my sleeve. I'm merely asking you if you see anything weird in the kitchen."

Durgan charged. *Guess not*, Mike thought as he put the handle up in a defensive manner. Durgan, either unbalanced from his physical or mental disease or more possibly from the half a bottle of rotgut he had consumed, clipped the corner of the couch and went sprawling past Mike. For good measure, Mike thwacked him once hard on the side of the face and, as previously concerned, it did little more than produce a welt which would sting for a day at the most, but Mike felt he would have been better off shooting a grizzly with a BB gun.

"That fucking hurt!" Durgan said, rubbing his cheek.

"Real sorry about that," Mike said as he moved away from Durgan and closer to the kitchen.

Mike was over halfway there when he felt Durgan's hand wrap around his calf and send him plunging to the ground.

"It's not really polite to eat without your guests," Durgan said as he began to pull Mike closer.

Mike reared back with his damaged leg and struck out for all he was worth into Durgan's forehead. The pain Mike felt was worth the shocked expression he saw on Durgan's face.

Durgan immediately let go of Mike's calf as his head whipped back from the blow. He seemed to be momentarily stunned and Mike saw no reason to waste the opportunity and admire his handiwork.

Mike propped himself up with the table. He finally turned, completely expecting Durgan to be right behind him, about to deliver a jaw cracking uppercut. Apparently, the kick had done a little more damage than he had originally assumed. Durgan was groggy and groaning. Mike decided to not give him an opportunity to recover quite so quickly. He stood up and took a quick two step walk before delivering a bone jarring impact from nose of boot to side of head. Durgan went slack.

"That's for the Hill, you *fuck*!" Mike spat. The oily blackness that was truly running the show bent over to see if its charge was still of this world when it was confident it still had a puppet to maneuver it stayed steadfast. "And fuck you, too," Mike said with a little less vehemence as he finished his entry into the kitchen.

Mike grabbed a large knife out of the sink, then noticed a small bottle next to a block of cheese. It looked like something out of an old apothecary shop, brown in color and a skull and crossbones sticker for a label.

Mike became outraged as he held the small vial up and then a wicked grin spread across his face. Durgan had not yet moved, but Mike figured it would be relatively soon. He grabbed his knife and the bottle and headed back to the prone man. The black figure pulling Durgan's strings had not suffered the same injury as its host; it stood silent over his body.

"Any chance you'll get the fuck out of my way?" Mike asked it. It did not acknowledge him. "Fine, we'll do this your way." Mike shivered as he moved in close, where his body made contact with the being, his skin burned from coldness.

When he was done pouring the contents of the bottle into the booze, Mike headed back to the kitchen table to sit down. It was long minutes before his skin warmed back up, he had thought about going back to the couch to get his blanket but didn't want to be near either one of the things that now inhabited his living room.

His left eye throbbed as if it were taking in too much information. The black mass around Durgan waited patiently at its station around the passed out man. Mike walked slowly upstairs to retrieve his eye patch, profusely apologizing for breaking his promise to Jandilyn about removing his contact. It wasn't long before Durgan began to stir. Mike was amazed; he figured he would have been dead if the roles had been reversed. That might not be a fair comparison, though, because Durgan's leg was probably twice the size of his.

Durgan rolled over and sat up. He placed his hand to the side of his head which was now rapidly swelling. "Looks like you won this round." He pressed the tequila bottle against his lips and took an extended draw. "You should have killed me, though."

"Night's young," Mike said, spinning the tip of a knife blade on the table.

"Jandilyn's mother funded my trip out here, you know. She hired private investigators to find you and then when I showed up at her doorstep she saw it as divine intervention."

"You know what divine means, don't you?" Mike asked him sardonically.

Durgan took another drag in response as he delayed speaking.

"I treated her daughter like the angel she truly was and that hag of a mother hated me for it," Mike said, anger starting to bubble to the surface.

"She hated you because she knew you were going to kill her!"

"Shut your mouth!" Mike yelled, standing up. He said it with such force, Durgan actually shied away; a sneer pulled the corners of Mike's lips back.

"Deny it!" Durgan challenged. "You can't because you know something's wrong with you or you wouldn't have that fucking demon eye! I can't tell you how many times I'd wished I had just caved your diseased skull in that day I ran into you."

Mike was shaking with impotence. Questions blazing

across his thoughts. *Would Jandilyn still be alive if I had died that night? Would she have been better off?*

Durgan had succeeded in his intentions to shake Mike's foundation, he was now riddled with self-doubt and should have been an easy target.

"They say better late than never," Durgan said, standing up and taking one choppy step toward Mike. "In this instance I'd have to disagree, but it's the only choice available" Durgan's next step was half as much as the previous one. He looked down at his traitorous legs before they turned on him and he folded in on himself. "What's going on?" Durgan said in alarm as he lost functional control over the rest of his body. He fell backward, his head bouncing twice off the hardwood floor.

Mike seemed to come out of his stupor, "Huh, I wonder what this shit is?" He held up the empty vial.

Durgan's eyes got huge, Mike laughed as Durgan appeared briefly cartoonish with his exaggerated gaze. "How much of that stuff did you give me?" Durgan asked as the corners of his mouth began to sag.

"All of it."

Durgan groaned.

"Well, it's not like there's dosage instructions on this," Mike said turning the small bottle over looking for some fine print. "How come you can still talk? I was really hoping to do the rest of this with you all glassy-eyed and a frozen look of terror on your face."

"What are you planning on doing?" Durgan asked in terror, his eyes now fixed on the ceiling.

"Oh…big plans, big plans," Mike said as he grabbed Durgan's left leg and began to slowly drag him across the floor toward the front door.

His injured leg screamed in pain, he barely noted it. Mike stopped to look back at Durgan, he lifted his patch quickly, hoping Jandilyn wasn't looking down at him at this inopportune time. The entity that had encircled Durgan had vacated, Mike wondered if it had done so when it realized its puppet's defeat.

"Mike, what are you doing?" Durgan asked in a panicked voice.

"Bet you're seeing the error of your ways right about now."

"This shit ain't funny!" Durgan screamed as Mike, with some effort, pulled him over the threshold his head striking the porch with a thud as he yanked him out. "I wasn't really trying to kill you, you know that, right? I was just trying to scare you."

"Scare me from what?" Mike pulled Durgan down the stairs taking satisfaction at every tread.

"Come on, Mike, we're friends now!" Durgan pleaded.

"Friends with benefits!" Mike laughed.

"Don't go getting all sick on me, man," Durgan cried, trying in desperation to move any muscle that might make a difference. He thought he might have wiggled a toe but he couldn't be sure. At least not until Mike reacted.

"Oooh, getting a little sensation back, are you? Well, maybe we should take care of that." Mike left Durgan where he was, half his body on the walkway leading up to the house and his head on the second to last stair. Durgan fought to wrest control of himself from the insidious drug that Mrs. Hollow had given him.

Make him suffer, she had said. His whole life he had been doing other people's wet work, and now he was going to pay for it. Mike's look of insanity far outshone even that of Mrs. Hollow and she had scared the shit out of him.

"Thirsty, buddy?" Mike asked as he came back down the stairs.

"I hope you fall and break your neck!" Durgan shouted.

"God might not like me all that much, but he sure isn't going to do you any favors," Mike said as he sat down next to Durgan's stationary head. "So if you can talk…I guess you can swallow," Mike said as he tipped the bottle of tequila into Durgan's lips. Durgan was powerless to stop him. The caustic liquid burned his throat as his swallow reflex forced the agave juice and poison into his system.

"Flucken slop!" Durgan shouted as Mike nearly drowned him.

"Well, that should be enough anyway. I want you cognizant enough to enjoy this."

"You're insane."

Mike stood. "I guess I probably am. Have I told you about my fridge?"

"Your what?" Durgan asked, his eyes rolling a little into the back of his head.

A loud thwack brought him back as Mike slapped him hard. "Don't you fucking pass out on me!" Mike shouted into his face.

"I have kids!" Durgan pleaded—a new tactic—as Mike again resumed the dragging. Durgan's head bounced twice more before striking the small cement walkway.

"Someone bred with you? Really? Was it consensual? They'll thank me for this someday." Mike labored as the big man's weight began to cause friction. That and the wound on his leg had busted open again.

Durgan began to full on cry. He knew there would be no reasoning with insanity. How many people had pleaded with him for some pity or mercy? He had never acquiesced to them.

"Oh, it's okay it'll all be over soon, I guess. I mean I really don't know how this is going to work out." Pulling Durgan became easier as he got him on the lawn and then onto the small path that led to the clearing he had been working so diligently on.

"Please," Durgan hitched. "What would Jandilyn think? She wouldn't want you to do this."

Mike stiffened, Durgan genuinely hoped Mike would

kick him into unconsciousness. "No, I guess not," Mike replied with stooped shoulders, but he did not stop his forward momentum as he finally dragged Durgan into the clearing and another ten feet into the center. "I don't know if it's big enough, but I guess we'll find out."

"Find out what?" Durgan was still looking straight up into the cloudless sky, he had never felt more alone and isolated than at this very moment.

"I think it's going to be better for me if I step out of here now."

"Why?" Durgan begged, trying to follow Mike's retreating footsteps. "What's happening? Are there wild animals? Please, Mike, I don't want to be eaten alive! Please!"

"Did you feel that?" Mike asked excitedly.

"No," Durgan said at first. "What is that?" He cried as a slight tremor rippled through the earth he was bedded on.

"My guess is that it's the end. I mean for you anyway."

The ground around the whole perimeter of the clearing began to vibrate, Mike took another step backward.

"I think it's an equal opportunity destroyer." Mike said as he began to laugh.

The vibration intensified and began to pull into a tighter circle around Durgan.

"Can you still save me?"

"Doubtful and I can't imagine for what reason I would want to."

"Mike, you don't want to release what's in here."

Mike's heart lurched once as he watched moss crisscross over Durgan's body like green lattice; wherever it touched, smoke began to steam up as it burned through Durgan's skin, muscle, sinew and finally bone. The screams stilled the rest of the creatures in the woods. At the end Mike turned away when all that was left was some one-inch-by-one-inch remains of humanity.

Mike vomited and headed back up the path and into the relative safety of his home, wondering if at the end Durgan was somehow trying to mind fuck him or was speaking the truth. "Never know now," Mike said aloud. *Unless of course whatever is in there comes down (or up) to let me know*, he thought.

Mike was exhausted, the events of the day had completely drained him and his leg was throbbing in pain. Any thoughts he had of the pain forcing sleep away were quickly dispelled as he fell immediately asleep.

CHAPTER SEVENTEEN – The Sheriff

The sun was again blazing across his cheek when he awoke, he was not sure if that caused him to stir or the sound of tires crushing rock coming up his driveway was the cause.

Durgan? he thought immediately, his heart fluttering wildly. He quickly whipped his legs over the side of the bed in preparation for round three. He was rewarded by a sharp pain in his leg for his efforts. "Damn!" he snorted loudly.

The car outside stopped. He heard a car door open and then close.

Mailman? Mike hoped. Odds weren't greatly in his favor considering it was a Sunday.

"Anyone home?"

Mike's heart sank, it was the sheriff.

"Whoa," Mike said as he was coming down the stairs, the sheriff was coming through the screen and in. "I don't remember inviting you in."

"You in the habit of leaving your front door open while you sleep?"

"I've been up for hours and what business is it of yours?"

"Up for hours?" the sheriff asked. "You've still got sleep lines on the side of your face."

"Can I help you with something?" Mike said as he went outside effectively keeping the sheriff from entering the house.

"This your car?" the sheriff asked, pointing to the newly deceased Durgan's Chevy Impala.

"Why? Are you interested in buying it?"

"I'm the one asking the questions here," the sheriff

said as a plume of red began to creep up his neck.

"Isn't there some person of color somewhere you can harass?"

The sheriff looked like he wanted to reach for his mace and give the snot-nosed punk in front of him a good dosing. "I received a call from a concerned citizen. Said there might be something going on around here."

"Roman orgy," Mike said.

"Excuse me?"

"There'll all the rage these days. Making a hell of a comeback. It gets messy sometimes, especially when someone pulls out the Olive Oil, all that thrusting and grunting, sometimes you just never know where things are going to end up if you know what I mean," Mike said, winking at the sheriff.

"I have no desire to know your twisted sexual preferences. Like I said this woman called and said I might find some trouble here and now you're talking about orgies and there's this car here, which she also described.

"Mrs. Hollow."

"What? How did you know?"

"Lucky guess," he told the cop. *Bitch*, he thought. *She knew Durgan was coming to kill me so she waited two days before reporting it. And then she was going to turn his ass in*, He had to salute her for that. "Leave no stone unturned."

"What's that?"

"I said that out loud?"

"Where is the owner of that car?"

"No idea," Mike said.

"I think you're lying."

"I really don't give a shit."

"I have probable cause to search the premises."

"You don't have shit. You have a random car and the ravings of a crazy bitch three thousand miles away who has hated my guts since the first time she laid eyes on me."

"Much like myself then?" the sheriff asked Mike.

"Are you done?" Mike asked wearily. "I have a book to write."

"I read it by the way. It sucked."

"I wouldn't figure someone like you would understand it anyway."

"What happened to your leg?"

"I cut myself shaving."

"What happened to your eye—eyeliner accident?"

Mike brought his hand up to his face, he felt the material and then realized that at some point last night he must have put his patch on, but for the life of him couldn't remember when. "You should leave."

"You know I'll be back with a search warrant," he said, walking back toward his car.

"Good, maybe when you come back we can discuss where you went wrong in life."

The sheriff stopped and looked long and hard at Mike. Mike could tell the man was debating if anyone would hear the shot. "Have a nice day," he said as he removed his hat and climbed back into his cruiser.

Mike waved and headed back into the house.

Patches was on the counter, boring holes into him as he approached. "*Et tu*?" he asked the bristling cat. Patches hopped off and headed back upstairs.

Mike was going to get a cold drink, but the fridge, which was still in its original spot, was now however turned completely around so that he was staring at the coolant tubes.

"Is this shit supposed to be funny?" he asked the house. There was no response.

Mike was fairly confident the sheriff would be back and soon, the house looked like a CSI's wet dream. Blood spray from both men was all over the floor and even Mike with his untrained eye could see the telltale signs of a person being dragged. He went outside and followed the path, constantly wondering how the sheriff had missed what was right in front of him.

"Blinded by hate," Mike said as he entered the woods. He found himself at the foot of the clearing. Nothing remained of Durgan, even the human lattice holes were now part of the enshrouding landscape. The moss where Durgan lay appeared somewhat greener than the rest, but Mike wasn't sure if that was just a trick of his eye. Mike began to lift the corner of his patch, no matter what he had promised Jandilyn, but quickly shut his eyelid. He didn't think he would like what he 'saw' at all. Instead, he let the blackness again fall back in place.

He turned to go back up the trail, Patches was watching him from the side of the woods. "What?" he asked the cat. "He was an asshole, he wouldn't have fed you." Patches bounded off. "Ingrate!" Mike called after her.

Mike felt a small tremor under his feet. *Time to go*, he thought, following the cat, the diffused light of twilight making it difficult to see the way ahead.

"When the hell did that happen?" Mike asked, looking up as the stars were becoming visible. "The sheriff showed up couldn't have been any later than nine, nine thirty tops. And now it's gotta be close to seven thirty."

A cold dank wind pressed against his back. The smell of old dirt and rot folded around him as he added another gear to his walk. His injured leg was slow to flex. *That's what happens when you stand for ten hours straight*, he thought sourly.

He was halfway down the path toward his yard when he heard the sound of roots tearing free from the earth. It was not a comforting noise. Whatever they had been holding down within their heavy wooden embrace had finally and forcefully been set free.

Something was coming, Mike knew it without having to turn around. The hairs on the back of his neck were standing straight out. His fight or flight response was pegged on flight and if he could get his legs to cooperate he would be gone. He finally stole a quick glance behind him once he made it to the edge of his yard and could see some of the trees down by the clearing swaying violently. He began to run and so did whatever was following him if the thrashing of the trees was any indication.

He was breathing heavy on the top of the porch, a steady flow of blood issuing from his leg again when she appeared, at least he *felt* her to be female. The figure stopped where Mike's backyard started, she/it was clothed in a large black hooded cloak. Mike thought she was unnaturally tall until he realized the creature was levitating a full foot off the ground, her black dirt-clod feet dangling uselessly below her.

The head which had been looking at the perimeter, deciding if it could cross the barrier finally looked up. Mike pressed himself up against the door as the yellow eyes radiated light. The twin orbs of fire froze his heart.

"What do you want with me?" Michael cried.

The figure looked back down and began to move silently and effortlessly toward him. Mike ripped the screen door off its hinges to get away. He was thankful the front door was open, he didn't think he had enough reasoning ability over the ever crowding terror to twist the knob.

He slammed the door shut and threw the deadbolt home. He turned and placed his back against the door, thankful he had shut out the nightmare. A deep scratching noise came from the other side of the heavy oak. Mike jumped away with a cry.

"Michael," seethed a voice choked with mud, rock, and moss.

Patches was at the top of the stairs, her ears pulled back, hissing violently at the sound.

The scratching continued, Mike could hear wood shavings striking the porch. "What do you want?" Mike screamed.

"You," came the solitary response. The word could have been issued from the depths of a tomb carried along an ill breeze.

Mike turned around to face the door and began to back away, his body was shaking with fear. He could barely control his movements. "You…you should leave, I…I have a gun," Mike voiced weakly.

The laugh that came was as dry as a funeral drum.

Something unholy was outside, the mere thought of which made Mike wish Durgan was back.

Mike's terrified gaze was ripped from the front door to the kitchen where he heard an even louder scraping sound. He thought his heart might stop beating when he looked down the hallway and could see a huge shadow approaching.

"She's coming," he said resignedly. *If I slit my throat now, will I be dead before she can torment me?* He had turned to flee up the stairs when the object of his nightmare came into view. His wayward fridge was making its way down the narrow corridor. "What the fuck?" was all he could muster. *It's trying to crash the door down and let it in.* But he couldn't find it in himself to go and inhibit its forward progress.

The appliance picked up speed as it got closer to the door. To Mike it was happening in two completely different speeds. On one level, it was happening so fast he could do little more than wonder how quickly his demise was going to be; and on the other, he watched in agonizingly slowly spaced segments of thought, the end of his existence as he knew it. Hell had submitted a remittance and now the note was due.

The stairs shook as the ice box was pushed up against the door but not with the terminal velocity needed to shatter the wood but rather as an aid to keep what was out, out.

Mike laughed. It had about as much mirth as the entity's only moments before, but what it lacked in merriment was more than made up for in maniacal insanity.

"You're on my side now?" Mike asked, looking up to the loft. "Is this a matter of who staked a claim first or are you as scared as I am?"

Mike waited for a response… nothing. At least the scratching had stopped, but now the utter and complete silence was worse. The thing now plaguing his house didn't look like it was the giving up type.

"It would be great if it was a vampire, because then I'd have to invite her in and there is no way I'd do that."

Mike shivered. He began to search through all his lore of what he knew about vampires, almost all of it from movies, and a smattering from fiction books. He didn't know how that was going to help him.

"I screwed up royally this time," Mike said to the still flat eared cat who took a quick second to acknowledge the words he had shouted.

Mike began to wonder if it was a matter of surviving until the dawn, at which point he would jump in his car and drive into the ocean if it got him out of this mess. Mike stared at the blocked door for a while longer, wondering what was happening. When he was somewhat confident it wasn't starting up again, he slowly headed back down the stairs, not remembering having ever climbed them, wishing he'd had the foresight to stock up on Holy Water.

He placed his hands against the front of the fridge. It was as cold as if it had been stored inside a meat locker. The sweat on his hands had bonded with the metal as if flash frozen. He pulled back quickly losing the top couple layers of skin. His breath was pluming around his head and whatever was out front was still there, he could feel it.

Patches looked like she was getting ready to bound off, not sure of her house mate's intentions. "Don't worry, cat," Mike said, "I'm not *that* insane."

Patches seemed to frown on the '*that*' part.

The presence had not left, but neither was it advancing. Mike felt that they were at an impasse.

What now? Mike wondered. As if in response, the front door rattled. "I guess that confirms that suspicion."

Mike's gaze was quickly brought skyward as he

looked to the ceiling some thirty-five feet above his head when he heard a loud thumping. "I doubt that's Santa," Mike said, doing his best to hold on to his fleeing nerve. Shingle-ripping scrapes above him kept him rooted to his spot. *Is it trying to come through the roof?* he wondered.

He did not know what he would do if he were to come face-to-face with the being. He was fairly certain his mind would fragment like a shattered mirror. He did not think anything living was supposed to gaze upon its countenance. Mike watched through the windows as debris rained down from above. "Homeowners insurance isn't going to cover this!" he shouted.

The clawing sounds went from end to end, back and forth more rapidly than Mike could keep up with. He could feel his senses starting to shut down from overload. It was too much; he couldn't even begin to process everything that was happening. When the scrabbling finally stopped, Mike looked heavenward, waiting for the next assault.

His neck began to ache and his injured leg was screaming for some relief when he thought he might have finally been issued a reprieve from the psychological torture. He hobbled over to the couch and immediately covered himself with the small blanket in the hopes the cotton blend would somehow repel the evil that had descended upon him, an evilness which he felt he had brought on himself. *Does God allow do-overs?*

Mike finally succumbed to the events of the day and laid his head down upon the armrest of the couch. He didn't think he had been asleep more than a few minutes, but that didn't seem right, the light in the house was somehow different, muted perhaps. Something was pulling the color from his surroundings. He sat up quickly when he heard the floorboards upstairs creaking.

"It's inside," he hissed.

He could feel it, he knew without a doubt whatever it was, had come in and was going to walk out onto the small landing and peer at him with its somehow burning, black pitiless eyes and he would go insane. His 'self' would be gone, replaced with something that would resemble him on the outside but would have none of the same inner workings.

"Go away!" Mike screamed.

It was as effective as he figured it would be. Which meant not at all. Mike twitched with every noise upstairs until finally he could not take it, it sounded like someone was tossing bowling balls around his room. Anger boiled over, this slow steady decline into the abyss was not how he wanted to go out. He ran up the stairs completely ignoring the pain. The noise ceased the moment his right foot touched the landing.

"You're chicken shit!" he screamed, hoping he was not talking about himself.

Sounds began to emanate from the far side of the house on the main floor. Patches was on the couch looking into the gloom.

"Attack, cat!" Mike prodded, she wasn't having anything to do with it and Mike couldn't blame her much. The bowling balls were preferable to the sound drifting toward him. It was a light tapping on glass.

"The windows…it wants in. No way," Mike said, shaking his head back and forth and finally placing his fingers in his eardrums in a useless gesture to block it out. The tapping became louder to the point where, Mike thought the glass was going to shatter. He could hear the whole frame rattling as if the entity were violently trying to shake the window free from its moorings.

What happened after the windows stopped shaking was worse. Mike could hear the glass being etched, he could imagine fine filaments of glass strings curling as they were shaved from the surface. *What could be doing that but can't get in?* he wondered for the tenth time. *Unless it's already in and is just tormenting me. Think 'OUT, it's out!' That's much better.*

Mike was rooted to the top of the steps. Whatever had propelled him there was now devoid of any power to get him moving again. Now he saw it as a precognitive lifesaving event. Something had got him to go upstairs to get away from what was most likely looking in his windows even now. Mike had the feeling of bugs crawling beneath the surface of his skin as he dwelled on that.

Mike felt he had somehow failed a test with Durgan; he now harbored guilt for the death of Durgan and for offering the man up as some sort of sacrifice. He had brought this retribution upon himself with his actions. Whatever doorway he had opened it would not close without him as a final payment. Somehow Mike was able to push the terror to the back or else his body had just decided it couldn't take any more as it began to shut down. Mike wrapped himself up in as tight a fetal position as he could at the top of the stairs.

Even in his near state of delirium he knew this for the bad idea it was, but he didn't move. At some point the night had to end no matter the blackness that was ensuing.

***

The sun did little to burn away the feelings Mike had. Patches was no more than a foot from his face, her loud meowing more effective than a rooster.

"Don't you have a shit to take or something?" Mike said half-heartedly, trying to push her away, she danced away from his attempts. Mike rolled on to his side and almost down the stairs before he realized where he was.

"I can't go through another night like that, cat," Mike said, sitting up, careful not to rise too quickly lest an ill-timed case of vertigo finish him off. As he got to his feet, Patches headed into the bedroom. "Might as well see how much of my deductible I will have to pay to cover this," he said as he followed after her.

Chunks of drywall littered his floor, large swaths of it

had been removed. It looked as if a grizzly bear had been caged in his room the destruction was that vast. His bed was cleaved in two. Patches was sitting on the half still within the bed frame.

"You're braver than I am," he told her.

She looked at him as if to say 'No shit.'

"I wish that had happened *before* Durgan decided to spend the night with me," Mike said, trying to inject some humor. He thought maybe if he had someone with whom he could disperse his terror he would be able to abate it. Bouncing it off of himself was only having so much affect and none of it really all that good.

Jandilyn would be able to talk me off this perch, he thought. *But really, would she even understand what was going on?*

Mike closed the bedroom door as he walked out. As he got to the stairs he noticed Patches was already downstairs. "I should have named you Houdini, cat, but that's not really a girl's name, I guess." He wondered what she was looking at as she stared at the ground in front of the windows. He came down to see what it was when he felt the fine silica snap under his shoe, he lifted up his foot to see the glass ground into the wood floor.

"What the hell?"

Mike looked up to the window pane. If he had the foresight to look at his reflection he would have witnessed how quickly he went from a robust tan color to that of bleached bone. Three scratches each about an inch apart from each other ran the width of the window. Mike rubbed his finger along one of the lines and was rewarded with a bleeding wound when a sliver of glass embedded itself deeply, the shard sent electric currents of pain through his nervous system.

"Fuck!" he yelled, pulling away quickly.

Fat droplets of blood splattered on the ground and began pooling around him, Patches moved away as the blood began to run in a small rivulet. Mike hurried to the kitchen and turned the water on, what spewed from the spigot was nearly identical in color to what poured from his finger. He waited for the rust to work its way through, at least that's what he hoped it was and then placed his finger underneath. By the time the seepage began to diminish, Mike was watching as the sheriff's car weaved its way up his long drive. His soured disposition was not going to improve in the least with his new guest.

Mike grabbed a bandage, wishing he had a few more moments to dig for the irritating splinter and headed down the hallway to the front door. He pushed the fridge out of the way to watch the approach of the sheriff. He did a quick scan of the area to make sure his night visitor was nowhere to be seen. It wasn't visible, but the damage was, sheets of shingles lay strewn around the yard, a micro-burst descending on his house would have had a hard time replicating the amount of damage he was looking at. When he was confident it was not close he turned back toward the sheriff who had just stopped his car and was getting out.

"Good to see you again, I was wondering when we might find some time to get together," Mike inflected with as much sarcasm as he could muster given that he was as stressed out as he had ever been in his life and hadn't slept much in at least two days.

The sheriff said nothing as he came up the stairs. When he got to the top he also surveyed the damage on the lawn. "Trouble?" he asked behind his mirrored glasses.

"Squirrels."

"Squirrels did this?"

"They're very angry. I think the previous owner built his house on an ancient native squirrel burial site."

"Do people really spend their hard earned cash on this shit you think up every day?"

"Well, I know it's not as impressive as harassing people and just generally being an asshole, but yeah, you'd be amazed. Already got the court order? That'd be monumental."

"Judge wouldn't sign off on it, seems that the ramblings of a distraught mother-in-law aren't probable cause."

"Damn shame."

"But I figured you'd invite me in because of good old Northwestern hospitality."

"Well, that's where you're wrong, because I'm from Boston and we're all pretty much dickheads there."

"I figured you'd say as much so I brought my persuader."

Mike was now staring at the chromed-out barrel of what appeared from his angle to be a howitzer. "Sheriff?" Mike asked. He was scared, but nothing approaching the level it had been only a few hours previous.

"You smell…wrong. You look…wrong. And something about this place is foul."

Mike found himself nodding in agreement.

"I'm going to find whatever I need in this place to get you thrown in jail."

"How you going to make it stick if it's illegally obtained?" Mike asked.

"Or you could just die in a struggle to escape, I guess." The sheriff smiled.

"Who really sent you here, Sheriff? I can't even begin to wrap my head around what is going on here much less be able to explain it."

"I'm sure I'll be able to figure it out. I'm not nearly as insane as you are." The sheriff motioned with the gun for Mike to go inside. "Another struggle?" he asked as he stepped to the side to avoid the screen door leaning up against the railing. "Doing a little woodworking?" he asked as he stopped to admire the wood carving on the door.

Three half inch deep claw marks were hewn into the wood. Mike reached up and traced them and pulled back quickly as a splinter lodged into his ring finger. "I've got mice," he said. The sheriff was not amused.

"Whatever you've done here, you won't be able to cover it up with an insanity plea or are you going to try to say you're researching a character for a new book? Because I'd love to get a sneak peek at that."

Me too, Mike thought, considering he hadn't written a word since Jandilyn died.

Mike kept looking from the door to the pathway and back again.

"Something out there?"

"I really don't know."

"Maybe we should take a look there first. Some folks think they can get away with anything out here in the wilderness, but that's not always the case."

"I think it'd be safer if you looked around the house."

"Are you afraid I'll find something."

"I'm more afraid something will find us."

Mike felt an iron grip on his shoulder as he was forcibly turned around. "Move," the sheriff said. Mike felt the barrel pressed firmly in between his shoulder blades. He involuntarily raised his hands.

"I'd rather you shoot me now and get it over with," Mike said hesitant to go any farther.

"That can be arranged, but I want to see your face first when I find out what has you so disturbed. Now move." He shoved Mike roughly forward.

Mike's steps were as small as he could make them while still making forward progress.

"You're beginning to piss me off, Mr. Talbot."

"Beginning?"

"You know what I mean. I would like to get to the crime scene while it's still light so I can get an investigative team up here and working."

The path down to the clearing was quiet and for the first time Mike could remember there were no flying insects present, anything that valued life was nowhere in the vicinity and this fact was not lost on him. The sheriff was completely oblivious, he was so wrapped up in the hunt for evidence.

"Been busy?" the sheriff asked over Mike's shoulder as he looked into the clearing. "Did you do all this?" he asked as he came abreast of Mike.

Mike nodded, but he wasn't so sure he had. The trees he had felled, but he had not removed the stumps and there wasn't so much as a hint they had ever existed despite the fact that some had been at least five feet around at the base.

The area where Durgan had been eroded was the same pale shade of green as the rest of the flooring, the greener pigmentation had faded to match the rest. The ground was uniform, whatever had ripped its way through the earth had not disturbed so much as a lone pine needle.

"What's wrong with this place?" the sheriff asked as he hesitantly held a foot above the edge as if he was now thinking better of entering into the opening.

Mike was fairly certain if he were to push the man in the same fate that had besot Durgan would happen to him. But did he deserve it? That was the question. Whatever residual vestiges of humanity he was still hanging onto would be pulled away. Mike instead grabbed the cop's shoulder and pulled him back from the brink.

"You afraid I'll find something?" the cop asked, but there was something else, he looked relieved.

"I think you'd die," Mike said flatly.

"From what?"

"Listen."

The cop was staring at him intently. "To what?"

"Do you hear anything—a cricket? A bird? A squirrel? Fucking Bigfoot?"

"No."

"There's something here sheriff, something evil."

"I think you're full of shit, like maybe you've read too many of your crappy stories."

"Durgan tried to kill me."

"The man who owns the car?" He formed it as a question but it was more a statement.

"Yes, I lucked out and was able to turn the tables."

"He's dead then?"

"Yes."

"Was it self-defense?"

"Up to a point," Mike said vaguely.

"What exactly does 'up to a point' mean?"

"It means I got the best of him and then kicked him while he was down."

"Was it in the heat of the moment?"

"Does that make a difference?" Mike asked.

The sheriff nodded.

"Then absolutely, couldn't have been any more heatier."

"Where's his body?"

"In there," Mike said pointing to the center of the clearing.

"This ground hasn't been disturbed recently—are you pulling my leg?"

"Yes, Sheriff, I just admitted to killing another man just to gauge your reaction."

"Did you bury him?"

"No, I didn't have to."

"Okay, we can play two hundred questions all damn day long if you want or you can just tell me what is going on."

"I'm not sure if I even know what's going on."

"Why don't you give it a shot and I'll decide whether you can sit in the front or back of my cruiser?"

Mike thought it would be option C, an ambulance equipped with a straight jacket but he kept that to himself.

"Let's go back up to the house and I'll tell you everything. You can decide then what you want to do with me. Jail might be preferable to another night here."

Mike spent the next couple of hours laying out the whole story, from his first introduction with the cat, to the being that seemed to reside in the loft. With each sentence Mike couldn't tell if he was drawing the sheriff in or alienating him. He told him about his encounter with death, the compulsion to make the clearing. Durgan showing up at his door to the fight and then even the dragging to the clearing where Durgan disappeared.

"Want something to drink?" Mike asked, heading to the fridge still parked midway in the hall.

"I think I'll pass on that. So you're saying he dissolved?" the sheriff asked. He was taking copious notes for his investigation. How much of what Mike was telling him would end up on any official report was anybody's guess.

"Dissolved sounds like sugar in coffee this was much more violent. He melted, it was horrific."

Mike didn't know when the transformation happened or even why for that matter, but for now he and the sheriff were no longer antagonistic towards each other. He wasn't sure he could trust the man completely, but it was nice to at least feel like the man wasn't going to shoot him and leave his body for the wolves.

"I'm having a hard time with this, Mike. It seems like you're laying the groundwork for an insanity plea. At trial I'll have to let them know how lucid you are right now."

"Should I start running around ranting, maybe do some cartwheels?"

"That won't help now."

"Well, then this might," Mike said relating the story of what came up through the clearing the previous night.

"You're saying this woman was floating and that she dug those claw marks into your door?"

Mike could tell the sheriff wasn't buying much of what he was selling, but the conviction with which he was saying it was having an effect. Mike saw ripples of goose bumps on the sheriff's forearms where he had rolled his sleeves up.

"And that brings us to the present, Sheriff."

"That's some imagination, I would think with all that running around in your head that your book would have been better."

Mike shrugged. "What now?"

"I'm going to have to take you into custody until we can do a full investigation and we can find Durgan's body."

"What if you can't?"

"Well, it will make prosecution more difficult, but not impossible. If he's in these woods, the bloodhounds will find him." The sheriff stood and reached behind his back to grab his handcuffs.

Mike's eyes widened.

"You're not planning on being any trouble, are you?" the sheriff asked warily.

"Nope, scout's honor," Mike said, turning around so that his arms were toward the sheriff.

"I've got a feeling you weren't in the Boy Scouts." The sheriff placed the cuffs on Mike's wrists.

Mike laughed. "Busted."

The sheriff was escorting Mike toward the front door, when the fridge slammed up against it.

"What did you do?" the sheriff yelled in Mike's ear.

"My hands are cuffed and I'm standing next to you, I didn't do shit. I'm thinking the house isn't quite willing to let us leave just yet."

"Bullshit. Do not move," the sheriff said as he pushed Mike up against the wall. He pulled his gun out of his holster and slowly approached the fridge which was vibrating hollowly. The sheriff looked around the fridge for some sort of device or cable system that would have moved it. "This is pretty elaborate. I don't see anything, so what's the trick?"

"I'm not an engineer, Sheriff, I didn't *do* anything."

"Fine, have it your way." The sheriff placed his

weapon back in its holster and attempted to move the appliance. It may as well have been cemented in place. "There's nothing holding this thing in here," the sheriff grunted.

"One would think that," Mike said, rubbing the side of his head and the patch up against a wall sconce so that he could move it out of the way. When he finally dislodged it enough to see out he was not excessively surprised to see a large black mist pressed against the fridge.

"What are you looking at?" the sheriff said, eyeing Mike.

"My other house guest is here. I guess that's not really the truth, though," Mike said, thinking. "More than likely, I'm the guest, he or it has been here longer than me."

The sheriff again pulled his revolver out of his holster and pointed it at Mike's chest. "Release whatever switch you have holding that thing in place or I'm going to make you considerably lighter."

"Do it," Mike begged. "I'm so tired of living, it's become so difficult since Jandilyn died. I feel like I'm going through the motions. Every night I go to sleep hoping to be released from this nightmare and each morning I wake up to the horror of realizing she's gone and I'll never hold her in my arms again. Do you know what that's like?"

The sheriff backed up a step from the power of Mike's words. "If that's the way you truly feel, why didn't you just let Durgan do you in?"

"Because he was an asshole sent by a bitch and I'd be damned if I was going to let them win. Although, somehow, Sheriff, I think I already am."

"Already am what?"

"Damned."

"Is there a back door?" the sheriff asked as he grabbed Mike's shoulder and turned him around, but not before he carefully placed the patch back in place. "Your eye creeps the shit out of me."

"You're not the only one. And no there's no back door."

"The basement then?"

"Never been down there."

"You're shitting me. You bought a house without going down the basement first—what if it was two feet under water?"

"I always got the feeling I wasn't going to be here long…didn't think it mattered much."

"Are all you authors as crazy as you?"

"I can't speak for the others, but I would imagine they have a slice of insanity running through them—how else could they have multiple worlds coursing through their heads?"

"Let's go." The sheriff pushed Mike back toward the kitchen and the door that led to the cellar stairs. "Light switch?" he asked, looking into the gloom pooling at the bottom of the stairs.

Mike shrugged. "No clue."

"Fantastic. Go slow."

The stairs creaked and shook as the duo descended. When Mike stopped on the basement floor he realized it was dirt by the uneven feel under his sneakers. Mike took another step in, his forehead bumped against a cool object which yielded to his advance.

"Think I found a light," Mike said as the sheriff got down behind him. "By my head there's a light hanging down."

The sheriff batted the side of Mike's head.

"Yeah, that wasn't it."

"Sorry," the sheriff told him.

Mike heard the click as the sheriff threw the switch. At first nothing happened, both thought the light must have been burned out. And then it began to flicker to life. "Must have had to warm up," Mike said, turning away from the slowly building light.

"What the fuck is this place?" the sheriff asked, moving past Mike and farther in.

Mike turned his head to follow the sheriff's steps. Steel tables lined the far wall, gleaming surgical tools hung on pegboards: bone saws, rib splitters, oversized scalpels.

"This looks like a mortuary," Mike said, panicking. "I really don't want to be down here." He backed up.

More than one table was bathed in a rusty brown substance. "Dried blood," the sheriff stated as he got closer.

Dried husks of what looked like internal organs were piled in the far corner from where Mike stood. Mike cramped and violently vomited. "I need to get out of here," he begged, still hunched over, long lines of spittle hanging from his mouth.

"How could you not know this was here?" the sheriff shouted in an accusatory tone.

Mike could only shake his head.

The sheriff went farther than the light could pierce. Mike thought for sure he would get swallowed up in the bleakness of the place.

"I think I found your Durgan," the sheriff said as he dragged something large toward the center of the room.

"What is it?" Mike asked not looking up.

"I'll play your game, but I'm winning. It's a body bag." The sheriff dragged it into the light.

Mike could feel his pulse quicken, his pupils began to contract and his sight started to tunnel so only pinpricks of light could enter. The sheriff grabbed the oversized zipper, a smile of satisfaction crossing his lips.

"Please, Sheriff…" Mike said, a wicked case of vertigo threatening to drop him on his ass. "Please don't open that."

"No desire to see your handiwork, I take it?" the sheriff asked as he pulled the zipper down. "Huh?" He stood.

Mike watched as a tress of dirty blonde locks spilled out from the bag. He knew without going any farther who was in that bag.

"Who the fuck is this, you sick fuck!" the sheriff was screaming from a million miles away.

Mike was rapidly losing consciousness as his back slid down the wall. "It's Jandilyn," he murmured moments before he blacked out. His respite from the horror was short-lived as the sheriff manhandled him to his feet and gave him a once over across the face to get him awake.

"Who is in that bag!" the sheriff was shaking Mike so hard the back of his head was making a sickening thwacking sound against the concrete wall. "That is not your month-long dead wife in that bag, it can't be." The sheriff seemed to be hoping at least that that was the case.

Mike couldn't bring himself to look over, but he didn't have to. "It is." he cried softly.

"The woman in that bag hasn't been dead more than a few minutes. Rigor mortis hasn't even set in. What have you done?" he asked as he slammed Mike hard against the wall again for good measure.

The sheriff finally let him go, Mike slid down halfway, tears the size of small marbles fell in his lap. The sheriff went back to the body and felt around in the woman's pockets until he found what he was looking for, he stood up quickly as if he didn't want to be this close to death.

"What the fuck is going on?" he asked as he swept his hand across the side of his face. He looked from the picture ID to the face in the bag and back again at least a dozen times.

Mike had already realized what was going on. "That's my Jandilyn."

"It can't be!" the sheriff said nearly hysterically. "Did you dig her up? But that can't be it...she looks like she just fell asleep. I have to call this in. Get your ass up."

He grabbed Mike by the shoulder and hauled him to his feet. Mike looked over his shoulder as he headed to the stairs. Jandilyn's arm fell out of the bag, her modest engagement and wedding rings shone brightly in the dim light.

Mike's sob caught in his throat. "I love you, Jandilyn," he said.

"Move!" the sheriff said, not wanting or willing to believe the body in the basement was anything but the fresh kill of a madman. To think on any other scenario opened up doors to places he had no wish or reason to visit.

Patches stood at the top of the stairs, her tail was going back and forth in an excessively agitated manner. Mike stopped two steps from the top.

"What are you doing?" the sheriff asked. Mike could sense the panic rising in the man much like his own had been.

"My cat won't get out of the way."

"Kick it, I don't care, they're all just bats with a 'c' at the beginning of their name."

"And no, wings. Move, cat," Mike said. But she wouldn't.

Patches hissed at the men as if in response.

"I'm going to shoot the thing if you don't hurry up and get out of here. I don't see anything," the sheriff said as he peered around the side of Mike.

Patches stared a second longer at Mike and then rounded the corner to go back upstairs Mike presumed. Mike got back to the top.

"I need to get to my cruiser, but that fridge is wedged tight. If I undo your cuffs will you behave?" the sheriff asked pleadingly.

"Would you believe anything I say, Sheriff?" Mike responded. "Even I wouldn't take the cuffs off me in this predicament."

The sheriff removed his hat and ran his hands through his thinning brown hair. "I'll shoot you dead if you try anything. You hear me?" He reached for his cuff key, his hands were visibly shaking. He had to grasp Mike's wrist to steady his own, but that was much like grabbing a handhold on a ship in a squall, Mike was no better off. "You're going to hang for this," the sheriff said as he removed the cuffs.

"This is a bad way to start an alliance," Mike said as he brought his hands to the front of his body and rubbed where the cuffs had chaffed him.

"This is no alliance, I…we just need to get out of here. I don't know how you did it, unless you just found some girl that looked like your wife or maybe just made a fake ID who knows what you sick fucks having going through your minds."

"I did not kill my wife."

"Maybe not your wife…but your fingerprints are all over whoever that unfortunate young lady in the basement is. I can get you some help, Mike, it looks like you've never recovered from the loss."

"So I'll be healthy when I swing?" Mike asked, a sick smile splashed on his face.

"Let's just get this thing out of the way."

"The suns almost setting, I don't think that's such a wise idea."

"Setting? I just got here."

"I'm thinking we were in the basement a lot longer than you realize."

The sheriff strode over to the windows in the living room. "It must be getting cloudy, it can't be any later than ten."

"The only reason it would be this dark at ten AM was if there was going to be a tornado."

"That's insane, there's no tornados in upstate Washington," the sheriff said as he peered through the window. "My watch says seven thirty, how can that be?"

"There still might be time, let's get out of here," Mike said, bolting down the hallway.

"Stop!" the sheriff shouted, thinking Mike was making an escape attempt. The sheriff's view was obstructed by the staircase but he could hear Mike rustling around in one of the cabinet's in the kitchen. "Stop what you're doing, Mike!" the sheriff yelled.

Mike paid no heed. "I thought it was in here!" he yelled triumphantly. "Sheriff, let's get out of here!" Mike ran back down the hallway.

The first thing the sheriff noticed was the octagonal steel of what appeared to be a rifle barrel. He fired his revolver once, placing one well-aimed shot between the third and fourth rib on Mike's right side. The round slammed Mike up against the wall as it shattered the two ribs and punctured his lung. The crow bar clanged to the ground and slid toward the fridge.

"A fucking crow bar? I thought it was a rifle," he said, placing his revolver back into his holster and running over toward Mike. Mike's complexion had paled considerably, he looked waxen. Questioning eyes looked up at the sheriff. Blood flowed freely from under Mike's arm.

Mike noted that he was again on the ground but this hit did not seem to pack as much punch as the earlier one when he saw Jandilyn in the body bag. "I thought it would hurt more," Mike rasped.

The sheriff ran to the laundry room and grabbed a handful of towels, he placed one tightly up against the wound, holding it in place. "What were you doing?" the sheriff asked him.

"I was going to help you pry the fridge away from the door."

"I told you to stop."

"It's better this way."

"You are not going to die on me, Talbot, you got that?"

"Do you really have that kind of pull in the afterlife?" Mike asked.

The sheriff couldn't tell if Mike was being sarcastic or the blood loss combined with shock was making him start to hallucinate. "Hold this tight," the sheriff, said moving Mike's arm over the wound with the towel in between. "I'm going out to my cruiser and radio for help."

"I think that window of opportunity has closed," Mike said.

The sheriff got chills. "You'll die when I give the say so."

"Comforting," Mike said with a small smile. "Jandilyn, is that you? Paul? Dennis?" Mike said as he stared off into space.

The sheriff ran to the fridge which moved effortlessly to the side. "What the hell?" The sheriff opened the front door and placed one foot on the porch when he saw something coming from the woods. He pulled his foot back into the house before he could even register the dread that rocketed through his system.

He swung his gaze from the cruiser to the thing coming at him.

"You won't make it," Mike said from the hallway.

"How…how can you know?"

"I've had the good fortune to meet it earlier."

"What is it?"

"Put the fridge back."

The fridge slid as effortlessly back into place as it had moved out. The sheriff did not seem convinced his stalwart defense would hold.

"Sheriff, please lift my patch off my face, I can't move my arm anymore." The towel was soaked dark red and was lying on the ground, Mike's arm hung uselessly by his side.

The sheriff did as Mike asked, the view from his damaged left eye now seemed to be the more prominent of the two. 'Reality' seemed to be taking a backseat as the shadows around him grew more substantial.

"I think I'm dying," Mike said as a shadow dislodged itself from the nearest wall and materialized into a familiar shape.

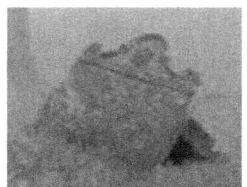

CHAPTER EIGHTEEN – The Sheriff Part Two

The sheriff was looking down at Mike, an ever increasing show of alarm spreading on his features. "What's out there, Mike? I need to radio for help!" the sheriff asked desperately.

It took Mike a moment to concentrate on the words the sheriff was speaking.

"Tell him she's a purveyor of souls," a familiar voice spoke.

"Paul?" Mike hitched, "You're alive?"

"Not quite, buddy," Paul said with a bittersweet smile.

"Who are you talking to?" the sheriff asked, following Mike's line of sight and not witnessing anything except a slight chill and a swirl of dust.

"She's a purveyor of souls," Mike spoke.

"What? Are you going into shock?"

"Would I be able to tell?" Mike asked the sheriff.

"No, I guess not. Here, lie down."

"There'll be plenty of time for that."

The sheriff's face fell when he realized the truth behind Mike's words.

"I wouldn't have taken the purveyor as a she," Mike said to Paul.

"It's not really either, just a label. Are you afraid?"

Mike nodded.

"It'll all be over soon, buddy."

"Am I going to hell?" Mike asked.

Both the sheriff and Paul answered simultaneously. "Absolutely not."

"I murdered a man."

"Self-defense goes a long way in the eyes of the law and with God," the sheriff said tenderly. "Is there anything else you'd like to confess?"

Mike could barely focus on the sheriff, the images in his right eye began to melt and blur around the edges.

"The girl in the basement, Mike," the sheriff said in clarification.

"That's my wife," Mike said, drifting in and out of consciousness.

"You never married," Paul said.

"That cannot be your wife, Mike, she's been gone for over a month. Don't die with this on your conscience."

"We didn't mean to kill her," Mike said.

"We?" the sheriff asked as Mike slumped over, his heartbeat making its last struggling effort to cling to a destroyed life. "No, you're staying with me!" the sheriff yelled, beating on Mike's chest. "I will not lose another one," he cried as he began compressions on Mike's chest and then pinching Mike's nose in an effort to get life-giving breath into the teenager.

***

The carnage on the roadway was unlike anything the sheriff had seen in his fourteen years on the job. A teenager who the sheriff was sure would fail a toxicology report had taken a turn too severely and had first plowed into a young couple out for a walk and then into a tree. The couple on the ground had died instantly, two teenagers had fried in the car and the one who had been ejected had struggled to hold onto life as long as he could but the massive trauma to the side of his head where he had struck the tree had been too much for his body to sustain life.

The Flight for Life helicopter which had just found a safe place to land was waved away once it was realized that no one that was a part of this tragedy would be walking away.

An EMT came up to the sheriff and pressed his fingers on the side of Mike's neck. He waited a few moments before shaking his head.

"He's dead, Al," the EMT said as he placed his hand on the sheriff's shoulder.

"This is the first day in all my years, Lawrence, that I wish I was anything but a sheriff," he said as he stood and walked away from the scene to get away for a moment.

Deputy Caldwell found him a hundred yards down the road. "I ran the plates sheriff, the car is registered to a Mr. and Mrs. Paul Ginson, I know them, that's most likely their son behind the wheel. Do you want me to make the call?"

"I'll do it," the sheriff said as he walked back toward his cruiser, his heart nearly dragging. "What about the two on the ground?" he asked the deputy.

"Jandilyn Hollow and Durgan O'Grady, they're locals, both graduated last year. Pretty sure they've been an item since school. I might have even seen an announcement in the newspaper about their engagement."

"Damn shame," the sheriff said as the two bodies were placed into body bags by the coroner and his assistant. "Finish getting statements by the witnesses, please," he said as he dragged his hand across his face.

"Mr. and Mrs. Planter, just a few more questions," the deputy stated.

"Please I'm Jed and this is my wife Grace," the old man said.

EPILOGUE

"It's good to see you, my friend," Mike said as he hugged his friend. Paul reciprocated. "What happened, Paul?" Mike asked as he watched the sheriff sit down in his cruiser and grab his radio to make a call that no one should ever have to make.

"I crashed," Paul said, putting his head down. "I killed us all, including Jandilyn and Durgan."

"You didn't kill my wife," Mike said. "She died in child birth."

"This might take a few minutes," Paul said, motioning to a log.

"What's the rush?" Dennis said, smiling as he came out of the backseat of Paul's car, looking as good as the day he had entered it some six years previous.

"Wags!" Mike shouted. "I've missed you, man, every fucking day I've missed you both so much." He stood to greet his grinning friend.

"He doesn't know?" Dennis asked Paul.

Paul shook his head.

"Buddy, how old do you think you are?" Paul asked.

"Twenty-one, twenty-two maybe." Mike responded without blinking.

"I know this is a lot to take in, but look around," Paul said, sweeping the landscape with his hand, a sad smile spread thinly on his lips.

"Why have you brought me back here, Paul?" Mike asked, clearly confused.

"I didn't bring you back, Mike, we never left."

"Come on. What's really going on?"

"We all died tonight."

"Paul, that can't be. I met Jandilyn after I got out of the hospital. Fell madly in love with her, she saved me from my constant thoughts of suicide. We moved to California, got married and were having a kid. And you want me to believe all of that didn't happen? I can't, that's almost as traumatic as dying as a teenager."

"I lived in Nova Scotia for a few years," Dennis said as he sat down next to Mike. "Started working on a sword fishing boat."

"When'd you do that?" Mike asked.

"Same time you were falling in love with Jandilyn," Dennis said.

"What about you, Paul?" Mike asked.

"I stayed here, I never left. The guilt was too much."

"How long, Paul?" Mike asked.

Paul put his head down.

"The whole time?" Mike asked Dennis.

"When the demon came I almost went willingly," Paul said with his head buried in his hands.

"I couldn't run fast enough or I guess swim," Dennis said, "I was sinking in the ocean. Fell off the damn boat in a swell. I loved that boat, it was the only place I was at peace."

"Was it haunted?" Mike asked.

"The cat saved me," Paul said before Dennis could respond.

"Cat? Was it a seven pound runt, with different colored fur?" Mike asked.

"That sounds like Patches," Dennis said, she was on the boat with me, weirdest thing too because don't cats hate water?"

"I thought she was going to rip my head off. The cat, not the demon," Paul added for clarification. "The purveyor wasn't even moving, I was heading toward it and the cat came tearing out of the woods, got right in front of me and was hissing and spitting. One small kick and I could have sent it tumbling away. When I stopped moving the demon started coming toward me. The cat whipped around and stood her ground against that thing. It was at that point I understood what was going on. The demon is just looking for opportunities to claim unfettered souls."

"Dude, what are you talking about?" Dennis asked.

"When you die before your time your soul is not allocated one way or the other, the Purveyor will do her best to gather you up and basically sell you off to the highest bidder."

"I'm not saying I believe all that, but what happens now? We're still unfettered," Mike said.

"It's our choice," Paul answered.

"Are there any brochures we can look over?" Mike asked.

"I didn't think sarcasm would travel over into death," Dennis said, stroking his chin.

"Free will, we all have it," Paul said.

"Do you know what was in my house with me?" Mike asked.

"Your soul, I would imagine," Paul answered.

"Isn't that what I am now?"

"But you didn't know it then," Dennis finished.

"I don't know if this is ever going to make sense."

Mike looked over at some movement, the sheriff was getting out of his car, it appeared that he was aging yearly per minute. The events of this night would haunt him for the rest of his days.

Mike's phantom heart slammed into his chest as he caught sight of Jandilyn coming around the front of the sheriff's cruiser, she was peering down at the body bag that contained her physical remains. Mike had a pang of jealousy when he saw Durgan standing behind her.

Tears were coming down her face as she clutched her distended belly.

"She's pregnant," Mike said softly.

She caught Mike looking at her and gave him a slow meaningful look as if they had shared something and then she turned to her fiancé, they clutched hands and walked down the road. Mike watched until he couldn't see them anymore.

"You alright?" Paul asked, putting his arm around Mike's shoulder.

"The best I've been in a while, Paul. I thought I was going insane."

"I'm sorry."

Mike didn't know what to say, he wasn't really angry that his life had been cut short. He was saddened for what his family was going to have to go through but they were tight-knit they would get through it. And it really did seem as if in the end they would all be reunited.

"What now?" Mike answered in repose.

"How about one more walk on Indian Hill?" Dennis asked. "And we'll decide from there."

The three friends laughed as if there were no tomorrow, soaking in the best of what the world of the living had to offer. When they parted, Mike and Dennis chose the light, Paul burdened with guilt, stayed to roam what the locals dubbed The Spirit Clearing. On occasion, a runtish, multicolored cat and her charge, a young sad man, could be seen wandering the road in the hopes to slow drivers down.

I hope you enjoyed the book. If you did please consider leaving a review.

For more in The Zombie Fallout Series by Mark Tufo:

Zombie Fallout 1

Zombie Fallout 2 A Plague Upon Your Family

Zombie Fallout 3 The End....

Zombie Fallout 3.5 Dr. Hugh Mann

Zombie Fallout 4 The End Has Come And Gone

Zombie Fallout 5 Alive In A Dead World

Zombie Fallout 6 Til Death Do Us Part

Zombie Fallout 7 For The Fallen

The newest Post Apocalyptic Horror by Mark Tufo:

Lycan Fallout Rise of the Werewolf

Fun with zombies in The Book of Riley Series by Mark Tufo

The Book Of Riley A Zombie Tale pt 1

The Book Of Riley A Zombie Tale pt 2

The Book Of Riley A Zombie Tale pt 3

The Book Of Riley A Zombie Tale pt 4

Or all in one neat package:

The Book Of Riley A Zombie Tale Boxed set plus a bonus short

Dark Zombie Fiction can be found in The Timothy Series by Mark Tufo

Timothy

Tim2

Michael Talbot is at it again in this Post Apocalyptic Alternative History series Indian Hill by Mark Tufo

Indian Hill 1 Encounters:
Coming soon from Permuted Press

Indian Hill 2 Reckoning
Coming Soon from Permuted Press

Indian Hill 3 Conquest

Indian Hill 4 From The Ashes

Writing as M.R. Tufo

Dystance Winter's Rising

The Spirit Clearing

Callis Rose

I love hearing from readers, you can reach me at:

email
mark@marktufo.com

website
www.marktufo.com

Facebook
https://www.facebook.com/pages/Mark-Tufo/133954330009843?ref=hl

Twitter
@zombiefallout

All books are available in audio version at Audible.com or itunes.

All books are available in print at Amazon.com or Barnes and Noble.com

I hope you enjoyed the book. If you did please consider leaving a review.

CPSIA information can be obtained at www.ICGtesting.com
Printed in the USA
LVOW04s1533010215

425237LV00027B/1211/P